THE YEAR'S BEST HORROR STORIES IX

...Back he swung in flight along the gallery, but this time he took the other way, making for the reading-cabinet at the end. He floundered in exhausted and slammed the screen door after him. Once in, he knew how futile this move was; there was no way out.

Already the hideous face was looking through the open woodwork at him. With nightmare fascination he watched it craning its gaunt head about as though blind, then squeeze between the carved foliage, straining its quivering legs against the sides. By some uncanny sense it came straight for him as he stood transfixed. It fastened on him without haste and though he raised his arms to beat it off, they fell limply down again and left him to his fate.

A fiery glow suffused all vision now as he felt the bristling tendons on his chest and saw the ghastly proboscis nosing up for his throat. . . .

Watch for these exciting DAW Anthologies:

ASIMOV PRESENTS THE GREAT SF STORIES
Classics of short fiction from the golden age through today.
Edited by Isaac Asimov and Martin H. Greenberg.

THE ANNUAL WORLD'S BEST SF
The finest stories of the current year.
Edited by Donald A. Wollheim with Arthur W. Saha.

THE YEAR'S BEST HORROR STORIES
The finest horror stories of the current year.
Edited by Karl Edward Wagner.

THE YEAR'S BEST FANTASY STORIES
An annual of fantastic tales.
Edited by Arthur W. Saha.

SWORD AND SORCERESS
Original tales of fantasy and adventure with female protagonists.
Edited by Marion Zimmer Bradley

THE YEAR'S BEST HORROR STORIES
IX

Edited by
KARL EDWARD WAGNER

DAW BOOKS, INC.
DONALD A. WOLLHEIM, PUBLISHER

1633 Broadway, New York, NY 10019

Copyright ©, 1981 by DAW Books, Inc.
All Rights Reserved.
Cover art by Michael Whelan.

For color prints of Michael Whelan paintings, please contact:

Glass Onion Graphics
P.O. Box 88
Brookfield, CT 06804

DAW Book Collectors No. 445.

First Printing, August 1981

3 4 5 6 7 8 9

PRINTED IN U.S.A.

ACKNOWLEDGMENTS

The Monkey by Stephen King. Copyright © 1980 by Stephen King for *Gallery*, November 1980. Reprinted by permission of the author and the author's agent, Kirby McCauley Ltd.

The Gay by Ramsey Campbell. Copyright © 1980 by Ramsey Campbell for *Fantasy Readers Guide* No. 2. Reprinted by permission of the author.

The Cats of Pere LaChaise by Neil Olonoff. Copyright © 1980 by Editions MSGD for *A Touch of Paris*, June 1980 (under the title, "I'll Tell Her You'll Be Late for Dinner"). Reprinted by permission of the author.

The Propert Bequest by Basil A. Smith. Copyright © 1980 by Stuart Schiff for *The Scallion Stone*. Reprinted by permission of the author's agent, Kirby McCauley Ltd.

On Call by Dennis Etchison. Copyright © 1980 by Paul C. Allen for *Fantasy Newsletter*, March 1980. Reprinted by permission of the author.

The Catacomb by Peter Shilston. Copyright © 1980 by Rosemary Pardoe for *More Ghosts & Scholars*. Reprinted by permission of the author.

Black Man With a Horn by T. E. D. Klein. Copyright © 1980 by Arkham House Publishers, Inc. for *New Tales of the Cthulhu Mythos*. Reprinted by permission of the author and the author's agent, Kirby McCauley Ltd.

The King by William Relling, Jr. Copyright © 1980 by Dugent Publishing Corp. for *Cavalier*. February 1980. Reprinted by permission of the author.

Footsteps by Harlan Ellison. Copyright © 1980 by The Kilimanjaro Corporation for *Gallery*, December 1980. Reprinted by permission of and arrangement with the author and the author's agent, Robert P. Mills, Ltd.

Without Rhyme or Reason by Peter Valentine Timlett. Copyright © 1980 by Peter Valentine Timlett for *New Terrors 1*. Reprinted by permission of the author and the author's agent, Carole Blake.

Table of Contents

Introduction by Karl Edward Wagner	11
The Monkey by Stephen King	15
The Gap by Ramsey Campbell	54
The Cats of Pere LaChaise by Neil Olonoff	67
The Propert Bequest by Basil A. Smith	77
On Call by Dennis Etchison	123
The Catacomb by Peter Shilston	132
Black Man with a Horn by T.E.D. Klein	144
The King by William Relling, Jr.	185
Footsteps by Harlan Ellison	194
Without Rhyme or Reason by Peter Valentine Timlett	208

To Barbara

Who loves a good shiver almost as much as she loves a good party.

Introduction: *The Year of the Anthology and Beyond*

by KARL EDWARD WAGNER

The year past, 1980, will go down in the annals of horror literature as the year of the blockbuster original anthology. One has to go back to those thousand-page super-dreadnought-class horror anthologies published in England during the 1930's—particularly those edited by John Gawsworth—to find a comparison.

Most visible was *Dark Forces*, edited by Kirby McCauley, a finely produced 550-page hardcover volume containing 23 stories by major authors, published by The Viking Press in the U.S. and by Macdonald in England. Less opulent but a far better value was Ramsey Campbell's two-volume paperback anthology, *New Terrors*, offering 37 original stories crammed into 670 pages. This was published by Pan Books in England; regrettably there has not yet been a U.S. edition, but on the brighter side there has been talk of continuing *New Terrors* as a series. The avowed intent of both of these anthologies was to showcase the cream of today's horror fiction—the genre's top writers creating *contemporary* tales of terror. How often and how well they succeed in achieving that is something each reader will enjoy deciding for himself.

Against these two shelf-benders, the other original horror anthologies of 1980 might well be unjustly overlooked. Charles L. Grant has edited *Shadows 3* for Doubleday—a collection that maintains the same level of his previous two entries in the series. Pan Books published *The 21st Pan Book of Horror*, edited by Herbert van Thal, which unfortunately maintains the level of that long-lived series. Perhaps best of 1980's crop of original anthologies was *New Tales of the Cthulhu Mythos,* edited by Ramsey Campbell for Arkham House. Instead of the inept and amateurish Lovecraftian pastiches one might have expected (Douglas E. Winter has pointed out in a review that "Cthulhu Mythos" has been given a pejorative connotation in recent years), Campbell asked his authors for (and for the most part received from them) genuinely original and intelligent contemporary interpretations of the underlying concepts of Lovecraft's synthesis.

Roy Torgeson edited *Other Worlds 2* and *Chrysalis 7* for Zebra Books—evidently the last for Zebra, as the series will now be published by Doubleday. From Berkley came the first two volumes of *The Berkley Showcase,* edited by Victoria Schochet and John Silbersack. Fantasy anthologies offering part original and part reprint fiction included *Mummy!* edited by Bill Pronzini, *Basilisk,* edited by Ellen Kushner, and *The Phoenix Tree,* edited by Robert H. Boyer and Kenneth J. Zahorski. Ostensibly science fiction but not entirely without interest to the horror fan were *Interfaces* and *Edges,* both edited by Ursula K. Le Guin and Virginia Kidd, and the continuing paperback series, *Destinies, New Dimensions,* and *Stellar.*

If it was a good year for original anthologies, it was a grim year for magazines. Two of the few surviving newsstand science fiction and fantasy magazines, *Galaxy* and *Fantastic,* published their final issues in 1980, as did a promising newcomer, *Galileo. Galaxy* had been around since 1950; *Fantastic* since 1952. For those fans who, like myself, discovered imaginative fiction through reading these magazines back when *they* were the bright new publications in the field, it's a sad feeling. Of the Golden Age pulps and Atomic Age digests, now only *Amazing, Analog,* and *The Magazine of Fantasy and Science Fiction* survive. Not all is gloom on the magazine front: 1981 promises the debut of *The Twilight Zone Magazine* as well as yet another reincarnation of *Weird Tales.*

The lively world of the amateur press continues to furnish us with what is perhaps the best new writing in horror fiction. These publications run the gamut from the crudely produced fanzines, which pay their contributors with a free copy or two, to the most lavish of the semi-prozines (amateur magazines that pay competitive rates for material but lack newsstand distribution), whose production values far outstrip those of the prozines (magazines you can find on your newsstand, if you're lucky).

Theirs is a fast-changing scene. Two of the best have ceased publication—*Midnight Sun* and *Copper Toadstool*. Two others long at the top of the field—*Whispers* and *Weirdbook*—did not have an issue during 1980 but promise to return in 1981. *Fantasy Tales*, Britain's top semi-prozine, had its sixth issue in 1980, and was joined by a new countryman, *Fantasy Macabre*. The British Fantasy Society continued to publish *The B.F.S. Bulletin*, expanded under new editor Carl Hiles, as well as *Dark Horizons*, its literary journal. Stephen Jones and David Sutton, editors of *Fantasy Tales*, published *Airgedlámh*, a beautifully produced fantasy magazine brought out as a posthumous tribute to its editor, Dave McFerran, whose untimely death cost fandom one of its brightest stars.

Space and Time published its fifty-seventh issue, *Dark Fantasy* its twenty-second, *Nyctalops* its fifteenth, *Sorcerer's Apprentice* its eighth, *Eldritch Tales* its seventh, *The Argonaut* its seventh. Many of the newer small press publications continued to show encouraging growth with their latest issues: *Night Voyages, Gothic, Just Pulp, Ogre, Cryptoc, 1985* (now *Alternates*), *Wax Dragon, Pandora*, to name just a few. New faces appeared: *Skullduggery*, devoted to mystery fiction; *Paragon*, from Chet Clingan who edited *The Diversifier; Kadath,* from Italy's Francesco Cova and including English-language fiction; *Dragonfields*, an amalgam of two Canadian fanzines.

As I said, the amateur press field is a lively one—and just as active outside the United States. Well, you can't tell the players without a program, and fortunately for the fantasy fan there *is* a program: *Fantasy Newsletter* (which itself publishes an occasional story) is a monthly magazine that keeps fans up to date on all that's happening within the fantasy genre. Subscriptions to *Fantasy Newsletter* are available from Paul C. Allen at P.O. Box 170A, Rochester, New York 14601. For those fans not fortunate enough to live close by a well-stocked science-fiction and fantasy bookstore, two established specialty dealers who issue regular catalogs are Robert Weinberg (15145 Oxford Drive, Oak Forest, Illinois 60452) and J. S. Hurst (P.O. Box 236, Vienna, Maryland 21869).

And so from the year of the anthology we come now to the anthology of the year, *The Year's Best Horror Stories: Series IX*, presenting the best of the best from 1980's bumper crop of horror fiction. The selection is never easy; in addition to everything else it demands a good bit of luck and not a little presumption. In selecting these stories I have tried to read all eligible material from this past year—basing my choices without regard to taboos or to story length, considering each story on its own merits without regard to the renown of the author or the prestige of the original publication. Some of these stories follow traditional guidelines, others reinterpret these patterns or move off to establish new models. My definition of horror fiction is a broad one, without quibbling over the various genres and subgenres. Most of these stories are fantasy, some are not; they all convey a convincing mood of fear.

Because a horror story asks its readers to accept as truth certain facts which the reader knows are contrary to the ordered universe (as he has been led to believe it exists), it is absolutely imperative that the author *convince* the reader of the reality within his story. Catsup isn't blood no matter how liberally it's spattered. Rubber monsters aren't frightening no matter how many fangs and tentacles. Cardboard sets and wooden characters don't scare us for all the cobwebs and screams. If you don't believe it, you aren't frightened.

These authors have brought all their considerable talents to bear for the purpose of convincing you, of frightening you. And they *will* frighten you. Believe me.

THE MONKEY
Stephen King

One of the bright spots for horror fans during the 1960's was a series of shoddily produced magazines edited by Robert A. W. Lowndes for something called Health Knowledge, Inc. Longest running of their several titles were *Magazine of Horror* and *Startling Mystery Stories;* for the most part they reprinted otherwise inaccessible stories from sources such as *Weird Tales* and *Strange Tales*—with an occasional original story, usually unreadable, by someone you'd never heard of. Ramsey Campbell, already with one book to his credit, was one of these obscure writers, and another was Stephen King, who sold his first two stories here (for a combined total of $65).

Born September 21, 1946, in Portland, Maine, King started writing at age twelve. Success was not instantaneous. After graduating from college, he worked in a laundromat for $60 a week before landing a $6400 a year high school teaching job. His first few novels earned only rejection slips, but in the men's magazines, particularly *Cavalier*, King found a ready market for short horror fiction, and he decided to try his luck with the popular horror novel. Here King fared somewhat better: his first novel, *Carrie*, was published in 1974, followed by *'Salem's Lot, The Shining, Night Shift* (a collection), *The Stand, The Dead Zone,* and *Firestarter*. These have done well enough that King is unlikely to need his job at the laundromat back. "The Monkey" was published as a separate booklet inserted in the November, 1980 issue of *Gallery*—one of the more unusual first editions for collectors to chase after. Since reading it, I've been trying to remember whatever happened to that wind-up toy monkey I had when I was a kid. Trying *hard* to remember. . . .

When Hal Shelburn saw it, when his son Dennis pulled it out of a moldering Ralston-Purina carton that had been pushed far back under one attic eave, such a feeling of horror and dismay rose in him that for one moment he thought he surely must scream. He put one fist to his mouth, as if to cram it back . . . and then merely coughed into his fist. Neither Terry nor Dennis noticed, but Petey looked around, momentarily curious.

"Hey, neat," Dennis said respectfully. It was a tone Hal rarely got from the boy anymore himself. Dennis was twelve.

"What is it?" Petey asked. He glanced at his father again before his eyes were dragged back to the thing his big brother had found. "What is it, Daddy?"

"It's a monkey, fartbrains," Dennis said. "Haven't you ever seen a monkey before?"

"Don't call your brother fartbrains," Terry said automatically, and began to examine a box of curtains. The curtains were slimy with mildew and she dropped them quickly. "Uck."

"Can I have it, Daddy?" Petey asked. He was nine.

"What do you mean?" Dennis cried. "*I* found it!"

"Boys, please," Terry said. "I'm getting a headache."

Hal barely heard them—any of them. The monkey glimmered up at him from his older son's hands, grinning its old familiar grin. The same grin that had haunted his nightmares as a child, haunted them until he had—

Outside a cold gust of wind rose, and for a moment lips with no flesh blew a long note through the old, rusty gutter outside. Petey stepped closer to his father, eyes moving uneasily to the rough attic roof through which nailheads poked.

"What was that, Daddy?" he asked as the whistle died to a guttural buzz.

"Just the wind," Hal said, still looking at the monkey. Its cymbals, crescents of brass rather than full circles in the weak light of the one naked bulb, were moveless, perhaps a foot apart, and he added automatically, "Wind can whistle, but it can't carry a tune." Then he realized that was a saying of his Uncle Will's, and a goose ran over his grave.

The long note came again, the wind coming off Crystal Lake in a long, droning swoop and then wavering in the gutter. Half a dozen small drafts puffed cold October air into Hal's face—God, this place was so much like the back closet of the house in Hartford that they might all have been transported thirty years back in time.

I won't think about that.

But the thought wouldn't be denied.

In the back closet where I found that goddammed monkey in that same box.

Terry had moved away to examine a wooden crate filled with knickknacks, duck-walking because the pitch of the eave was so sharp.

"I don't like it," Petey said, and felt for Hal's hand. "Dennis c'n have it if he wants. Can we go, Daddy?"

"Worried about ghosts, chickenguts?" Dennis inquired.

"Dennis, you stop it," Terry said absently. She picked up a wafer-thin cup with a Chinese pattern. "This is nice. This—"

Hal saw that Dennis had found the wind-up key in the monkey's back. Terror flew through him on dark wings.

"Don't do that!"

It came out more sharply than he had intended, and he had snatched the monkey out of Dennis's hands before he was really aware he had done it. Dennis looked around at him, startled. Terry had also glanced back over her shoulder, and Petey looked up. For a moment they were all silent, and the wind whistled again, very low this time, like an unpleasant invitation.

"I mean, it's probably broken," Hal said.

It used to be broken . . . except when it wanted to be fixed.

"Well, you didn't have to *grab*," Dennis said.

"Dennis, shut up."

Dennis blinked at him and for a moment looked almost uneasy. Hal hadn't spoken to him so sharply in a long time. Not since he had lost his job with National Aerodyne in California two years before and they had moved to Texas. Dennis decided not to push it . . . for now. He turned back to the Ralston-Purina carton and began to root through it again, but the other stuff was nothing but shit. Broken toys bleeding springs and stuffings.

The wind was louder now, hooting instead of whistling. The attic began to creak softly, making a noise like footsteps.

"Please, Daddy?" Petey asked, only loud enough for his father to hear.

"Yeah," he said. "Terry, let's go."

"I'm not through with this—"

"I said let's *go*."

It was her turn to look startled.

They had taken two adjoining rooms in a motel. By ten that night the boys were asleep in their room and Terry was asleep in the adults' room. She had taken two Valium on the ride back from the home place in Casco. To keep her nerves from giving her a migraine. Just lately she took a lot of Valium. It had started around the time National Aerodyne had laid Hal off. For the last two years he had been working for Texas Instruments—it was $4,000 less a year, but it was work. He told Terry they were lucky. She agreed. There were plenty of software architects drawing unemployment, he said. She agreed. The company housing in Arnette was every bit as good as the place in Fresno, he said. She agreed, but he thought her agreement was a lie.

And he had been losing Dennis. He could feel the kid going, achieving a premature escape velocity, so long, Dennis, bye-bye stranger, it was nice sharing this train with you. Terry said she thought the boy was smoking reefer. She smelled it sometimes. You have to talk to him, Hal. And *he* agreed, but so far he had not.

The boys were asleep. Terry was asleep. Hal went into the bathroom and locked the door and sat down on the closed lid of the john and looked at the monkey.

He hated the way it felt, that soft brown nappy fur, worn bald in spots. He hated its grin—*that monkey grin just like a nigger*, Uncle Will had said once, but it didn't grin like a nigger, or like anything human. Its grin was all teeth, and if you wound up the key, the lips would move, the teeth would seem to get bigger, to become vampire teeth, the lips would writhe and the cymbals would bang, stupid monkey, stupid clockwork monkey, stupid, stupid—

He dropped it. His hands were shaking and he dropped it.

The key clicked on the bathroom tiles as it struck the floor. The sound seemed very loud in the stillness. It grinned at him

THE MONKEY

with its murky amber eyes, doll's eyes, filled with idiot glee, its brass cymbals poised as if to strike up a march for some black band from hell, and on the bottom the words MADE IN HONG KONG were stamped.

"You can't be here," he whispered. "I threw you down the well when I was nine."

The monkey grinned up at him.

Hal Shelburn shuddered.

Outside in the night, a black capful of wind shook the motel.

Hal's brother Bill and Bill's wife Collette met them at Uncle Will's and Aunt Ida's the next day. "Did it ever cross your mind that a death in the family is a really lousy way to renew the family connection?" Bill asked him with a bit of a grin. He had been named for Uncle Will. Will and Bill, champions of the rodayo, Uncle Will used to say, and ruffle Bill's hair. It was one of his sayings . . . like the wind can whistle but it can't carry a tune. Uncle Will had died six years before, and Aunt Ida had lived on here alone, until a stroke had taken her just the previous week. Very sudden, Bill had said when he called long distance to give Hal the news. As if he could know; as if anyone could know. She had died alone.

"Yeah," Hal said. "The thought crossed my mind."

They looked at the place together, the home place where they had finished growing up. Their father, a merchant mariner, had simply disappeared as if from the very face of the earth when they were young; Bill claimed to remember him vaguely, but Hal had no memories of him at all. Their mother had died when Bill was ten and Hal eight. They had come to Uncle Will's and Aunt Ida's from Hartford, and they had been raised here, and gone to college here. Bill had stayed and now had a healthy law practice in Portland.

Hal saw that Petey had wandered off toward the blackberry tangles that lay on the eastern side of the house in a mad jumble. "Stay away from there, Petey," he called.

Petey looked back, questioning. Hal felt simple love for the boy rush him . . . and he suddenly thought of the monkey again.

"Why, Dad?"

"The old well's in there someplace," Bill said. "But I'll be damned if I remember just where. Your dad's right, Petey—those blackberry tangles are a good place to stay away from. Thorns'll do a job on you. Right, Hal?"

"Right," Hal said automatically. Pete moved away, not looking back, and then started down the embankment toward the small shingle of beach where Dennis was skipping stones over the water. Hal felt something in his chest loosen a little.

Bill might have forgotten where the old well had been, but late that afternoon Hal went to it unerringly, shouldering his way through the brambles that tore at his old flannel jacket and hunted for his eyes. He reached it and stood there, breathing hard, looking at the rotted, warped boards that covered it. After a moment's debate, he knelt (his knees fired twin pistol shots) and moved two of the boards aside.

From the bottom of that wet, rock-lined throat a face stared up at him, wide eyes, grimacing mouth, and a moan escaped him. It was not loud, except in his heart. There it had been very loud.

It was his own face, reflected up from dark water.

Not the monkey's. For a moment he had thought it was the monkey's.

He was shaking. Shaking all over.

I threw it down the well. I threw it down the well, please God don't let me be crazy, I threw it down the well.

The well had gone dry the summer Johnny McCabe died, the year after Bill and Hal came to stay at the home place with Uncle Will and Aunt Ida. Uncle Will had borrowed money from the bank to have an artesian well sunk, and the blackberry tangles had grown up around the old dug well. The dry well.

Except the water had come back. Like the monkey.

This time the memory would not be denied. Hal sat there helplessly, letting it come, trying to go with it, to ride it like a surfer riding a monster wave that will crush him if he falls off his board, just trying to get through it so it would be gone again.

He had crept out here with the monkey late that summer, and the blackberries had been out, the smell of them thick and cloying. No one came in here to pick, although Aunt Ida would sometimes stand at the edge of the tangles and pick a cupful of berries into her apron. In here the blackberries had gone past ripe to overripe, some of them were rotting, sweating a thick white fluid like pus, and the crickets sang maddeningly in the high grass underfoot, their endless cry: *Reeeeeee—*

The thorns tore at him, brought dots of blood onto his bare arms. He made no effort to avoid their sting. He had been blind with terror—so blind that he had come within inches of stumbling onto the boards that covered the well, perhaps within inches of crashing thirty feet to the well's muddy bottom. He had pinwheeled his arms for balance, and more thorns had branded his forearms. It was that memory that had caused him to call Petey back sharply.

That was the day Johnny McCabe had died—his best friend. Johnny had been climbing the rungs up to his treehouse in his back yard. The two of them had spent many hours up there that summer, playing pirate, seeing make-believe galleons out on the lake, unlimbering the cannons, preparing to board. Johnny had been climbing up to the treehouse as he had done a thousand times before, and the rung just below the trap door in the bottom of the treehouse had snapped off in his hands and Johnny had fallen thirty feet to the ground and had broken his neck and it was the monkey's fault, the monkey, the goddam hateful monkey. When the phone rang, when Aunt Ida's mouth dropped open and then formed an O of horror as her friend Milly from down the road told her the news, when Aunt Ida said, "Come out on the porch, Hal, I have to tell you some bad news—," he had thought with sick horror, *The monkey! What's the monkey done now?*

There had been no reflection of his face trapped at the bottom of the well that day, only the stone cobbles going down into the darkness and the smell of wet mud. He had looked at the monkey lying there on the wiry grass that grew between the blackberry tangles, its cymbals poised, its grinning teeth huge between its splayed lips, its fur, rubbed away in balding, mangy patches here and there, its glazed eyes.

"I hate you," he had hissed at it. He wrapped his hand around its loathsome body, feeling the nappy fur crinkle. It grinned at him as he held it up in front of his face. "Go on!" he dared it, beginning to cry for the first time that day. He shook it. The poised cymbals trembled minutely. It spoiled everything good. Everything. "Go on, clap them! Clap them!"

The monkey only grinned.

"Go on and clap them!" His voice rose hysterically. "Fraidy-cat, fraidy-cat, go on and clap them! I dare you!"

Its brownish-yellow eyes. Its huge and gleeful teeth.

He threw it down the well then, mad with grief and terror. He saw it turn over once on its way down, a simian acrobat doing a trick, and the sun glinted one last time on those cymbals. It struck the bottom with a thud, and that must have jogged its clockwork, for suddenly the cymbals *did* begin to beat. Their steady, deliberate, and tinny banging rose to his ears, echoing and fey in the stone throat of the dead well: *jang-jang-jang-jang*—

Hal clapped his hands over his mouth, and for a moment he could see it down there, perhaps only in the eye of imagination . . . lying there in the mud, eyes glaring up at the small circle of his boy's face peering over the lip of the well (as if marking its shape forever), lips expanding and contracting around those grinning teeth, cymbals clapping, funny wind-up monkey.

Jang-jang-jang-jang, who's dead? *Jang-jang-jang-jang*, is it Johnny McCabe, falling with his eyes wide, doing his own acrobatic somersault as he falls through the bright summer vacation air with the splintered rung still held in his hands to strike the ground with a single bitter snapping sound? Is it Johnny, Hal? Or is it you?

Moaning, Hal had shoved the boards across the hole, getting splinters in his hands, not caring, not even aware of them until later. And still he could hear it, even through the boards, muffled now and somehow all the worse for that: it was down there in stone-faced dark, clapping its cymbals and jerking its repulsive body, the sounding coming up like the sound of a prematurely buried man scrabbling for a way out.

Jang-jang-jang-jang, who's dead this time?

He fought and battered his way back through the blackberry creepers. Thorns stitched fresh lines of welling blood briskly across his face and burdocks caught in the cuffs of his jeans, and he fell full-length once, his ears still jangling, as if it had followed him. Uncle Will found him later, sitting on an old tire in the garage and sobbing, and he had thought

Hal was crying for his dead friend. So he had been; but he had also cried in the aftermath of terror.

He had thrown the monkey down the well in the afternoon. That evening, as twilight crept in through a shimmering mantle of ground-fog, a car moving too fast for the reduced visibility had run down Aunt Ida's manx cat in the road and gone right on. There had been guts everywhere, Bill had thrown up, but Hal had only turned his face away, his pale, still face, hearing Aunt Ida's sobbing (this on top of the news about the McCabe boy had caused a fit of weeping that was almost hysterics, and it was almost two hours before Uncle Will could calm her completely) as if from miles away. In his heart there was a cold and exultant joy. It hadn't been his turn. It had been Aunt Ida's manx, not him, not his brother Bill or his Uncle Will (just two champions of the rodayo). And now the monkey was gone, it was down the well, and one scruffy manx cat with ear mites was not too great a price to pay. If the monkey wanted to clap its hellish cymbals now, let it. It could clap and clash them for the crawling bugs and beetles, the dark things that made their home in the well's stone gullet. It would rot down there in the darkness and its loathsome cogs and wheels and springs would rust in darkness. It would die down there. In the mud and the darkness. Spiders would spin it a shroud.

But . . . it had come back.

Slowly, Hal covered the well again, as he had on that day, and in his ears he heard the phantom echo of the monkey's cymbals: *Jang-jang-jang-jang, who's dead, Hal? Is it Terry? Dennis? Is it Petey, Hal? He's your favorite, isn't he? Is it him? Jang-jang-jang—*

"Put that *down!*"

Petey flinched and dropped the monkey, and for one nightmare moment Hal thought that would do it, that the jolt would jog its machinery and the cymbals would begin to beat and clash.

"Daddy, you scared me."

"I'm sorry. I just . . . I don't want you to play with that."

The others had gone to see a movie, and he had thought he would beat them back to the motel. But he had stayed at the home place longer than he would have guessed; the old, hateful memories seemed to move in their own eternal time zone.

Terry was sitting near Dennis, watching "The Beverly Hillbillies." She watched the old, grainy print with a steady, bemused concentration that spoke of a recent Valium pop. Dennis was reading a rock magazine with the group Styx on the cover. Petey had been sitting cross-legged on the carpet, goofing with the monkey.

"It doesn't work anyway," Petey said. *Which explains why Dennis let him have it,* Hal thought, and then felt ashamed and angry at himself. He seemed to have no control over the hostility he felt toward Dennis more and more often, but in the aftermath he felt demeaned and tacky . . . helpless.

"No," he said. "It's old. I'm going to throw it away. Give it to me."

He held out his hand and Petey, looking troubled, handed it over.

Dennis said to his mother, "Pop's turning into a friggin schizophrenic."

Hal was across the room even before he knew he was going, the monkey in one hand, grinning as if in approbation. He hauled Dennis out of his chair by the shirt. There was a purring sound as a seam came adrift somewhere. Dennis looked almost comically shocked. His copy of *Tiger Beat* fell to the floor.

"Hey!"

"You come with me," Hal said grimly, pulling his son toward the door to the connecting room.

"Hal!" Terry nearly screamed. Petey just goggled.

Hal pulled Dennis through. He slammed the door and then slammed Dennis against the door. Dennis was starting to look scared. "You're getting a mouth problem," Hal said.

"Let *go* of me! You tore my shirt, you—"

Hal slammed the boy against the door again. "Yes," he said. "A real mouth problem. Did you learn that in school? Or back in the smoking area?"

Dennis flushed, his face momentarily ugly with guilt. "I wouldn't be in that shitty school if you didn't get canned!" he burst out.

Hal slammed Dennis against the door again. "I didn't get canned, I got laid off, you know it, and I don't need any of your shit about it. You have problems? Welcome to the world, Dennis. Just don't you lay off all your problems on me. You're eating. Your ass is covered. At eleven, I don't

... need any ... shit from you." He punctuated each phrase by pulling the boy forward until their noses were almost touching and then slamming him back into the door. It was not hard enough to hurt, but Dennis was scared—his father had not laid a hand on him since they moved to Texas—and now he began to cry with a young boy's loud, braying, healthy sobs.

"Go ahead, beat me up!" he yelled at Hal, his face twisted and blotchy. "Beat me up if you want, I know how much you fucking hate me!"

"I don't hate you. I love you a lot, Dennis. But I'm your dad and you're going to show me respect or I'm going to bust you for it."

Dennis tried to pull away. Hal pulled the boy to him and hugged him. Dennis fought for a moment and then put his face against Hal's chest and wept as if exhausted. It was the sort of cry Hal hadn't heard from either of his children in years. He closed his eyes, realizing that he felt exhausted himself.

Terry began to hammer on the other side of the door. "Stop it, Hal! Whatever you're doing to him, stop it!"

"I'm not killing him," Hal said. "Go away, Terry."

"Don't you—"

"It's all right, Mom," Dennis said, muffled against Hal's chest.

He could feel her perplexed silence for a moment, and then she went. Hal looked at his son again.

"I'm sorry I badmouthed you, Dad," Dennis said reluctantly.

"When we get home next week, I'm going to wait two or three days and then I'm going to go through all your drawers, Dennis. If there's something in them you don't want me to see, you better get rid of it."

That flash of guilt again. Dennis lowered his eyes and wiped away snot with the back of his hand.

"Can I go now?" He sounded sullen once more.

"Sure," Hal said, and let him go. *Got to take him camping in the spring, just the two of us. Do some fishing, like Uncle Will used to do with Bill and me. Got to get close to him. Got to try.*

He sat down on the bed in the empty room and looked at

the monkey. *You'll never be close to him again, Hal,* its grin seemed to say. *Never again. Never again.*

Just looking at the monkey made him feel tired. He laid it aside and put a hand over his eyes.

That night Hal stood in the bathroom, brushing his teeth, and thought: *It was in the same box. How could it be in the same box?*

The toothbrush jabbed upward, hurting his gums. He winced.

He had been four, Bill, six, the first time he saw the monkey. Their missing father had bought a house in Hartford, and it had been theirs, free and clear, before he died or disappeared or whatever it had been. Their mother worked as a secretary at Holmes Aircraft, the helicopter plant out in Westville, and a series of sitters came in to stay with the boys, except by then it was just Hal that the sitters had to mind through the day—Bill was in first grade, big school. None of the babysitters stayed for long. They got pregnant and married their boyfriends or got work at Holmes, or Mrs. Shelburn would discover they had been at the cooking sherry or her bottle of brandy which was kept in the sideboard for special occasions. Most of them were stupid girls who seemed only to want to eat or sleep. None of them wanted to read to Hal as his mother would do.

The sitter that long winter was a huge, sleek black girl named Beulah. She fawned over Hal when Hal's mother was around and sometimes pinched him when she wasn't. Still, Hal had some liking for Beulah, who once in awhile would read him a lurid tale from one of her confession or true-detective magazines ("Death Came for the Voluptuous Redhead," Beulah would intone ominously in the dozey daytime silence of the living room, and pop another Reese's Peanut Butter Cup into her mouth while Hal solemnly studied the grainy tabloid pictures and drank his milk from his Wish-Cup). And the liking made what happened worse.

He found the monkey on a cold, cloudy day in March. Sleet ticked sporadically off the windows, and Beulah was asleep on the couch, a copy of *My Story* tented open on her admirable bosom.

So Hal went into the back closet to look at his father's things.

THE MONKEY 27

The back closet was a storage space that ran the length of the second floor on the left side, extra space that had never been finished off. One got into the back closet by using a small door—a down-the-rabbit-hole sort of door—on Bill's side of the boys' bedroom. They both liked to go in there, even though it was chilly in winter and hot enough in summer to wring a bucketful of sweat out of your pores. Long and narrow and somehow snug, the back closet was full of fascinating junk. No matter how much stuff you looked at, you never seemed to be able to look at it all. He and Bill had spent whole Saturday afternoons up here, barely speaking to each other, taking things out of boxes, examining them, turning them over and over so their hands could absorb each unique reality, putting them back. Now Hal wondered if he and Bill hadn't been trying, as best they could, to somehow make contact with their vanished father.

He had been a merchant mariner with a navigator's certificate, and there were stacks of charts back there, some marked with neat circles (and the dimple of the compass' swing-point in the center of each). There were twenty volumes of something called *Barron's Guide to Navigation*. A set of cockeyed binoculars that made your eyes feel hot and funny if you looked through them too long. There were touristy things from a dozen ports of call—rubber hula-hula dolls, a black cardboard bowler with a torn band that said YOU PICK A GIRL AND I'LL PICKADILLY, a glass globe with a tiny Eiffel Tower inside—and there were also envelopes with foreign stamps tucked carefully away inside, and foreign coins; there were rock samples from the Hawaiian island of Maui, a glassy black—heavy and somehow ominous, and funny records in foreign languages.

That day, with the sleet ticking hypnotically off the roof just above his head, Hal worked his way all the way down to the far end of the back closet, moved a box aside, and saw another box behind it—a Ralston-Purina box. Looking over the top was a pair of glassy hazel eyes. They gave him a start and he skittered back for a moment, heart thumping, as if he had discovered a deadly pygmy. Then he saw its silence, the glaze in those eyes, and realized it was some sort of toy. He moved forward again and lifted it carefully from the box.

It grinned its ageless, toothy grin in the yellow light, its cymbals held apart.

Delighted, Hal had turned it this way and that, feeling the crinkle of its nappy fur. Its funny grin pleased him. Yet hadn't there been something else? An almost instinctive feeling of disgust that had come and gone almost before he was aware of it? Perhaps it was so, but with an old, old memory like this one, you had to be careful not to believe too much. Old memories could lie. But . . . hadn't he seen that same expression on Petey's face, in the attic of the home place?

He had seen the key set into the small of its back, and turned it. It had turned far too easily; there were no winding-up clicks. Broken, then. Broken, but still neat.

He took it out to play with it.

"Whatchoo got, Hal?" Beulah asked, waking from her nap.

"Nothing," Hal said. "I found it."

He put it up on the shelf on his side of the bedroom. It stood atop his Lassie coloring books, grinning, staring into space, cymbals poised. It was broken, but it grinned nonetheless. That night Hal awakened from some uneasy dream, bladder full, and got up to use the bathroom in the hall. Bill was a breathing lump of covers across the room.

Hal came back, almost asleep again . . . and suddenly the monkey began to beat its cymbals together in the darkness.

Jang-jang-jang-jang—

He came fully awake, as if snapped in the face with a cold, wet towel. His heart gave a staggering leap of surprise, and a tiny, mouselike squeak escaped his throat. He stared at the monkey, eyes wide, lip trembling.

Jang-jang-jang-jang—

Its body rocked and humped on the shelf. Its lips spread and closed, spread and closed, hideously gleeful, revealing huge and carnivorous teeth.

"Stop," Hal whispered.

His brother turned over and uttered a loud, single snore. All else was silent . . . except for the monkey. The cymbals clapped and clashed, and surely it would wake his brother, his mother, the world. It would wake the dead.

Jang-jang-jang-jang—

Hal moved toward it, meaning to stop it somehow, perhaps put his hand between its cymbals until it ran down (*but it was broken, wasn't it?*), and then it stopped on its own. The cymbals came together one last time—*Jang!*—and then

THE MONKEY

spread slowly apart to their original position. The brass glimmered in the shadows. The monkey's dirty yellowish teeth grinned their improbable grin.

The house was silent again. His mother turned over in her bed and echoed Bill's single snore. Hal got back into his bed and pulled the covers up, his heart still beating fast, and he thought: *I'll put it back in the closet again tomorrow. I don't want it.*

But the next morning he forgot all about putting the monkey back because his mother didn't go to work. Beulah was dead. Their mother wouldn't tell them exactly what happened. "It was an accident, just a terrible accident" was all she would say. But that afternoon Bill bought a newspaper on his way home from school and smuggled page four up to their room under his shirt (TWO KILLED IN APARTMENT SHOOT-OUT, the headline read) and read the article haltingly to Hal, following along with his finger, while their mother cooked supper in the kitchen. Beulah McCaffery, 19, and Sally Tremont, 20, had been shot by Miss McCaffery's boyfriend, Leonard White, 25, following an argument over who was to go out and pick up an order of Chinese food. Miss Tremont had expired at Hartford Receiving; Beulah McCaffery had been pronounced dead at the scene.

It was like Beulah just disappeared into one of her own detective magazines, Hal Shelburn thought, and felt a cold chill race up his spine and then circle his heart. And then he realized the shootings had occurred about the same time the monkey—

"Hal?" It was Terry's voice, sleepy. "Coming to bed?"

He spat toothpaste into the sink and rinsed his mouth. "Yes," he said.

He had put the monkey in his suitcase earlier, and locked it up. They were flying back to Texas in two or three days. But before they went, he would get rid of the damned thing for good.

Somehow.

"You were pretty rough on Dennis this afternoon," Terry said in the dark.

"Dennis has needed somebody to start being rough on him

for quite a while now, I think. He's been drifting. I just don't want him to start falling."

"Psychologically, beating the boy isn't a very productive—"

"I didn't *beat* him, Terry—for Christ's sake!"

"—way to assert parental authority—"

"Oh, don't give me any of that encounter-group shit," Hal said angrily.

"I can see you don't want to discuss this." Her voice was cold.

"I told him to get the dope out of the house, too."

"You did?" Now she sounded apprehensive. "How did he take it? What did he say?"

"Come on, Terry! What *could* he say? 'You're fired'?"

"Hal, what's the *matter* with you? You're not like this—what's *wrong*?"

"Nothing," he said, thinking of the monkey locked away in his Samsonite. Would he hear it if it began to clap its cymbals? Yes, he surely would. Muffled, but audible. Clapping doom for someone, as it had for Beulah, Johnny McCabe, Uncle Will's dog Daisy. *Jang-jang-jang*, is it you, Hal? "I've just been under a strain."

"I *hope* that's all it is. Because I don't like you this way."

"No?" And the words escaped before he could stop them; he didn't even want to stop them. "So pop a few Valium and everything will look okay again, right?"

He heard her draw breath in and let it out shakily. She began to cry then. He could have comforted her (maybe), but there seemed to be no comfort in him. There was too much terror. It would be better when the monkey was gone again, gone for good. Please God, gone for good.

He lay wakeful until very late, until morning began to gray the air outside. But he thought he knew what to do.

Bill had found the monkey the second time.

That was about a year and a half after Beulah McCaffery had been pronounced dead at the scene. It was summer. Hal had just finished kindergarten.

He came in from playing with Stevie Arlingen and his mother called, "Wash your hands, Hal, you're filthy like a pig." She was on the porch, drinking an iced tea and reading a book. It was her vacation; she had two weeks.

Hal gave his hands a token pass under cold water and printed dirt on the hand towel. "Where's Bill?"

"Upstairs. You tell him to clean his side of the room. It's a mess."

Hal, who enjoyed being the messenger of unpleasant news in such matters, rushed up. Bill was sitting on the floor. The small down-the-rabbit-hole door leading to the back closet was ajar. He had the monkey in his hands.

"That don't work," Hal said immediately. "It's busted."

He was apprehensive, although he barely remembered coming back from the bathroom that night, and the monkey suddenly beginning to clap its cymbals. A week or so after that, he had had a bad dream about the monkey and Beulah—he couldn't remember exactly what— and had awakened screaming, thinking for a moment that the soft weight on his chest was the monkey, that he would open his eyes and see it grinning down at him. But of course the soft weight had only been his pillow, clutched with panicky tightness. His mother came in to soothe him with a drink of water and two chalky-orange baby aspirins, those Valium for childhood's troubled times. She thought it was the fact of Beulah's death that had caused the nightmare. So it was, but not in the way she thought.

He barely remembered any of this now, but the monkey still scared him, particularly its cymbals. And its teeth.

"I know that," Bill said, and tossed the monkey aside. "It's stupid." It landed on Bill's bed, staring up at the ceiling, cymbals poised. Hal did not like to see it there. "You want to go down to Teddy's and get Popsicles?"

"I spent my allowance already," Hal said. "Besides, Mom says you got to clean up your side of the room."

"I can do that later," Bill said. "And I'll loan you a nickel, if you want." Bill was not above giving Hal an Indian rope burn sometimes, and would occasionally trip him up or punch him for no particular reason, but mostly he was okay.

"Sure," Hal said gratefully. "I'll just put that busted monkey back in the closet first, okay?"

"Nah," Bill said, getting up. "Let's go-go-go."

Hal went. Bill's moods were changeable, and if he paused to put the monkey away, he might lose his Popsicle. They went down to Teddy's and got them, then down to the Rec where some kids were getting up a baseball game. Hal was too small to play, but he sat far out in foul territory, sucking his root beer Popsicle and chasing what the big kids called "Chinese home runs." They didn't get home until almost dark, and their mother whacked Hal for getting the hand towel dirty and whacked Bill for not cleaning up his side of the room, and after supper there was TV, and by the time all of that had happened, Hal had forgotten all about the monkey. It somehow found its way up onto *Bill's* shelf, where it stood right next to Bill's autographed picture of Bill Boyd. And there it stayed for nearly two years.

By the time Hal was seven, babysitters had become an extravagance, and Mrs. Shelburn's last word to the two of them each morning was, "Bill, look after your brother."

That day, however, Bill had to stay after school for a Safety Patrol Boy meeting and Hal came home alone, stopping at each corner until he could see absolutely no traffic coming in either direction and then skittering across, shoulders hunched, like a doughboy crossing no man's land. He let himself into the house with the key under the mat and went immediately to the refrigerator for a glass of milk. He got the bottle, and then it slipped through his fingers and crashed to smithereens on the floor, the pieces of glass flying everywhere, as the monkey suddenly began to beat its cymbals together upstairs.

Jang-jang-jang-jang, on and on.

He stood there immobile, looking down at the broken glass and the puddle of milk, full of a terror he could not name or understand. It was simply there, seeming to ooze from his pores.

He turned and rushed upstairs to their room. The monkey stood on Bill's shelf, seeming to stare at him. He had knocked the autographed picture of Bill Boyd face-down onto Bill's bed. The monkey rocked and grinned and beat its cymbals together. Hal approached it slowly, not wanting to, not able to stay away. Its cymbals jerked apart and crashed together and jerked apart again. As he got closer, he could hear the clockwork running in the monkey's guts.

Abruptly, uttering a cry of revulsion and terror, he swatted it from the shelf as one might swat a large, loathsome bug. It struck Bill's pillow and then fell on the floor, cymbals still beating together, *jang-jang-jang,* lips flexing and closing as it lay there on its back in a patch of late April sunshine.

Then, suddenly, he remembered Beulah. The monkey had clapped its cymbals that night, too.

Hal kicked it with one Buster Brown shoe, kicked it as hard as he could, and this time the cry that escaped him was one of fury. The clockwork monkey skittered across the floor, bounced off the wall, and lay still. Hal stood staring at it, fists bunched, heart pounding. It grinned saucily back at him, the sun a burning pinpoint in one glass eye. *Kick me all you want*, it seemed to tell him. *I'm nothing but cogs and clockwork and a worm-gear or two, kick me all you feel like, I'm not real, just a funny clockwork monkey is all I am, and who's dead? There's been an explosion at the helicopter plant! What's that rising up into the sky like a big bloody bowling ball with eyes where the finger-holes should be? Is it your mother's head, Hal? Down at Brook Street Corner! The car was going too fast! The driver was drunk! There's one Patrol Boy less! Could you hear the crunching sound when the wheels ran over Bill's skull and his brains squirted out of his ears? Yes? No? Maybe? Don't ask me, I don't know, I can't know, all I know how to do is beat these cymbals together jang-jang-jang, and who's dead, Hal? Your mother? Your brother? Or is it you, Hal? Is it you?*

He rushed at it again, meaning to stomp on it, smash its loathsome body, jump on it until cogs and gears flew and its horrible glass eyes rolled across the floor. But just as he reached it, its cymbals came together once more, very softly ... *(jang)* ... as a spring somewhere inside expanded one final, minute notch ... and a sliver of ice seemed to whisper its way through the walls of his heart, impaling it, stilling its fury and leaving him sick with terror again. The monkey almost seemed to know—how gleeful its grin seemed!

He picked it up, tweezing one of its arms between the thumb and first finger of his right hand, mouth drawn down in a bow of loathing, as if it were a corpse he held. Its mangy fake fur seemed hot and fevered against his skin. He fumbled open the tiny door that led to the back closet and turned on the bulb. The monkey grinned at him as he crawled down the length of the storage area between boxes piled on top of boxes, past the set of navigation books and the photograph albums with their fume of old chemicals and the souvenirs and the old clothes, and Hal thought: *If it begins to clap its cymbals together now and move in my hand, I'll scream, and if I scream, it'll do more than grin, it'll start to laugh, to laugh at me, and then I'll go crazy and they'll find me in here, drooling and laughing, crazy, I'll be crazy, oh please dear God, please dear Jesus, don't let me go crazy—*

He reached the far end and clawed two boxes aside, spilling one of them, and jammed the monkey back into the Ralston-Purina box in the farthest corner. And it leaned in there, comfortably, as if home at last, cymbals poised, grinning its simian grin, as if the joke were still on Hal. Hal crawled backward, sweating, hot and cold, all fire and ice, waiting for the cymbals to begin, and when they began, the monkey would leap from its box and scurry beetlelike toward him, clockwork whirring, cymbals clashing madly, and—

—and none of that happened. He turned off the light and slammed the small down-the-rabbit-hole door and leaned on it, panting. At last he began to feel a little better. He went downstairs on rubbery legs, got an empty bag, and began carefully to pick up the jagged shards and splinters of the broken milk bottle, wondering if he was going to cut himself and bleed to death, if that was what the clapping cymbals had meant. But that didn't happen, either. He got a towel and wiped up the milk and then sat down to see if his mother and brother would come home.

His mother came first, asking, "Where's Bill?"

In a low, colorless voice, now sure that Bill must be dead, Hal started to explain about the Patrol Boy meeting, knowing that, even given a very long meeting, Bill should have been home half an hour ago.

His mother looked at him curiously, started to ask what was wrong, and then the door opened and Bill came in—only it was not Bill at all, not really. This was a ghost-Bill, pale and silent.

"What's wrong?" Mrs. Shelburn exclaimed. "Bill, what's wrong?"

Bill began to cry and they got the story through his tears. There had been a car, he said. He and his friend Charlie Silverman were walking home together after the meeting and the car came around Brook Street corner too fast and Charlie had frozen, Bill had tugged Charlie's hand once but had lost his grip and the car—

Bill began to bray out loud, hysterical sobs, and his mother hugged him to her, rocking him, and Hal looked out on the porch and saw two policemen standing there. The squad car in which they had conveyed Bill home was at the curb. Then he began to cry himself . . . but his tears were tears of relief.

It was Bill's turn to have nightmares now—dreams in which Charlie Silverman died over and over again, knocked out of his Red Ryder cowboy boots, and flipped onto the hood of the old Hudson Hornet the drunk had been driving. Charlie Silverman's head and the Hudson's windshield had met with an explosive noise, and both had shattered. The drunk driver, who owned a candy store in Milford, suffered a heart attack shortly after being taken into custody (perhaps it was the sight of Charlie Silverman's brains drying on his pants), and his lawyer was quite successful at the trial with his "this man has been punished enough" theme. The drunk was given sixty days (suspended) and lost his privilege to operate a motor vehicle in the state of Connecticut for five years . . . which was about as long as Bill Shelburn's nightmares lasted. The monkey was hidden away again in the back closet. Bill never noticed it was gone from his shelf . . . or if he did, he never said.

Hal felt safe for a while. He began to forget about the monkey again, or to believe it had only been a bad dream. But when he came home from school on the afternoon his mother died, it was back on his shelf, cymbals poised, grinning down at him.

He approached it slowly, as if from outside himself—as if his own body had been turned into a wind-up toy at the sight of the monkey. He saw his hand reach out and take it down. He felt the nappy fur crinkle under his hand, but the feeling was muffled; mere pressure, as if someone had shot him full of Novocaine. He could hear his breathing, quick and dry, like the rattle of wind through straw.

He turned it over and grasped the key and years later he would think that his drugged fascination was like that of a man who puts a six-shooter with one loaded chamber against a closed and jittering eyelid and pulls the trigger.

No don't—let it alone throw it away don't touch it—

He turned the key and in the silence he heard a perfect tiny series of winding-up clicks. When he let the key go, the monkey began to clap its cymbals together and he could feel its body jerking, bend-and-*jerk*, bend-and-*jerk*, as if it were alive, it *was* alive, writhing in his hand like some loathsome pygmy, and the vibration he felt through its balding brown fur was not that of turning cogs but the beating of its black and cindered heart.

With a groan, Hal dropped the monkey and backed away, fingernails digging into the flesh under his eyes, palms pressed to his mouth. He stumbled over something and nearly lost his balance (then he would have been right down on the floor with it, his bulging blue eyes looking into its glassy hazel ones). He scrambled toward the door, backed through it, slammed it, and leaned against it. Suddenly he bolted for the bathroom and vomited.

It was Mrs. Stukey from the helicopter plant who brought the news and stayed with them those first two endless nights, until Aunt Ida got down from Maine. Their mother had died of a brain embolism in the middle of the afternoon. She had been standing at the water cooler with a cup of water in one hand and had crumpled as if shot, still holding the paper cup in one hand. With the other she had clawed at the water cooler and had pulled the great glass bottle of Poland water down with her. It had shattered . . . but the plant doctor, who came on the run, said later that he believed Mrs. Shelburn was dead before the water had soaked through her dress and her underclothes to wet her skin. The boys were never told any of this, but Hal knew anyway. He dreamed it again and again on the long nights following his mother's death. *You still have trouble gettin to sleep, little brother?* Bill had asked him, and Hal supposed Bill thought all the thrashing and bad dreams had to do with their mother dying so suddenly, and that was right . . . but only partly right. There was the guilt: the certain, deadly knowledge that he had killed his mother by winding the monkey up on that sunny after-school afternoon.

When Hal finally fell asleep, his sleep must have been deep. When he awoke, it was nearly noon. Petey was sitting cross-legged in a chair across the room, methodically eating an orange section by section and watching a game show on TV.

Hal swung his legs out of bed, feeling as if someone had punched him down into sleep . . . and then punched him back out of it. His head throbbed. "Where's your mom, Petey?"

Petey glanced around. "She and Dennis went shopping. I said I'd stay with you. Do you always talk in your sleep, Dad?"

Hal looked at his son cautiously. "No, I don't think so. What did I say?"

"It was all muttering, I couldn't make it out. It scared me, a little."

"Well, here I am in my right mind again," Hal said, and managed a small grin. Petey grinned back, and Hal felt simple love for the boy again, an emotion that was bright and strong and uncomplicated. He wondered why he had always been able to feel so good about Petey, to feel he understood Petey and could help him, and why Dennis seemed a window too dark to look through, a mystery in his ways and habits, the sort of boy he could not understand because he had never been that sort of boy. It was too easy to say that the move from California had changed Dennis, or that—

His thoughts froze. The monkey. The monkey was sitting on the windowsill, cymbals poised. Hal felt his heart stop dead in his chest and then suddenly begin to gallop. His vision wavered, and his throbbing head began to ache ferociously.

It had escaped from the suitcase and now stood on the windowsill, grinning at him. *Thought you got rid of me, didn't you? But you've thought that before, haven't you?*

Yes, he thought sickly. Yes, I have.

"Pete, did you take that monkey out of my suitcase?" he asked, knowing the answer already. He had locked the suitcase and had put the key in his overcoat pocket.

Petey glanced at the monkey, and something—Hal thought it was unease—passed over his face. "No," he said. "Mom put it there."

"Mom did?"

"Yeah. She took it from you. She laughed."

"Took it from me? What are you talking about?"

"You had it in bed with you. I was brushing my teeth, but Dennis saw. He laughed, too. He said you looked like a baby with a teddy bear."

Hal looked at the monkey. His mouth was too dry to swallow. He'd had it in *bed* with him? In *bed*? That loathsome fur against his cheek, maybe against his *mouth*, those glass eyes staring into his sleeping face, those grinning teeth near his neck? Dear *God*.

He turned abruptly and went to the closet. The Samsonite was there, still locked. The key was still in his overcoat pocket.

Behind him, the TV snapped off. He came out of the closet slowly. Peter was looking at him soberly. "Daddy, I don't like that monkey," he said, his voice almost too low to hear.

"Nor do I," Hal said.

Petey looked at him closely, to see if he was joking, and saw that he was not. He came to his father and hugged him tight. Hal could feel him trembling.

Petey spoke into his ear, then, very rapidly, as if afraid he might not have courage enough to say it again . . . or that the monkey might overhear.

"It's like it looks at you. Like it looks at you no matter where you are in the room. And if you go into the other room, it's like it's looking through the wall at you. I kept feeling like it . . . like it wanted me for something."

Petey shuddered. Hal held him tight.

"Like it wanted you to wind it up," Hal said.

Pete nodded violently. "It isn't really broken, is it, Dad?"

"Sometimes it is," Hal said, looking over his son's shoulder at the monkey. "But sometimes it still works."

"I kept wanting to go over there and wind it up. It was so quiet, and I thought, I can't, it'll wake up Daddy, but I still wanted to, and I went over and I . . . I *touched* it and I hate the way it feels . . . but I liked it, too . . . and it was like it was saying, Wind me up, Petey, we'll play, your father isn't going to wake up, he's never going to wake up at all, wind me up, wind me up . . ."

The boy suddenly burst into tears.

"It's bad, I know it is. There's something wrong with it. Can't we throw it out, Daddy? Please?"

The monkey grinned its endless grin at Hal. He could feel Petey's tears between them. Late morning sun glinted off the monkey's brass cymbals—the light reflected upward and put sunstreaks on the motel's plain white stucco ceiling.

"What time did your mother think she and Dennis would be back, Petey?"

"Around one." He swiped at his red eyes with his

THE MONKEY

shirtsleeve, looking embarrassed at his tears. But he wouldn't look at the monkey. "I turned on the TV," he whispered. "And I turned it up loud."

"That was all right, Petey."

"I had a crazy idea," Petey said. "I had this idea that if I wound that monkey up, you . . . you would have just died there in bed. In your sleep. Wasn't that a crazy idea, Daddy?" His voice had dropped again, and it trembled helplessly.

How would it have happened? Hal wondered. *Heart attack? An embolism, like my mother? What? It doesn't really matter, does it?*

And on the heels of that, another, colder thought: *Get rid of it, he says. Throw it out. But can it be gotten rid of? Ever?*

The monkey grinned mockingly at him, its cymbals held apart. Did it suddenly come to life on the night Aunt Ida died? he wondered suddenly. Was that the last sound she heard, the muffled *jang-jang-jang* of the monkey beating its cymbals together up in the black attic while the wind whistled along the drainpipe?

"Maybe not so crazy," Hal said slowly to his son. "Go get your flight bag, Petey."

Petey looked at him uncertainly. "What are we going to do?"

Maybe it can be got rid of. Maybe permanently, maybe just for a while . . . a long while or a short while. Maybe it's just going to come back and come back and that's what all this is about . . . but maybe I—we—can say good-bye to it for a long time. It took twenty years to come back this time. It took twenty years to get out of the well . . .

"We're going to go for a ride," Hal said. He felt fairly calm, but somehow too heavy inside his skin. Even his eyeballs seemed to have gained weight. "But first I want you to take your flight bag out there by the edge of the parking lot and find three or four good-sized rocks. Put them inside the bag and bring it back to me. Got it?"

Understanding flickered in Petey's eyes. "All right, Daddy."

Hal glanced at his watch. It was nearly 12:15. "Hurry. I want to be gone before your mother gets back."

"Where are we going?"

"To Uncle Will's and Aunt Ida's," Hal said. "To the home place."

Hal went into the bathroom, looked behind the toilet, and got the bowl brush leaning there. He took it back to the window and stood there with it in his hand like a cut-rate magic wand. He looked out at Petey in his melton shirt-jacket, crossing the parking lot with his flight bag, DELTA showing clearly in white letters against a blue field. A fly bumbled in an upper corner of the window, slow and stupid with the end of the warm season. Hal knew how it felt.

He watched Petey hunt up three good-sized rocks and then start back across the parking lot. A car came around the corner of the motel, a car that was moving too fast, much too fast, and without thinking, reaching with the kind of reflex a good short-stop shows going to his right, his hand flashed down, as if in a karate chop . . . and stopped.

The cymbals closed soundlessly on his intervening hand, and he felt something in the air. Something like rage.

The car's brakes screamed. Petey flinched back. The driver motioned to him impatiently, as if what had almost happened was Petey's fault, and Petey ran across the parking lot with his collar flapping and into the motel's rear entrance.

Sweat was running down Hal's chest; he felt it on his forehead like a drizzle of oily rain. The cymbals pressed coldly against his hand, numbing it.

Go on, he thought grimly. *Go on, I can wait all day. Until hell freezes over, if that's what it takes.*

The cymbals drew apart and came to rest. Hal heard one faint *click!* from inside the monkey. He withdrew his hand and looked at it. On both the back and the palm there were grayish semicircles printed into the skin, as if he had been frostbitten.

The fly bumbled and buzzed, trying to find the cold October sunshine that seemed so close.

Pete came bursting in, breathing quickly, cheeks rosy. "I got three good ones, Dad, I—" He broke off. "Are you all right, Daddy?"

"Fine," Hal said. "Bring the bag over."

Hal hooked the table by the sofa over to the window with his foot, so it stood below the sill, and put the flight bag on it. He spread its mouth open like lips. He could see the stones Petey had collected glimmering inside. He used the toilet-bowl brush to hook the monkey forward. It teetered for a moment and then fell into the bag. There was a faint *jing!* as one of its cymbals struck one of the rocks.

"Dad? Daddy?" Petey sounded frightened. Hal looked around at him. Something was different; something had changed. What was it?

Then he saw the direction of Petey's gaze and he knew. The buzzing of the fly had stopped. It lay dead on the windowsill.

"Did the monkey do that?" Petey whispered.

"Come on," Hal said, zipping the bag shut. "I'll tell you while we ride out to the home place."

"How can we go? Mom and Dennis took the car."

"I'll get us there," Hal said, and ruffled Petey's hair.

He showed the desk clerk his driver's license and a twenty-dollar bill. After taking Hal's Texas Instruments digital watch as further collateral, the clerk handed Hal the keys to his own car—a battered AMC Gremlin. As they drove east on Route 302 toward Casco, Hal began to talk, haltingly at first, then a little faster. He began by telling Petey that his father had probably brought the monkey home with him from overseas, as a gift for his sons. It wasn't a particularly unique toy; there was nothing strange or valuable about it. There must have been hundreds of thousands of wind-up monkeys in the world, some made in Hong Kong, some in Taiwan, some in Korea. But somewhere along the line—perhaps even in the dark back closet of the house in Connecticut where the two boys had begun their growing up—something had happened to the monkey. Something bad, evil. It might be, Hal told Petey as he tried to coax the clerk's Gremlin up past forty (he was very aware of the zipped-up flight bag on the back seat, and Petey kept glancing around at it), that some evil—maybe even most evil—isn't even sentient and aware of what it is. It might be that most evil is very much like a monkey full of clockwork that you wind up; the clockwork turns, the cymbals begin to beat, the teeth grin, the stupid glass eyes laugh . . . or appear to laugh . . .

He told Petey about finding the monkey, but he found himself skipping over large chunks of the story, not wanting to terrify his already scared boy any more than he was already. The story thus became disjointed, not really clear, but

Petey asked no questions; perhaps he was filling in the blanks for himself, Hal thought, in much the same way that he had dreamed his mother's death over and over, although he had not been there.

Uncle Will and Aunt Ida had both been there for the funeral. Afterward, Uncle Will had gone back to Maine—it was harvest-time—and Aunt Ida had stayed on for two weeks with the boys to neaten up her sister's affairs. But more than that, she spent the time making herself known to the boys, who were so stunned by their mother's sudden death that they were nearly sleepwalking. When they couldn't sleep, she was there with warm milk; when Hal woke at three in the morning with nightmares (nightmares in which his mother approached the water cooler without seeing the monkey that floated and bobbed in its cool sapphire depths, grinning and clapping its cymbals, each converging pair of sweeps leaving trails of bubbles behind); she was there when Bill came down with first a fever and then a rash of painful mouth sores and then hives three days after the funeral; she was there. She made herself known to the boys, and before they rode the New England Flyer from Hartford to Portland with her, both Bill and Hal had come to her separately and wept on her lap while she held them and rocked them, and the bonding began.

The day before they left Connecticut for good to go "down Maine" (as it was called in those days), the rag-man came in his great old rattly truck and picked up the huge pile of useless stuff that Bill and Hal had carried out to the sidewalk from the back closet. When all the junk had been set out by the curb for pick-up, Aunt Ida had asked them to go through the back closet again and pick out any souvenirs or remembrances they wanted specially to keep. We just don't have room for it all, boys, she told them, and Hal supposed Bill had taken her at her word and had gone through all those fascinating boxes their father had left behind one final time. Hal did not join his older brother. Hal had lost his taste for the back closet. A terrible idea had come to him during those first two weeks of mourning: perhaps his father hadn't just disappeared, or run away because he had an itchy foot and had discovered marriage wasn't for him.

Maybe the monkey had gotten him.

When he heard the rag-man's truck roaring and farting and

THE MONKEY

backfiring its way down the block, Hal nerved himself, snatched the scruffy wind-up monkey from his shelf where it had been since the day his mother died (he had not dared to touch it until then, not even to throw it back into the closet), and ran downstairs with it. Neither Bill nor Aunt Ida saw him. Sitting on top of a barrel filled with broken souvenirs and mouldy books was the Ralston-Purina carton, filled with similar junk. Hal had slammed the monkey back into the box it had originally come out of, hysterically daring it to begin clapping its cymbals (*go on, go on, I dare you, dare you, DARE YOU*), but the monkey only waited there, leaning back nonchalantly, as if expecting a bus, grinning its awful, knowing grin.

Hal stood by, a small boy in old corduroy pants and scuffed Buster Browns, as the rag-man, an Italian gent who wore a crucifix and whistled through the space in his teeth, began loading boxes and barrels into his ancient truck with the high wooden sides. Hal watched as he lifted both the barrel and the Ralston-Purina box balanced atop it; he watched the monkey disappear into the maw of the truck; he watched as the rag-man climbed back into the cab, blew his nose mightily into the palm of his hand, wiped his hand with a huge red handkerchief, and started the truck's engine with a mighty roar and a stinking blast of oily blue smoke; he watched the truck draw away. And a great weight had dropped away from his heart—he actually felt it go. He had jumped up and down twice, as high as he could jump, his arms spread, palms held out, and if any of the neighbors had seen him, they would have thought it odd almost to the point of blasphemy, perhaps—*why is that boy jumping for joy* (for that was surely what it was; a jump for joy can hardly be disguised) *with his mother not even a month in her grave?*

He was jumping for joy because the monkey was gone, gone forever. Gone forever, but not three months later Aunt Ida had sent him up into the attic to get the boxes of Christmas decorations, and as he crawled around looking for them, getting the knees of his pants dusty, he had suddenly come face to face with it again, and his wonder and terror had been so great that he had to bite sharply into the side of his hand to keep from screaming . . . or fainting dead away. There it was, grinning its toothy grin, cymbals poised apart and ready to clap, leaning nonchalantly back against one corner of a Ralston-Purina carton as if waiting for a bus, seeming to say: *Thought you got rid of me, didn't you? But I'm not that easy to get rid of, Hal. I like you, Hal. We were made for each other, just a boy and his pet monkey, a couple of good old buddies. And somewhere south of here there's a stupid old Italian rag-man lying in a claw-foot tub with his eyeballs bulging and his dentures half-popped out of his mouth, his screaming mouth, a rag-man who smells like a burned-out Exide battery. He was saving me for his grandson, Hal, and he put me on the shelf with his soap and his razor and his Burma-Shave and the Philco radio he listened to the Brooklyn Dodgers on, and I started to clap, and one of my cymbals hit that old radio and into the tub it went, and then I came to you, Hal, I worked my way along country roads at night and the moonlight shone off my teeth at three in the morning and I left death in my wake, Hal, I came to you, I'm your Christmas present, Hal, wind me up, who's dead? Is it Bill? Is it Uncle Will? Is it you, Hal? Is it you?*

Hal had backed away, grimacing madly, eyes rolling, and nearly fell going downstairs. He told Aunt Ida he hadn't been able to find the Christmas decorations—it was the first lie he had ever told her, and she had seen the lie on his face but had not asked him why he had told it, thank God—and later when Bill came in she asked him to look and he brought the Christmas decorations down. Later, when they were alone, Bill hissed at him that he was a dummy who couldn't find his own ass with both hands and a flashlight. Hal said nothing. Hal was pale and silent, only picking at his supper. And that night he dreamed of the monkey again, one of its cymbals striking the Philco radio as it babbled out Dean Martin singing Whenna da moon hitta you eye like a big pizza pie *ats-a moray*, the radio tumbling into the bathtub as the monkey grinned and beat its cymbals together with a *JANG* and a *JANG* and a *JANG*; only it wasn't the Italian rag-man who was in the tub when the water turned electric.

It was him.

Hal and his son scrambled down the embankment behind the home place to the boathouse that jutted out over the water on its old pilings. Hal had the flight bag in his right hand. His throat was dry, his ears were attuned to an unnaturally keen pitch. The bag seemed very heavy.

"What's down here, Daddy?" Petey asked.

Hal didn't answer. He set down the flight bag. "Don't touch that," he said, and Petey backed away from it. Hal felt in his pocket for the ring of keys Bill had given him and found one neatly labeled B'HOUSE on a scrap of adhesive tape.

The day was clear and cold, windy, the sky a brilliant blue. The leaves of the trees that crowded up to the verge of the lake had gone every bright fall shade from blood red to sneering yellow. They rattled and talked in the wind. Leaves swirled around Petey's sneakers as he stood anxiously by, and Hal could smell November on the wind, with winter crowding close behind it.

The key turned in the padlock and he pulled the swing doors open. Memory was strong: he didn't even have to look to kick down the wooden block that held the door open. The smell in here was all summer: canvas and bright wood, a lingering, musty warmth.

Uncle Will's rowboat was still here, the oars neatly shipped as if he had last loaded it with his fishing tackle and two six-packs of Black Label on ice yesterday afternoon. Bill and Hal had both gone out fishing with Uncle Will many times, but never together: Uncle Will maintained the boat was too small for three. The red trim, which Uncle Will had touched up each spring, was now faded and peeling, though, and spiders had spun their silk in the boat's bow.

Hal laid hold of it and pulled it down the ramp to the little shingle of beach. The fishing trips had been one of the best parts of his childhood with Uncle Will and Aunt Ida. He had a feeling that Bill felt much the same. Uncle Will was ordinarily the most taciturn of men, but once he had the boat positioned to his liking, some sixty or seventy yards offshore, lines set and bobbers floating on the water, he would crack a beer for himself and one for Hal (who rarely drank more than half of the one can Uncle Will would allow, always with the ritual admonition from Uncle Will that Aunt Ida must never be told because "she'd shoot me for a stranger if she knew I was givin you boys beer, don't you know"), and wax expansive. He would tell stories, answer questions, rebait Hal's hook when it needed rebaiting; and the boat would drift where the wind and the mild current wanted it to be.

"How come you never go right out to the middle, Uncle Will?" Hal had asked once.

"Look over the side there, Hal," Uncle Will had answered.

Hal did. He saw blue water and his fish line going down into black.

"You're looking into the deepest part of Crystal Lake," Uncle Will said, crunching his empty beer can in one hand and selecting a fresh one with the other. "A hundred feet if she's an inch. Amos Culligan's old Studebaker is down there somewhere. Damn fool took it out on the lake one early December, before the ice was made. Lucky to get out of it alive, he was. They'll never get that Studebaker out, nor see it until Judgment Trump blows. Lake's one deep son of a whore right here, it is. Big ones are right here, Hal. No need to go out no further. Let's see how your worm looks. Reel that son of a whore right in."

Hal did, and while Uncle Will put a fresh crawler from the old Crisco tin that served as his bait box on his hook, he stared into the water, fascinated, trying to see Amos Culligan's old Studebaker, all rust and waterweed drifting out of the open driver's side window through which Amos had escaped at the absolute last moment, waterweed festooning the steering wheel like a rotting necklace, waterweed dangling from the rearview mirror and drifting back and forth in the currents like some strange rosary. But he could see only blue shading to black, and there was the shape of Uncle Will's nightcrawler, the hook hidden inside its knots, hung up there in the middle of things, its own sun-shafted version of reality. Hal had a brief, dizzying vision of being suspended over a mighty gulf, and he had closed his eyes for a moment until the vertigo passed. That day, he seemed to recollect, he had drunk his entire can of beer.

. . . the deepest part of Crystal Lake . . . a hundred feet if she's an inch.

He paused a moment, panting, and looked up at Petey, still watching anxiously. "You want some help, Daddy?"

"In a minute."

He had his breath again, and now he pulled the rowboat across the narrow strip of sand to the water, leaving a groove. The paint had peeled, but the boat had been kept under cover and it looked sound.

THE MONKEY

When he and Uncle Will went out, Uncle Will would pull the boat down the ramp, and when the bow was afloat, he would clamber in, grab an oar to push with, and say: "Push me off, Hal . . . this is where you earn your truss!"

"Hand that bag in, Petey, and then give me a push," he said. And, smiling a little, he added: "This is where you earn your truss."

Petey didn't smile back. "Am I coming, Daddy?"

"Not this time. Another time I'll take you out fishing, but . . . not this time."

Petey hesitated. The wind tumbled his brown hair and a few yellow leaves, crisp and dry, wheeled past his shoulders and landed at the edge of the water, bobbing like boats themselves.

"You should have muffled them," he said, low.

"What?" But he thought he understood what Petey had meant.

"Put cotton over the cymbals. Taped it on. So it couldn't . . . make that noise."

Hal suddenly remembered Daisy coming toward him—not walking but lurching—and how, quite suddenly, blood had burst from both of Daisy's eyes in a flood that soaked her ruff and pattered down on the floor of the barn, how she had collapsed on her forepaws . . . and on the still, rainy spring air of that day he had heard the sound, not muffled but curiously clear, coming from the attic of the house fifty feet away: *Jang-jang-jang-jang*!

He began to scream hysterically, dropping the armload of wood he had been getting for the fire. He ran for the kitchen to get Uncle Will, who was eating scrambled eggs and toast, his suspenders not even up over his shoulders yet.

She was an old dog, Hal, Uncle Will had said, his face haggard and unhappy—he looked old himself. *She was twelve, and that's old for a dog. You mustn't take on, now—old Daisy wouldn't like that.*

Old, the vet had echoed, but he had looked troubled all the same, because dogs don't die of explosive brain hemorrhages, even at twelve ("like as if someone had stuck a firecracker in his head," Hal overheard the vet saying to Uncle Will as Uncle Will dug a hole in the back of the barn not far from the place where he had buried Daisy's mother in 1950; "I never seen the beat of it, Will").

And later, terrified almost out of his mind but unable to help himself, Hal had crept up to the attic.

Hello, Hal, how you doing? the monkey grinned from its shadowy corner. Its cymbals were poised, a foot or so apart. The sofa cushion Hal had stood on end between them was now all the way across the attic. Something—some force—had thrown it hard enough to split its cover, and stuffing foamed out of it. *Don't worry about Daisy*, the monkey whispered inside his head, its glassy hazel eyes fixed on Hal Shelburn's wide blue ones. *Don't worry about Daisy, she was old, old, Hal, even the vet said so, and by the way, did you see the blood coming out of her eyes, Hal? Wind me up, Hal. Wind me up, let's play, and who's dead, Hal? Is it you?*

And when he came back to himself he had been crawling toward the monkey as if hypnotized. One hand had been outstretched to grasp the key. He scrambled backward then, and almost fell down the attic stairs in his haste—probably would have if the stairwell had not been so narrow. A little whining noise had been coming from his throat.

Now he sat in the boat, looking at Petey. "Muffling the cymbals doesn't work," he said. "I tried it once."

Petey cast a nervous glance at the flight bag. "What happened, Daddy?"

"Nothing I want to talk about now," Hal said, "and nothing you want to hear about. Come on and give me a push."

Petey bent to it, and the stern of the boat grated along the sand. Hal dug in with an oar, and suddenly that feeling of being tied to the earth was gone and the boat was moving lightly, its own thing again after years in the dark boathouse, rocking on the light waves. Hal unshipped the oars one at a time and clicked the oarlocks shut.

"Be careful, Daddy," Petey said. His face was pale.

"This won't take long," Hal promised, but he looked at the flight bag and wondered.

He began to row, bending to the work. The old, familiar ache in the small of his back and between his shoulder blades began. The shore receded. Petey was magically eight again, six, a four-year-old standing at the edge of the water. He shaded his eyes with one infant hand.

Hal glanced casually at the shore but would not allow himself to actually study it. It had been nearly fifteen years, and if he studied the shoreline carefully, he would see the changes

THE MONKEY

rather than the similarities and become lost. The sun beat on his neck, and he began to sweat. He looked at the flight bag, and for a moment he lost the bend-and-pull rhythm. The flight bag seemed . . . seemed to be bulging. He began to row faster.

The wind gusted, drying the sweat and cooling his skin. The boat rose and the bow slapped water to either side when it came down. Hadn't the wind freshened, just in the last minute or so? And was Petey calling something? Yes. Hal couldn't make out what it was over the wind. It didn't matter. Getting rid of the monkey for another twenty years—or maybe forever (please God, forever)—that was what mattered.

The boat reared and came down. He glanced left and saw baby whitecaps. He looked shoreward again and saw Hunter's Point and a collapsed wreck that must have been the Burdon's boathouse when he and Bill were kids. Almost there, then. Almost over the spot where Amos Culligan's Studebaker had plunged through the ice one long-ago December. Almost over the deepest part of the lake.

Petey was screaming something; screaming and pointing. Hal still couldn't hear. The rowboat rocked and bucked, flatting off clouds of thin spray to either side of its peeling bow. A tiny rainbow glowed in one, was pulled apart. Sunlight and shadow raced across the lake in shutters and the waves were not mild now; the whitecaps had grown up. His sweat had dried to gooseflesh, and spray had soaked the back of his jacket. He rowed grimly, eyes alternating between the shoreline and the flight bag. The boat rose again, this time so high that for a moment the left oar pawed at air instead of water.

Petey was pointing at the sky, his screams now only a faint, bright runner of sound.

Hal looked over his shoulder.

The lake was a frenzy of waves. It had gone a deadly dark shade of blue sewn with white seams. A shadow raced across the water toward the boat and something in its shape was familiar, so terribly familiar, that Hal looked up and then the scream was there, struggling in his tight throat.

The sun was behind the cloud, turning it into a hunched working shape with two gold-edged crescents held apart. Two holes were torn in one end of the cloud, and sunshine poured through in two shafts.

As the cloud crossed over the boat, the monkey's cymbals, barely muffled by the flight bag, began to beat. *Jang-jang-jang-jang, it's you, Hal, it's finally you, you're over the deepest part of the lake now and it's your turn, your turn, your turn—*

All the necessary shoreline elements had clicked into their places. The rotting bones of Amos Culligan's Studebaker lay somewhere below, this was where the big ones were, this was the place.

Hal shipped the oars to the locks in one quick jerk, leaned forward unmindful of the wildly rocking boat, and snatched the flight bag. The cymbals made their wild, pagan music; the bag's sides bellowed as if with tenebrous respiration.

"*Right here, you sonofabitch!*" Hal screamed. "*RIGHT HERE!*"

He threw the bag over the side.

It sank fast. For a moment he could see it going down, sides moving, and for that endless moment *he could still hear the cymbals beating*. And for a moment the black waters seemed to clear and he could see down into that terrible gulf of waters to where the big ones lay; there was Amos Culligan's Studebaker, and Hal's mother was behind its slimy wheel, a grinning skeleton with a lake bass staring coldly from the skull's nasal cavity. Uncle Will and Aunt Ida lolled beside her, and Aunt Ida's gray hair trailed upward as the bag fell, turning over and over, a few silver bubbles trailing up: *jang-jang-jang-jang . . .*

Hal slammed the oars back into the water, scraping blood from his knuckles (*and ah God the back of Amos Culligan's Studebaker had been full of dead children! Charlie Silverman . . . Johnny McCabe . . .*), and began to bring the boat about.

There was a dry pistol-shot crack between his feet, and suddenly clear water was welling up between two boards. The boat was old; the wood had shrunk a bit, no doubt; it was just a small leak. But it hadn't been there when he rowed out. He would have sworn to it.

The shore and lake changed places in his view. Petey was at his back now. Overhead, that awful, simian cloud was breaking up. Hal began to row. Twenty seconds was enough to convince him he was rowing for his life. He was only a

THE MONKEY

so-so swimmer, and even a great one would have been put to the test in this suddenly angry water.

Two more boards suddenly shrank apart with that pistol-shot sound. More water poured into the boat, dousing his shoes. There were tiny metallic snapping sounds that he realized were nails breaking. One of the oarlocks snapped and flew off into the water—would the swivel itself go next?

The wind now came from his back, as if trying to slow him down or even to drive him into the middle of the lake. He was terrified, but he felt a crazy kind of exhilaration through the terror. The monkey was gone for good this time. He knew it somehow. Whatever happened to him, the monkey would not be back to draw a shadow over Dennis's life, or Petey's. The monkey was gone, perhaps resting on the roof or the hood of Amos Culligan's Studebaker at the bottom of Crystal Lake. Gone for good.

He rowed, bending forward and rocking back. That cracking, crimping sound came again, and now the rusty old bait can that had been lying in the bow of the boat was floating in three inches of water. Spray blew in Hal's face. There was a louder snapping sound, and the bow seat fell in two pieces and floated next to the bait box. A board tore off the left side of the boat, and then another, this one at the waterline, tore off at the right. Hal rowed. Breath rasped in his mouth, hot and dry, and his throat swelled with the coppery taste of exhaustion. His sweaty hair flew.

Now a crack ran directly up the bottom of the rowboat, zig-zagged between his feet, and ran up to the bow. Water gushed in; he was in water up to his ankles, then to the swell of calf. He rowed, but the boat's shoreward movement was sludgy now. He didn't dare look behind him to see how close he was getting.

Another board tore loose. The crack running up the center of the boat grew branches, like a tree. Water flooded in.

Hal began to make the oars sprint, breathing in great, failing gasps. He pulled once . . . twice . . . and on the third pull both oar swivels snapped off. He lost one oar, held onto the other. He rose to his feet and began to flail at the water with it. The boat rocked, almost capsized, and spilled him back onto his seat with a thump.

Moments later more boards tore loose, the seat collapsed, and he was lying in the water which filled the bottom of the boat, astounded at its coldness. He tried to get on his knees, desperately thinking: *Petey must not see this, must not see his father drown right in front of his eyes, you're going to swim, dog-paddle if you have to, but do, do something—*

There was another splintering crack—almost a crash—and he was in the water, swimming for the shore as he never had swum in his life . . . and the shore was amazingly close. A minute later he was standing waist-deep in water, not five yards from the beach.

Petey splashed toward him, arms out, screaming and crying and laughing. Hal started toward him and floundered. Petey, chest-deep, floundered.

They caught each other.

Hal breathed in great, winded gasps, nevertheless hoisted the boy into his arms and carried him up to the beach where both of them sprawled, panting.

"Daddy? Is it really gone? That monkey?"

"Yes. I think it's really gone."

"The boat fell apart. It just . . . fell apart all around you."

Disintegrated, Hal thought, and looked at the boards floating loose on the water forty feet out. They bore no resemblance to the tight, handmade rowboat he had pulled out of the boathouse.

"It's all right now," Hal said, leaning back on his elbows. He shut his eyes and let the sun warm his face.

"Did you see the cloud?" Petey whispered.

"Yes. But I don't see it now . . . do you?"

They looked at the sky. There were scattered white puffs here and there, but no large dark cloud. It was gone, as he had said.

Hal pulled Petey to his feet. "There'll be towels up at the house. Come on." But he paused, looking at his son. "You were crazy, running out there like that."

Petey looked at him solemnly. "You were brave, Daddy."

"Was I?" The thought of bravery had never crossed his mind. Only his fear. The fear had been too big to see anything else. If anything else had indeed been there. "Come on, Pete."

"What are we going to tell Mom?"

Hal smiled. "I dunno, big guy. We'll think of something."

He paused a moment longer, looking at the boards floating on the water. The lake was calm again, sparkling with small wavelets. Suddenly Hal thought of summer people he didn't even know—a man and his son, perhaps, fishing for the big one. *I've got something, Dad!* the boy screams. *Well reel it up and let's see,* the father says, and coming up from the depths, weeds draggling from its cymbals, grinning its terrible, welcoming grin ... the monkey.

He shuddered—but those were only things that might be.

"Come on," he said to Petey again, and they walked up the path through the flaming October woods toward the home place.

From the Bridgton News
October 24, 1980:

MYSTERY OF THE DEAD FISH

By BETSY MORIARTY

HUNDREDS of dead fish were found floating belly-up on Crystal Lake in the neighboring township of Casco late last week. The largest numbers appeared to have died in the vicinity of Hunter's Point, although the lake's currents make this a bit difficult to determine. The dead fish included all types commonly found in these waters—bluegills, pickerel, sunnies, carp, brown and rainbow trout, even one landlocked salmon. Fish and Game authorities say they are mystified, and caution fishermen and women not to eat any sort of fish from Crystal Lake until tests have determined ...

THE GAP

Ramsey Campbell

Born January 4, 1946 in Liverpool, Ramsey Campbell has devoted most of his life to frightening tourists away from that city; Campbell is a writer of urban horrors who revels in deteriorating neighborhoods and industrial slums, and not surprisingly Liverpool has been the setting of many of his stories and novels. Campbell's first book, *The Inhabitant of the Lake & Less Welcome Tenants,* was published by Arkham House in 1964. Since this teenage infatuation with the works of H. P. Lovecraft, Campbell moved rapidly to establish his own approach to horror fiction and is now considered one of this genre's foremost stylists. Campbell is versatile. His books include collections of his own stories: *Demons by Daylight, The Height of the Scream;* original anthologies that he has edited: *Superhorror* (retitled *The Far Reaches of Fear* in paperback), *New Tales of the Cthulhu Mythos,* and the two-volume *New Terrors;* as well as novels: *The Doll Who Ate His Mother, The Face That Must Die, To Wake the Dead* (which was retitled *The Parasite* for the U.S. edition and given an alternate ending).

Campbell lives with his wife, Jenny, in cannibal-haunted Liverpool, where for the past several years he has worked full time as a writer—evoking unexpected horrors from territories that threaten to expand worldwide. Currently Campbell is at work on a horror novel set in Chapel Hill, North Carolina. "The Gap" was published in the second number of *Fantasy Readers Guide,* subtitled *The File on Ramsey Campbell;* this booklet contains an index to all of Campbell's fiction to date, along with several commentaries and appreciations, and I recommend it to serious fans of fantasy literature.

Tate was fitting a bird into the sky when he heard the car. He hurried to the window. Sunlit cars blazed, a double-stranded necklace on the distant main road; clouds transformed above the hills, assembling the sky. Yes, it was the Dewhursts: he could see them, packed into the front seat of their Fiat as it ventured into the drive. On his table, scraps of cloud were scattered around the jigsaw. The Dewhursts weren't due for an hour. He glanced at the displaced fragments and then, resigned, went to the stairs.

By the time he'd strolled downstairs and opened the front door, they were just emerging from the car. David's coat buttons displayed various colors of thread. Next came his wife Dottie: her real name was Carla, but they felt that Dave and Dottie looked a more attractive combination on book covers —a notion with which millions of readers seemed to agree. She looked like a cartoonist's American tourist: trousers bulging like sausages, carefully silvered hair. Sometimes Tate wished that his writer's eye could be less oppressively alert to telling details.

Dewhurst gestured at his car like a conjuror unveiling an astonishment. "And here are our friends that we promised you."

Had it been a promise? It had seemed more a side effect of inviting the Dewhursts. And when had their friend turned plural? Still, Tate was unable to feel much resentment; he was too full of having completed his witchcraft novel.

The young man's aggressive bony face was topped with hair short as turf; the girl's face was almost the color and texture of chalk. "This is Don Skelton," Dewhurst said. "Don, Lionel Tate. You two should have plenty to talk about, you're in the same field. And this is Don's friend, er—" Skelton stared at the large old villa as if he couldn't believe he was meant to be impressed.

He let the girl drag his case upstairs; she refused to yield it to Tate when he protested. "This is your room," he told Skelton, and felt like a disapproving landlady. "I had no idea you wouldn't be alone."

"Don't worry, there'll be room for her."

If the girl had been more attractive, if her tangled hair had been less inert and her face less hungry, mightn't he have envied Skelton? "There'll be cocktails before dinner, if that's your scene," he said to the closed door.

The jigsaw helped him relax. Evening eased into the house, shadows deepened within the large windows. The table glowed darkly through the last gap, then he snapped the piece home. Was that an echo of the snap behind him? He turned, but nobody was watching him.

As he shaved in one of the bathrooms he heard someone go downstairs. Good Lord, he wasn't a very efficient host. He hurried down, achieving the bow of his tie just as he reached the lounge, but idling within were only Skelton and the girl. At least she now wore something like an evening dress; the top of her pale chest was spattered with freckles. "We generally change before going out for dinner," Tate said.

Skelton shrugged his crumpled shoulders. "Go ahead."

Alcohol made Skelton more talkative. "I'll have somewhere like this," he said, glancing at the Victorian carved mahogany suite. After a calculated pause he added, "But better."

Tate made a last effort to reach him. "I'm afraid I haven't read anything of yours."

"There won't be many people who'll be able to say that." It sounded oddly threatening. He reached in his briefcase for a book. "I'll give you something to keep."

Tate glimpsed carved boxes, a camera, a small round gleam that twinged him with indefinable apprehension before the case snapped shut. Silver letters shone on the paperback, which was glossy as coal: *The Black Road*.

A virgin was being mutilated, gloated over by the elegant prose. Tate searched for a question that wouldn't sound insulting. At last he managed "What are your themes?"

"Autobiography." Perhaps Skelton was one of those writers of the macabre who needed to joke defensively about their work, for the Dewhursts were laughing.

Dinner at the inn was nerve-racking. Candlelight made food hop restlessly on plates, waiters loomed beneath the low beams and flung their vague shadows over the tables. The Dewhursts grew merry, but couldn't draw the girl into the conversation. When a waiter gave Skelton's clothes a withering glance he demanded of Tate, "Do you believe in witchcraft?"

"Well, I had to do a lot of research for my book. Some of the things I read made me think."

"No," Skelton said impatiently. "Do you *believe* in it—as a way of life?"

"Good heavens no. Certainly not."

"Then why waste your time writing about it?" He was still watching the disapproving waiter. Was it the candlelight that twitched his lips? "He's going to drop that," he said.

The waiter's shadow seemed to lose its balance before he did. His trayful of food crashed onto a table. Candles broke, flaring; light swayed the oak beams. Flaming wax spilled over the waiter's jacket, hot food leapt into his face.

"You're a writer," Skelton said, ignoring the commotion, "yet you've no idea of the power of words. There aren't many of us left who have." He smiled as waiters guided the injured man away. "Mind you, words are only part of it. Science hasn't robbed us of power, it's given us more tools. Telephones, cameras—so many ways to announce power."

Obviously he was drunk. The Dewhursts gazed at him as if he were a favorite, if somewhat irrepressible, child. Tate was glad to head home. Lights shone through his windows, charms against burglary; the girl hurried toward them, ahead of the rest of the party. Skelton dawdled, happy with the dark.

After his guests had gone to bed, Tate carried Skelton's book upstairs with him. Skelton's contempt had fastened on the doubts he always felt on having completed a new book. He'd see what sort of performance Skelton had to offer, since he thought so much of himself.

Less than halfway through he flung the book across the room. The narrator had sought perversions, taken all the drugs available, sampled most crimes in pursuit of his power; his favorite pastime was theft. Most of the scenes were pornographic. So this was autobiography, was it? Certainly drugs would explain the state of the speechless girl.

Tate's eyes were raw with nights of revision and typing. As he read *The Black Road*, the walls had seemed to waver and advance; the furniture had flexed its legs. He needed sleep, not Skelton's trash.

Dawn woke him. Oh God, he knew what he'd seen gleaming in Skelton's case—an eye. Surely that was a dream, born of a particularly disgusting image in the book. He tried to turn his back on the image, but he couldn't sleep. Unpleasant glimpses jerked him awake: his own novel with an oily black cover, friends snubbing him, his incredulous disgust on rereading his own book. Could his book be accused of Skelton's sins? Never before had he been so unsure about his work.

There was only one way to reassure himself, or otherwise. Tying himself into his dressing gown, he tiptoed past the closed doors to his study. Could he reread his entire novel before breakfast? Long morning shadows drew imperceptibly into themselves. A woman's protruded from his open study.

Why was his housekeeper early? In a moment he saw that he had been as absurdly trusting as the Dewhursts. The silent girl stood just within the doorway. As a guard she was a failure, for Tate had time to glimpse Skelton at his desk, gathering pages from the typescript of his novel.

The girl began to shriek, an uneven wailing sound that seemed not to need to catch breath. Though it was distracting as a police car's siren, he kept his gaze on Skelton. "Get out," he said.

A suspicion seized him. "No, on second thoughts—stay where you are." Skelton stood, looking pained like the victim of an inefficient store detective, while Tate made sure that all the pages were still on his desk. Those which Skelton had selected were the best researched. In an intolerable way it was a tribute.

The Dewhursts appeared, blinking as they wrapped themselves in dressing gowns. "What on earth's the matter?" Carla demanded.

"Your friend is a thief."

"Oh, dear me," Dewhurst protested. "Just because of what he said about his book? Don't believe everything he says."

"I'd advise you to choose your friends more carefully."

"I think we're perfectly good judges of people. What else do you think could have made our books so successful?"

Tate was too angry to restrain himself. "Technical competence, fourth-form wit, naive faith in people and a promise of life after death. You sell your readers what they want—anything but the truth."

He watched them trudge out. The girl was still making a sound, somewhere between panting and wailing, as she bumped the case downstairs. He didn't help her. As they squeezed into the car, only Skelton glanced back at him. His smile seemed almost warm, certainly content. Tate found it insufferable, and looked away.

When they'd gone, petrol fumes and all, he read through his novel. It seemed intelligent and unsensational—up to his standard. He hoped his publishers thought so. How would it read in print? Nothing of his ever satisfied him—but he was his least important reader.

Should he have called the police? It seemed trivial now. Pity about the Dewhursts—but if they were so stupid, he was well rid of them. The police would catch up with Skelton if he did much of what his book boasted.

After lunch Tate strolled toward the hills. Slopes blazed green; countless flames of grass swayed gently. The horizon was dusty with clouds. He lay enjoying the pace of the sky. At twilight the large emptiness of the house was soothing. He strolled back from the inn after a meal, refusing to glance at the nodding shapes that creaked and rustled beside him.

He slept well. Why should that surprise him when he woke? The mail waited at the end of his bed, placed there quietly by his housekeeper. The envelope with the blue and red fringe was from his New York agent—a new American paperback sale, hurrah. What else? A bill peering through its cellophane window, yet another circular, and a rattling carton wrapped in brown paper.

His address was anonymously typed on the carton; there was no return address. The contents shifted dryly, waves of shards. At last he stripped off the wrapping. When he opened the blank carton, its contents spilled out at him and were what he'd thought they must be: a jigsaw.

Was it a peace offering from the Dewhursts? Perhaps they'd chosen one without a cover picture because they thought he might enjoy the difficulty. And so he would. He broke up the sky and woodland on the table, and scooped them into their box. Beyond the window, trees and clouds wavered.

He began to sort out the edge of the jigsaw. Ah, there was the fourth corner. A warm breeze fluttered in the curtains. Behind him the door inched open on the emptiness of the house.

Noon had withdrawn most shadows from the room by the time he had assembled the edge. Most of the jumbled fragments were glossily brown, like furniture; but there was a human figure—no, two. He assembled them partially—one dressed in a suit, one in denim—then went downstairs to the salad his housekeeper had left him.

The jigsaw had freed his mind to compose. A story of rivalry between authors—a murder story? Two collaborators, one of whom became resentful, jealous, determined to achieve fame by himself? But he couldn't imagine anyone collaborating with Skelton. He consigned the idea to the bin at the back of his mind.

He strolled upstairs. What was his housekeeper doing? Had she knocked the jigsaw off the table? No, of course not; she had gone home hours ago—it was only the shadow of a tree fumbling about the floor.

The incomplete figures waited. The eye of a fragment gazed up at him. He shouldn't do all the easy sections first. Surely there must be points at which he could build inward from the edge. Yes, there was one: the leg of an item of furniture. At once he saw three more pieces. It was an Empire cabinet. The shadow of a cloud groped toward him.

Connections grew clear. He'd reached the stage where his subconscious directed his attention to the appropriate pieces. The room was fitting together: a walnut canterbury, a mahogany table, a whatnot. When the shape leaned toward him he started, scattering fragments, but it must have been a tree outside the window. It didn't take much to make him nervous now. He had recognized the room in the jigsaw.

Should he break it up unfinished? That would be admitting that it had disturbed him: absurd. He fitted the suited figure into place at the assembled table. Before he had put together the face, with its single eye in profile, he could see that the figure was himself.

He stood finishing a jigsaw, and was turning to glance behind him. When had the photograph been taken? When had the figure in denim crept behind him, unheard? Irritably resisting an urge to glance over his shoulder, he thumped the figure into place and snapped home the last pieces.

Perhaps it was Skelton: its denims were frayed and stained enough. But all the pieces which would have composed the face were missing. Reflected sunlight on the table within the gap gave the figure a flat pale gleam for a face.

"Damned nonsense!" He whirled, but there was only the

unsteady door edging its shadow over the carpet. Skelton must have superimposed the figure; no doubt he had enjoyed making it look menacing—stepping eagerly forward, its hands outstretched. Had he meant there to be a hole where its face should be, to obscure its intentions?

Tate held the box like a waste-bin, and swept in the disintegrating jigsaw. The sound behind him was nothing but an echo of its fall; he refused to turn. He left the box on the table. Should he show it to the Dewhursts? No doubt they would shrug it off as a joke—and really, it was ridiculous to take it even so seriously.

He strode to the inn. He must have his housekeeper prepare dinner more often. He was early—because he was hungry, that was all; why should he want to be home before dark? On the path, part of an insect writhed.

The inn was serving a large party. He had to wait, at a table hardly bigger than a stool. Waiters and diners, their faces obscured, surrounded him. He found himself glancing compulsively each time candlelight leapt onto a face. When eventually he hurried home, his mind was muttering at the restless shapes on both sides of the path: go away, go away.

A distant car blinked and was gone. His house's were the only lights to be seen. They seemed less heartening than lost in the night. No, his housekeeper hadn't let herself in. He was damned if he'd search all the rooms to make sure. The presence he sensed was only the heat, squatting in the house. When he tired of trying to read, the heat went to bed with him.

Eventually it woke him. Dawn made the room into a charcoal drawing. He sat up in panic. Nothing was watching him over the foot of the bed, which was somehow the trouble: beyond the bed, an absence hovered in the air. When it rose, he saw that it was perched on shoulders. The dim figure groped rapidly around the bed. As it bore down on him its hands lifted, alert and eager as a dowser's.

He screamed, and the light was dashed from his eyes. He lay trembling in absolute darkness. Was he still asleep? Had he been seized by his worst nightmare, of blindness? Very gradually a sketch of the room gathered about him, as though developing from fog. Only then did he dare switch on the light. He waited for the dawn before he slept again.

When he heard footsteps downstairs, he rose. It was idiotic

that he'd lain brooding for hours over a dream. Before he did anything else he would throw away the obnoxious jigsaw. He hurried to its room, and faltered. Flat sunlight occupied the table.

He called his housekeeper. "Have you moved a box from here?"

"No, Mr. Tate." When he frowned, dissatisfied, she said haughtily, "Certainly not."

She seemed nervous—because of his distrust, or because she was lying? She must have thrown away the box by mistake and was afraid to own up. Questioning her further would only cause unpleasantness.

He avoided her throughout the morning, though her sounds in other rooms disturbed him, as did occasional glimpses of her shadow. Why was he tempted to ask her to stay? It was absurd. When she'd left, he was glad to be able to listen to the emptiness of the house.

Gradually his pleasure faded. The warmly sunlit house seemed too bright, expectantly so, like a stage awaiting a first act. He was still listening, but less to absorb the silence than to penetrate it: in search of what? He wandered desultorily. His compulsion to glance about infuriated him. He had never realized how many shadows each room contained.

After lunch he struggled to begin to organize his ideas for his next book, at least roughly. It was too soon after the last one. His mind felt empty as the house. In which of them was there a sense of intrusion, of patient, distant lurking? No, of course his housekeeper hadn't returned. Sunlight drained from the house, leaving a congealed residue of heat. Shadows crept imperceptibly.

He needed an engrossing film—the Bergman at the Academy. He'd go now, and eat in London. Impulsively he stuffed *The Black Road* into his pocket, to get the thing out of the house. The slam of the front door echoed through the deserted rooms. From trees and walls and bushes, shadows spread; their outlines were restless with grass. A bird dodged about to pull struggling entrails out of the ground.

Was the railway station unattended? Eventually a shuffling, hollow with wood, responded to his knocks at the ticket window. As he paid, Tate realized that he'd let himself be driven from his house by nothing more than doubts. There were drawbacks to writing fantastic fiction, it seemed.

His realization made him feel vulnerable. He paced the short platform. Flowers in a bed spelt the station's name; lampposts thrust forward their dull heads. He was alone but for a man seated in the waiting room on the opposite platform. The window was dusty, and bright reflected clouds were caught in the glass; he couldn't distinguish the man's face. Why should he want to?

The train came dawdling. It carried few passengers, like the last exhibits of a run-down waxworks. Stations passed, displaying empty platforms. Fields stretched away toward the sinking light.

At each station the train halted, hoping for passengers but always disappointed—until, just before London, Tate saw a man striding in pursuit. On which platform? He could see only the man's reflection: bluish clothes, blurred face. The empty carriage creaked around him; metal scuttled beneath his feet. Though the train was gathering speed, the man kept pace with it. Still he was only striding; he seemed to feel no need to run. Good Lord, how long were his legs? A sudden explosion of foliage filled the window. When it fell away, the strider had gone.

Charing Cross Station was still busy. A giant's voice blundered among its rafters. As Tate hurried out, avoiding a miniature train of trolleys, silver gleamed at him from the bookstall. *The Black Road*, and there again, at another spot on the display: *The Black Road*. If someone stole them, that would be a fair irony. Of the people around him, several wore denim.

He ate curry in the Wampo Egg on the Charing Cross Road. He knew better restaurants nearby, but they were on side streets; he preferred to stay on the main road—never mind why. Denimed figures peered at the menu in the window. The menu obscured his view of their faces.

He bypassed Leicester Square Underground. He didn't care to go down into that dark, where trains burrowed, clanking. Besides, he had time to stroll; it was a pleasant evening. The colors of the bookshops cooled.

He glimpsed books of his in a couple of shops, which was heartening. But Skelton's title glared from Booksmith's window. Was that a gap beside it in the display? No, it was a reflected alley, for here came a figure striding down it. Tate turned and located the alley, but the figure must have stepped aside.

He made for Oxford Street. Skelton's book was there too, in Claude Gill's. Beyond it, on the ghost of the opposite pavement, a denimed figure watched. Tate whirled, but a bus idled past, blocking his view. Certainly there were a good many strollers wearing denim.

When he reached the Academy Cinema he had glimpsed a figure several times, both walking through window displays and, most frustratingly, pacing him on the opposite pavement, at the edge of his vision. He walked past the cinema, thinking how many faces he would be unable to see in its dark.

Instinctively drawn toward the brightest lights, he headed down Poland Street. Twilight had reached the narrow streets of Soho, awakening the neon. SEX SHOP. SEX AIDS. SCANDINAVIAN FILMS. The shops cramped one another, a shoulder-to-shoulder row of touts. In one window framed by livery neon, between *Spanking Letters* and *Rubber News*, he saw Skelton's book.

Pedestrians and cars crowded the streets. Whenever Tate glanced across, he glimpsed a figure in denim on the other pavement. Of course it needn't be the same one each time—it was impossible to tell, for he could never catch sight of the face. He had never realized how many faces you couldn't see in crowds. He'd made for these streets precisely in order to be among people.

Really, this was absurd. He'd allowed himself to be driven among the seedy bookshops in search of company, like a fugitive from Edgar Allan Poe—and by what? An idiotic conversation, an equally asinine jigsaw, a few stray glimpses? It proved that curses could work on the imagination—but good heavens, that was no reason for him to feel apprehensive. Yet he did, for behind the walkers painted with neon a figure was moving like a hunter, close to the wall. Tate's fear tasted of curry.

Very well, his pursuer existed. That could be readily explained: it was Skelton, skulking. How snugly those two words fitted together! Skelton must have seen him gazing at *The Black Road* in the window. It would be just like Skelton to stroll about admiring his own work in displays. He must have decided to chase Tate, to unnerve him.

He must glimpse Skelton's face, then pounce. Abruptly he crossed the street, through a break in the sequence of cars. Neon, entangled with neon after-images, danced on his eyed. Where was the skulker? Had he dodged into a shop? In a moment Tate saw him, on the pavement he'd just vacated. By the time Tate's vision struggled clear of after-images, the face was obscured by the crowd.

Tate dashed across the street again, with the same result. So Skelton was going to play at maneuvering, was he? Well, Tate could play too. He dodged into a shop. Amplified panting pounded rhythmically beyond an inner doorway. "Hardcore film now showing, sir," said the Indian behind the counter. Men, some wearing denim, stood at racks of magazines. All kept their faces averted from Tate.

He was behaving ridiculously—which frightened him: he'd let his defenses be penetrated. How long did he mean to indulge in this absurd chase? How was he to put a stop to it?

He peered out of the shop. Passers-by glanced at him as though he was touting. Pavements twitched, restless with neon. The battle of lights jerked the shadows of the crowd. Faces shone green, burned red.

If he could just spot Skelton. . . . What would he do? Next to Tate's doorway was an alley, empty save for darkness. At the far end, another street glared. He could dodge through the alley and lose his pursuer. Perhaps he would find a policeman; that would teach Skelton—he'd had enough of this poor excuse for a joke.

There was Skelton, lurking in a dark doorway almost opposite. Tate made as if to chase him, and at once the figure sneaked away behind a group of strollers. Tate darted into the alley.

His footsteps clanged back from the walls. Beyond the scrawny exit, figures passed like a peepshow. A wall grazed his shoulder; a burden knocked repetitively against his thigh. It was *The Black Road*, still crumpled in his pocket. He flung it away. It caught at his feet in the dark until he trampled on it; he heard its spine break. Good riddance.

He was halfway down the alley, where its darkness was strongest. He looked back to confirm that nobody had followed him. Stumbling a little, he faced forward again, and the hands of the figure before him grabbed his shoulders.

He recoiled gasping. The wall struck his shoulder blades.

Darkness stood in front of him, but he felt the body clasp him close, so as to thrust its unseen face into his. His face felt seized by ice; he couldn't distinguish the shape of what touched it. Then the clasp had gone, and there was silence.

He stood shivering. His hands groped at his sides, as though afraid to move. He understood why he could see nothing—there was no light so deep in the alley—but why couldn't he hear? Even the taste of curry had vanished. His head felt anesthetized, and somehow insubstantial. He found that he didn't dare turn to look at either lighted street. Slowly, reluctantly, his hands groped upward toward his face.

THE CATS OF PERE LACHAISE

Neil Olonoff

Perhaps the most fascinating aspect of editing such an anthology as *The Year's Best Horror Stories* is that I'm continually coming upon horror stories which were published in some of the least likely places. "The Cats of Pere LaChaise" is one such story: it was published in France in *A Touch of Paris*, an English-language magazine aimed at tourists in that city, and I should never have encountered it had not another writer, Tim Sullivan, called it to my attention.

Neil Olonoff was born in Brooklyn in 1950, graduated from the University of Oklahoma, and currently resides in Miami, Florida. He was living in Paris at the time he wrote this story, teaching English and writing articles for a news magazine, *Metro*. The editor of *A Touch of Paris* expressed interest in fiction relating to Paris, and Olonoff responded with "The Cats of Pere LaChaise." The editor there retitled the story, to no good effect, and I have restored the author's title at his request. Olonoff has also worked as a psychiatric aide and as an exporter, among other jobs, and had lived a year in Sao Paulo, Brazil. Hardly one to let the grass grow under his feet. Just now, Olonoff writes, "I'm finishing my first novel, begun four years ago. It's about death."

Bateman hated to be late. He was irritated, after wasting half the morning trying to convince his wife to come to Oscar's funeral. Now, ascending to the entrance of the Pere LaChaise Crematorium, he was further annoyed at having to weave his way among a group of large cats sunning themselves on the broad steps. Near the top, tired of watching his feet, he carelessly trod on a tail. The yowl was quite loud enough, he thought with amusement, to wake the dead. But the cats did not scatter with alarm. Instead, they arched their backs and glared at him with malevolence. With a nervous backward glance at the cats, Bateman passed into the cool gloom of the crematorium.

He delayed a moment in the doorway of the crematory chamber. Pierre was seated among the small clot of mourners who faced the door of the funerary oven. It reminded Bateman of the time he peered into the courtroom during Pierre and Alicia's divorce, twelve years before. Now he hesitated, preparing an explanation for Alicia's absence. Damn her stubbornness! The children were a good excuse, of course, or perhaps she could have a cold. A cold, he decided. Let him mention the children first. Perhaps he could avoid Pierre's reproachful glances, which always made him feel so guilty.

The furnace door was rising to reveal the red glow within. With a whine of automatic machinery the plain pine coffin slid inwards. Bateman seated himself behind Pierre and his sister. The door descended. That was it. As the group rose with a collective sigh, Pierre turned and saw Bateman. He noticed Pierre's disappointment at not seeing Alicia by his side. Bateman said, "We're really very sorry, Pierre."

Pierre answered almost rudely with a perfunctory nod and told his sister to go along home, that he would wait to receive the ashes alone. The group left, and the two men stepped out of the crematorium and strolled across the broad paved plaza.

Oscar, the deceased, had been Pierre's brother-in-law. He had died of drink, one might say, but in a most macabre way. Oscar drowned after passing out cold under the Pont Neuf during a rainstorm; the river simply rose around him. The police found him there with no *carte d'identité*. They took fingerprints, but Oscar was born in Toulouse, and before they reached the family the body had been bound over to the public crematorium at Pere LaChaise, the famous cemetery in the 20th *arrondissement*. It was simpler to go ahead with the pauper's funeral.

"We were lucky they did him alone," Pierre said to Bateman. "They usually cremate indigents four at a time."

Bateman looked up in surprise, but said nothing. They

scuffed along one of the gravel paths of the cemetery, blinking at puddles of light stippled on the ground. It was a lovely late afternoon, and the leaves of the ancient trees rustled above their heads.

"How is she feeling?" asked Pierre, meaning Alicia.

"She's fine," said Bateman, reflecting that he was no more certain of her feelings than Allan Kardek's, the long-dead spirit medium whose granite tomb they were passing.

"And Janine?" asked Pierre.

"She's fine, too," said Bateman. Janine was Pierre's daughter. She had been just a baby when Alicia divorced him.

Pierre was a morose, silent man by nature, but today he seemed to be groping for a way to prolong the conversation. Bateman felt sorry for him, knowing Pierre found it difficult to overcome his shyness and self-restriction. But Bateman wasn't feeling his usual voluble self, either.

Their path was crossed then by one of the enormous cats which resided in the cemetery. They seemed to be everywhere, peeking at one from behind tombstones, skulking in the musty vaults. They were huge, and Bateman supposed they made their diet on field mice and other rodents.

Pierre said, "Look at the cats. They are so large."

Bateman smiled. He felt he could predict each thing Pierre said. The man's mind was that of an engineer, he thought, strictly oriented to the concrete and the real. Bateman could look ahead and pick the most remarkable features of the cemetery's paths. As they passed, Pierre was sure to remark on each. Bateman was amused at this confirmation, not for the first time, of the difference in their characters. Bateman had always been able to ignore the obvious, to act as though the real conditions of life and requirements of propriety simply did not exist.

Alicia was like that, too. When their affair had begun in a small gallery on the rue du Bac, the rest of the world had seemed to fade into the background. Her marriage to Pierre, their child and Pierre's position in her father's brick and tile factory were all secondary to the paramount fact in their lives: Their love for one another.

Bateman had been on a buying trip, adding to the art collection of a man who owned several department stores in New York City. For many months he and Alicia burned up the telephone lines between Paris and New York. He used up his savings on air fares. Finally, Bateman convinced the wealthy New Yorker to station him permanently in Paris. A few years later, Bateman opened his own gallery. But the period before the divorce was painful for all of them.

Pierre stayed with Alicia all that time for Janine's sake, preparing baby bottles and coping with early morning colic. Alicia pursued both her blossoming career as an artist and her American lover, and somehow between the two found time for her baby.

Bateman imagined that Pierre had preferred to have them near him, even without Alicia's love, than to have neither. Afterwards, Pierre never found another woman who suited him. It was an act of sacrifice of which Bateman would not have been capable. Because of it, Janine grew up a happy child.

During that year Bateman and Alicia shocked their friends and family by carrying on an open affair. She often brought Janine around to his apartment or the galleries, but often as not would leave the infant with her father. When Bateman would call her from New York, it was inevitable that Pierre would sometimes answer. Bateman hung up the first few times that happened, but as they became somewhat inured to the situation, he began asking for her and even leaving messages. Pierre bore it all with not a single word of protest to Bateman.

Bateman looked at Pierre, reflecting that it was probably that same repressed, unimaginative quality which had allowed him to survive that trying period, to say nothing of the last twelve, lonely years. He saw the tail of a cat disappear behind a tree. "I wonder what the cats eat?" he asked. "Do you suppose someone feeds them?"

Pierre laughed in that muffled way of his, a kind of tight-lipped bobbing of the head, from which no sound of mirth came out. His eyes kept their eternal sad expression but there was, for once, a twinkle of animation. He said, "I was talking to one of the men who work in the crematorium before you came. I asked how things were with the ovens and so on."

"What do you mean?" Bateman asked.

"DeLaye did an overhaul on the brick linings," said Pierre. DeLaye was Alicia's maiden name and the name of her father's company, for which Pierre still worked.

"Oh, I see."

"The bricks must be replaced every four years or so. It wasn't a very big job."

"My God, look at the size of that cat!" Bateman said. "He must weigh a good ten kilos."

Pierre looked at the tabby cat. "He's a big one, all right," he said. "The fellow told me a funny story about the cats. I don't know whether or not to believe it."

"What was that?" The tabby cat was gazing at Bateman with that manic expression they acquire when they are hungry.

"The ovens have gas burners," said Pierre. "They reach twelve hundred degrees, but gas is so expensive these days that they try to economize by reducing the time between cremations, so the ovens don't have a chance to cool down."

"That makes sense."

"Yes, except it means they must remove the previous corpse sooner. Often, with a large body, especially one that has been frozen, the bones aren't completely reduced to ashes."

"You're joking," Bateman said. "What do they do then?"

"Well, generally, they break the bones with the *raclette*."

"A *raclette*? Like the bakers use?"

"More or less. But that's not the worst of it. The skull and brain are a bigger problem."

"The brain?"

"Oh, yes. You can imagine. It's enclosed and surrounded by fluid. It's very difficult to burn. And, you know, in summer, the bodies must be kept frozen. It takes much longer to burn a frozen corpse."

"I do see what you mean," said Bateman, a vague nausea beginning in his chest.

"At any rate, the fellow was saying . . ." Pierre fell silent as they rounded the corner. They had come to a section of the graves covered by graffiti, much of it obscene. "I want to fuck you, Jim," "The Snake," "Patrick, Harley Davidson, 1984," and, finally, sprayed in day-glo colors across an unmarked granite slab, the explanation: "Jim Morrison, The Doors."

They stood staring at the hundreds of chalked, painted and scratched inscriptions. Some had been there for years but others seemed quite fresh. It was appalling to Bateman. They seemed mindless. He was ashamed of his own country, even after all that time away.

There was a small group of bicyclists relaxing at this curve in the path. The bicycle was a nice way to see the cemetery. The paths were smooth and free of traffic but one couldn't wander among the stones. They had left their bikes locked together and gone off a little way among the weedstrewn graves. Bateman and Pierre could hear their laughter as they examined the old-fashioned inscriptions. The bicyclists came toward them speaking English, two boys and two girls walking straight across the graves without regard for the path between. Bateman looked away. The sun went behind a cloud and he thought to look at his watch. Five-thirty already? It was getting late. He walked a little way down the path, not wanting to see the desecrations performed here to commemorate an American rock star. Pierre remained at the spot, reading the names and comments. A few minutes later Bateman looked back to see Pierre kneeling by the bicycles, talking to one of the boys, no doubt about the machines.

Bateman could see the plaza of the Crematorium and across from it the Columbarium, where the urns of ashes were installed. His eyes were caught by a strange scene. In the middle of the plaza a large German shepherd dog stood motionless. Even at that distance he could see the bared fangs and the tail lowered between the dog's legs. Surrounding the dog were about a dozen large cats. One of them advanced on the dog, and the ring of cats contracted toward him. The closest cat swatted at the dog and it appeared they were on the point of attacking him *en masse* when a man came out of the Crematorium and brandished a long stick at the crouching cats. They backed off and watched the man pull the dog away.

There were sounds of laughter and some sort of a tussle among the boys and girls at the bend in the path. He wasn't paying them much attention. Pierre was still back there. Bateman knew that the sepulcher which held the ashes of Victor Hugo was somewhere in this area. A little farther down he could find Rothschild and Gertrude Stein.

The sepulchers were quaint. Some were furnished with a sort of low chair with a padded backrest, designed for kneeling in prayer, called a *prie-dieu*. A few had hooks on the walls for hanging wreaths. Though most of the vaults were securely locked, many were open, and he peered into the shadows of one which had been used as a shelter by generations of winos, to judge from the amount of green bottle glass on the floor. Curled on the faded seat of the ancient *prie-dieu* was a large gray cat with yellow eyes.

Was it his imagination or was that cat staring at him with a particularly feral look? He had never been fond of cats. When they open their mouths, showing the tips of their tongues, their eyes glazed over in some humanly unimaginable feline ecstasy, he found them positively loathsome. He wanted to be out of the place. He looked at his watch again. Nearly six! He really had to be going. He turned around to call to Pierre and found himself staring into his face. He covered his shock with a nervous laugh. "Oh, so there you are!" Bateman said. "I thought you had bicycled off with them."

"No," said Pierre, frowning.

"I really must be getting along," Bateman said. "I told my wife we'd go out to dinner tonight." For the moment he had forgotten to whom he was speaking. But it was too late to recover gracefully. "Of course, I mean Alicia," he said.

"Of course," said Pierre. "Myself as well. I've . . . I've some work to do."

"Look, Pierre," said Bateman. "I'm sorry."

"For what?" asked Pierre, his eyes flaring suddenly. He was angry, Bateman realized. Bateman was quite taken aback. It was the first time he had seen Pierre show his temper. Pierre had something, a bit of metal, in his hand, and he was worrying at it with his fingers.

In tense silence they walked a shortcut between the rows of decrepit graves and thick foliage. The shadows were lengthening and Bateman felt uncomfortable walking ahead of Pierre. There was a tingling in his scalp. Was he afraid that Pierre might, after all these years, take some sort of physical revenge? He had never uttered a word against Bateman, never hung up a telephone, never left a message go untransmitted. As cuckolds went, Bateman thought, he had been as cooperative as could be imagined. Bateman regretted this thought immediately. Pierre was ten times more generous than he was. He deserved his sympathy, his help, not derision. "You were telling me something before," said Bateman turning around.

Pierre was walking with his eyes downcast, his hands

clasped behind, and Bateman was even more regretful of his unspoken mockery. Pierre looked up slowly. It seemed Bateman had disturbed an interior monologue. "Yes," he said, "but I don't believe it myself. Still, I suppose it would be interesting to know the truth."

"I'm not following you," said Bateman.

"The cats," he said. "You asked how they had gotten so fat. You would expect them to be starving. And there are so many."

"Yes."

"Still, I expect you are right," he said. "Someone else probably feeds them. Though the man in the Crematorium seemed serious."

"Pierre," he said, "you are talking in circles. I wish you would just come out and say what you mean."

"The way you do?" asked Pierre.

"I don't know what you are talking about," he said.

"Never mind. Come on. Maybe I can show you what the cats eat."

They had come, via the back way, to the Columbarium. It was nothing more than a wall of niches in which the urns were placed. A plaque engraved with the name and dates was fixed in each place. Some were empty and were marked *"Réservée."* They strode across the broad courtyard fronting the Crematorium, the massive building now backlit by the reddening sunset.

They left the plaza and continued toward the exit through an older section of graves, terraced to several levels. This was now a "low-rent" district, with many more abandoned graves and fewer splendid, well-kept ones.

"He said he put it somewhere around here," said Pierre, scaling an incline to reach a higher level. They were among large trees which blocked the sun. Twice, Bateman stumbled on creepers as he tried to trace Pierre's footsteps.

"Incredible," he heard Pierre say, "the guy was telling the truth!"

Bateman emerged into an overgrown area nearly hidden from the main grounds. There was a small cluster of ancient family sepulchers, with doors of rusty iron grillwork. Pierre was kneeling on the worn cushion of the prayer stool in one of the vaults, examining the contents of a small dish. He gingerly backed out of the small stone structure.

"Take a look," he said. "Watch out, there's cat shit all over."

"I don't wonder," said Bateman. "Look over there." There were no fewer than twenty-five large cats congregated around the doorway of another sepulcher. He shuddered and peered into the gloom of the vault, trying to make out what was in the small ceramic dish. He had no desire to dirty his pants on that floor.

"You won't be able to see it from here," said Pierre. "It's too dark in there."

Bateman stooped into the confined darkness. There was a withered wreath and plastic cross suspended from hooks on his right. He had to kneel on the *prie-dieu* to get a look at what was in the dish. He recognized it immediately. Nothing looks quite like brain tissue, with its twisting convolutions. But he had never seen a brain this large before, and it had already been partially consumed, by the cats, he assumed.

He was violently startled by a spider crawling across his hand. He crushed it against the stone wall with the back of his hand. There was a gentle thump and the rustling of leaves above him as something landed on the roof, a large cat, no doubt. Someone blew a whistle. It was closing time. He started to rise from the *prie-dieu* and heard a loud creak. He felt the tomb door close against his shoe soles. That was no accident. There was a loud, metallic click. He turned around, difficult in the confined space. He looked down at the door latch and saw the glint of a sturdy combination lock, the kind used with bicycle chains. It had to be Pierre, but he could see no one.

He shouted, "Open it up, Pierre!"

There was no reply. He was sure Pierre was still nearby. He remembered him kneeling with the boys at Jim Morrison's grave. After they had gone he had a bit of shiny metal in his hand.

"Mrkgnao," he heard, along with the muted thuds of several pairs of padded paws. The huge face of a cat appeared in the window grating opposite the locked door, its insane eyes glowing gold in the dying light.

He threw all of his two hundred pounds against the iron grating. It looked as though it would shatter with one lunge, but did not. Again he heaved into it with his shoulder. It was no use. He couldn't back up enough to get up momentum.

The cat in the window jumped down beside him. The faces of two others appeared in its place.

The huge cat on the floor took a swat at his ankle, cocking his head as though curious to see his reaction. He felt a sharp pain and kicked out at the cat. It arched its back and hissed, sounding very loud in the tiny space. What if they all attacked him at once, as they had been about to do in the plaza? He wouldn't be able to hold them off in the claustrophobic space. He could barely move his arms and legs.

"Pierre!" he screamed. "For God's sake!"

There were several loud thuds. Three cats were suddenly on the floor with him. Another, a huge black one, was in the window. It leaped at him. He felt the stab of claws in the back of his neck and a forepaw raked his right eye. With all his strength, ignoring the claws, sharp as needles, he wrenched the animal off and hurled it against the wall, while kicking out at the others, which had begun to attack his legs.

"Help, anyone!" he screamed. Then he saw Pierre a few meters away from the grating, wearing on his face his mournful expression which almost never changed. Bateman was quite hysterical. "They're attacking me!" he shouted. "Please, open this thing!"

"They're only cats," Pierre said. "Besides, I don't know the combination." There was the beginning of a smile tugging at his lips, though his eyes remained pitying.

One of the cats nipped Bateman's ankle and he winced in pain.

Pierre turned and started down the path toward the exit.

"For heaven's sake," Bateman screamed. "Think of Alicia!"

Pierre's steps slowed. He appeared to be reconsidering.

Bateman gripped the rusty bars of his cage, watching Pierre disappear from sight and he heard, "Don't worry Bateman. I'll tell her you'll be late for dinner."

THE PROPERT BEQUEST
Basil A. Smith

It may seem at first a contradiction for a best-of-the-year anthology to include a story by an author who has been dead for a number of years. However, 1980 saw the first publication of an important collection of supernatural stories by Basil A. Smith, *The Scallion Stone*, from Whispers Press. Although Smith died in 1969, only the title story had previously been published, and the story behind all this seems itself a bit like the start of an M. R. James ghost story.

Basil A. Smith was an English clergyman, for many years Rector of Holy Trinity, Micklegate, York. The rectory grounds covered the graveyard of a medieval priory, and monks' bones were forever surfacing in the Smiths' garden. The church itself, with its twelfth-century nave, was reputedly haunted by apparitions whose silhouettes passed against a great stained-glass window. A scholar and antiquary as well, Smith was author of *Dean Church: the Anglican Response to Newman* (Oxford University Press: 1958) and was active in numerous drives to preserve York's rich architectural heritage. At the time of his death he was Canon Treasurer of York Minster. Smith was also interested in ghost stories, and he tried his hand at writing several himself—evidently for his own amusement alone. Fortunately he showed his manuscripts to his friend, Russell Kirk, the noted author and critic, who rescued them from oblivion after Smith's death. These came to the attention of editor Stuart David Schiff, who published "The Scallion Stone" in *Whispers* (Doubleday: 1977), and then collected all of Smith's stories in a beautifully produced hardcover volume with an introduction by Russell Kirk and illustrations by Stephen Fabian. Although structurally Smith's stories immediately call to mind the English ghost story tradition of M. R. James, Smith was no slavish pasticheur. Indeed, "The Propert Bequest" is a masterpiece in its own right, and makes one wish Smith had had a bit more time to indulge his hobby.

I

As a typical English estate Peryford Priory would be difficult to surpass. The house, designed by Carr in his best manner amid a majestic grouping of beech trees, is well placed to dominate the wide expanse of park which sweeps gently away southwestward with its formal plantations and cattle browsing in the pasture. The way from the outer world into this haven of tranquility is by a gravel drive curving leisurely for half a mile and terminating in a balustraded terrace before the hall itself.

It was from the vantage point of this terrace that Courtleigh, accompanied by Mr. Sanderton, the Rector of Peryford, looked across the park one pleasant evening in the summer of 18—. The rectory, where they had recently dined, adjoined the priory grounds and there was access by a private walk beside the kitchen gardens. This was a very convenient arrangement as Dr. Propert, the owner of Peryford, and Mr. Sanderton were on terms of constant intercourse.

Courtleigh, who had only arrived a little before dinner, was to spend the night with his clerical friend and then resume his journey to London. Legal business had called him away from the academic routine of Durham, and he had taken the opportunity of breaking his journey at York and driving out to Peryford which was about ten miles away. He had long wanted to know more about this secluded place that his friend had tumbled into. And now at last he was here to see for himself the priory and parish.

It was indeed well worth seeing, and the evening was perfect. The monastic ruins (which gave the name "Priory" to the modern residence) lay in a corner of the park beyond the cypress walk. Birds were trilling sleepily among the mossy stonework of the dilapidated columns and archways, and a sluggish brook was glinting in the willows beyond, as the two friends left the ornamental seat and resumed their stroll.

"You've got an eye for landscape in these parts," murmured the professor, drinking in the mellow scene. "There's quite a last-century tone about it—except perhaps that chapel yonder looks a bit out of period!"

"Yes," assented Sanderton, "that's the library I told you about in my letter. Originally it was part of the old Peryford Priory—the monks' frater, in fact. Then it was the family chapel. Rather magnificent, too, though I grant you it's been over-restored. Some of your enthusiasts for the mediaeval are nothing if not drastic. Still, like some of the ladies of the parish, it may not be much to look at—but it's full of good works within!"

"And the greatest of these—" added Courtleigh with a laugh, "is the *Peryford Household Book*. What a stir its discovery made! I wonder the British Museum has not been after it. I've always wanted to see it for myself."

"I'm afraid," said the rector, now suddenly gloomy, "you'll be disappointed. It's not here now."

"What? Sold, you mean, or away on loan?" asked Courtleigh, a little annoyed.

"No. Not that," replied Sanderton in evident misery. "I fear it's stolen—or at any rate it disappeared some time back. But, please, please, don't say a word about it. I perhaps shouldn't have told you. Dr. Propert still thinks to find it again without any public inquiries and excitement. And I hope he will, poor man, for the loss of it has weighed on him considerably."

The professor could only gasp at the news. "And how long do you suppose you're going to keep a thing like this quiet?" he said at length. "Why, it's a matter of national interest."

"Oh, I don't know," pleaded the harassed clergyman. "Only the doctor especially wants nothing to be done as yet. He thinks it will turn up."

"Well, well," sighed Courtleigh at length. "I suppose he is the one most concerned and must have his way. But, thank heaven, you've got some valuable items still. I say," he brightened, "while I'm here I must have a peep at some of them. I'd dearly like to see that Flemish missal and the freak psalter you spoke about."

Sanderton reflected for a moment, anxious to please his friend, but again looked doubtful. "I'm afraid the place is locked for the night," he said despondently, "or else I would have been delighted. Can't you take a later train in the morning and give us time to look round together?"

"It's really most important I should go first thing," answered Courtleigh with genuine regret. "I suppose we couldn't get the key and just have a rapid glance at things now? It won't be dark for an hour yet."

"Very well, I'll go and get the keys while you have a look round the outside," declared his friend at last. "Dr. Propert is rather averse to anyone's going into the library after dusk, but for once I think we might."

So saying, the good little man hurried off and left Courtleigh strolling round to survey the exterior features of the building.

It certainly bore signs of having been "restored" and heightened by nineteenth-century hands. This was specially evident at the east end where a fine large window took up almost the whole height from ground to gable point. The sides were flanked by wide and heavy buttresses, apparently strengthened in recent years but ivy-clad to tone with the older stonework. It looked as if parts of the choir window of the priory had been incorporated here, but for some reason the upper tracery had been replaced by a great wheel-window of the type so dear to Gothic architects of Queen Victoria's reign.

Such atrocious treatment of an old building made Courtleigh shake his head, and he was glad to give up stumbling among the bushes and get back to the pathway to wait for Sanderton's return. Standing in the library doorway in loitering mood, he was surprised when the door opened and a man came out bearing a bag of tools. The man was apparently also surprised for as he went off toward the lodge he looked back more than once at the professor.

But, whoever he was, he had not locked the door. So after a moment Courtleigh took the heavy iron ring in both hands and let himself in. Sanderton was not in sight and his friend smiled to think what he would say when he returned. Entering, he found himself in a churchlike hall of oblong shape, running east and west. The entrance was on the north side, and just within was a staircase leading up to a gallery. This upper floor both formed a sort of vestibule by the doorway and also ran the full length of the wall. The south side had

THE PROPERT BEQUEST

no gallery, but a flight of stone steps led eastward up to the stout door of what appeared to be a raised vestry in the corner. ("A good strong-room for scarce volumes," thought Courtleigh as he noted this last feature.) The whole western end was taken up with a chapel shut off by an oak screen. It was rather dingy as most of the light came from the window at the farther end, and the evening sun was getting faint by now.

The walls, both in the gallery and below, were lined with shelves of books and, his attention drawn toward some rich bindings, Courtleigh had soon forgotten all about the architecture as he wandered from case to case taking down and replacing various books that his interest lighted on.

Thus occupied, he kept moving gently about on the ground floor till he became aware that he was not alone. He was by this time at the western end of the building where the library proper was terminated by the little oratory or chapel we have mentioned. It was somewhere above that he heard a snuffling sound. He looked up to the gallery and noticed that the end of it which overlooked the oratory was also partitioned off by a wooden screen, evidently so as to form a compartment for more private study. Yes, there was someone in there, for a chair was pushed back, and through the balusters Courtleigh saw a person rise and move slowly to the staircase.

Presently a tall man descended, nodding his head with the involuntary gravity of old age, and mouthing somewhat as he went. Courtleigh was wondering how to address him, but the old man seemed not to have noticed his presence. Indeed, having reached the ground floor, he passed straightway into the little oratory and closed the screen again. For the next few minutes there followed a rapid muttering and much sighing from within, while Courtleigh pretended to be examining an antiquated commentary. Then, his devotion ended, the old man re-emerged and, catching sight of the stranger, turned halting as if to inquire what brought him there.

"Ah! Good day, sir. A visitor, I presume?" he cried in a sharp, old-fashioned tone.

"A good evening to you, sir," replied Courtleigh. "My friend Mr. Sanderton's left me here while . . ."

"Yes, yes, yes," chattered the other with a comprehending wag of the head as he moved away to end the conversation without more ado. "He will tell you sufficient of the vanities and vicissitudes of the place."

Before Courtleigh had time to do more than mutter some word of thanks, the old man had trotted past him and up the stone stairs at the other side to the strong-room which he unlocked and entered, returning presently with a heavy quarto volume under his arm. He relocked the place and descended again to leave the library, and was in the act of letting himself out when he returned a pace or two as with an afterthought.

"It is, I believe," said he, "my duty to commend to you as a stranger our little oratory there. Should you be in need of ghostly succor it is a very present help."

He cocked a shrewd eye intently upon the stranger, pausing a moment as if he might say more. As he stood, the faint light falling upon his aged face gave its drawn quizzical grimace an air most cryptic. But presently the door had closed behind him, and Courtleigh, with a fading smile upon his lips, was left alone.

The twilight was thickening now, hardly a good time to be examining the east window, but it compelled attention. For what a gigantic window it was: the dimensions were almost cathedral. Indeed, the additional mullions, standing off from the glasswork to give vertical support on the inner side, reminded Courtleigh of the great window at York Minster. So also did the two transoms whose horizontal lines divided the whole space into three separate areas. The lower lights—up to where the outline of the window curved away from the oblong to the arch—were filled with countless fragments of mediaeval glass. By dint of twisting his head about, Courtleigh could decipher broken scraps of mitred heads, ships' prows, rich canopies and flowing robes, all jumbled into a mosaic of dull tinctures glowing ever so faintly against the library's interior gloom. There were heraldic medallions among all this but any effort to identify the arms at that hour was bound to be in vain. It remained but to scan the topmost section above the upper transom. Here the original tracery had disappeared and a rose-window been inserted in its place. No wonder the antiquary shook his head. With some impatience he too found himself trying to make out the motif of the pattern in this glass. For, though the coloring was fearsome, the emblems had a barbaric vigor unlike the jejeune conventions

THE PROPERT BEQUEST

usually found in imitations of this sort. With a sigh of frustration, though, he soon turned away to explore elsewhere.

And then it was that he had to jerk himself together. Perhaps he had been craning upward too long and made his head a little giddy. But, just for the moment when his back was turned, something had clattered on the glass, and a sudden shadow seemed to swoop down from across the window and behind him. He ducked involuntarily as from a stealthy blow, and swung around with his arm upraised.

Then he laughed softly at the idea. The appearance of the old man and his morbid-sounding words had probably reacted on his mind. After all, what more likely than that this queer old gentleman had thought it was not mere curiosity, but a troubled mind in need of spiritual comfort, that brought a stranger into the chapel library at that hour? It was all very natural. No doubt there was a tree outside swayed by the wind, and the sound he had heard would be the twigs scrabbled against the glass. Certainly there was nothing to be seen now. And so, jeering inwardly at himself to find his nerves so jumpy, he turned his attention once more from the glass and decided to have a look inside the eccentric's place of retreat.

He was quite composed again as he pushed back the screen door and entered this dim and poky oratory. It was, though small, elaborately fitted out in High Church style. Above the altar a votive lamp, burning steadfastly and low, cast a slumbering gleam upon the gilded finery. At one side there stood a curious Sanctus bell, and at the other an antique prayer-desk where, it seemed, the old man said his frequent orisons. His lighted candle, fixed in an iron bracket, was still flickering before an image of the Virgin.

As Courtleigh was engrossed with these things, Sanderton returned, apologizing for being away so long. "What a chase I've had," he exclaimed. "When I got up to the house they told me Dr. Propert was down here. I met him on the way back. He said there was a friend of mine in the library when he came out!"

"So that was the doctor!" murmured Courtleigh. "He didn't give me much chance to explain myself and I felt a bit of a trespasser. He seems a queer man."

"Yes," returned the rector, "he is a bit diffident with strangers. Anyway, it's lucky you tried the door."

"In point of fact, I didn't," confessed Courtleigh. "It was a mechanic coming out that made me realize it was open. An elderly man with some joiner's tools; and he looked a bit suspicious of me too!"

"That would be Hook, I should think," said the rector. "I heard the doctor had sent for him again but I don't know what for—some little repair job, I expect. It's a bit surprising, though, for he used to work for Faik."

"Faik? Who's Faik?" asked the professor as they left the oratory together.

"Oh, he's the man responsible for altering this place and turning it into a library. I'll tell you about him afterward when we've had a glance through some of the books. It's getting dark so we shall have to be quick: there's no artificial light in the place. But fancy my going for the key while the door was open all the time!"

So saying, the rector escorted his friend rapidly around the shelves in the gallery and below. There was not enough time to do more than pick out a few unusual volumes here and there.

"The best of our treasures are in the Muniment Room, as we call it," said he next, leading up the stone steps and unlocking the strong-room. "And it will hardly be possible to see them to advantage now, I fear." It was indeed so dark inside that Courtleigh could only catch a tantalizing glimpse of heavy oak presses filled with shadowy volumes. In order to get at least some idea of its rich contents they took one or two items to the doorway—a sixteenth-century herbal by Nicholas Huby; a Book of Hours, said to have belonged to the mother of Lady Jane Grey; a volume or so of an early set of the Greek Fathers; a treatise on the Court of Piepowder (the only known copy) by Spelman; some seventeenth-century manuscripts on Church Law; and an abstruse work on casuistry, ascribed to Charles I.

"And all these go to Oxford when Dr. Propert dies. I shall have to come along again and have a proper look at them before long," said Courtleigh with a sigh, thinking of psalters and missals yet unseen. As they locked the doors and emerged into the park again, he added: "But what a pity the *Household Book* should be missing. The flower of the collection."

"Good gracious me! I was going to tell you about that,"

exclaimed Sanderton, suddenly remembering. "When I met Dr. Propert on the terrace I mentioned your special interest in it and said I had often wondered about it myself. Imagine my astonishment when the doctor smiled at me in that strange way of his and said, 'My dear Sanderton, have no fear. It's safe all right in spite of the devices of the ungodly. *It's here, Sanderton, it's here!*' he hissed, tapping a heavy volume which he was carrying under his arm.

" 'Oh, that's wonderful!' I exclaimed. 'When did you find it? I am itching to examine it, and I'm also sure my friend would be delighted.' 'So you shall, both of you, but not just yet. There's more about this matter than you know of. One day you will understand why I say this, but meanwhile we must be patient—patient and secret.' With that he left me. And that's all I can tell you," concluded Sanderton.

"Ah," said Courtleigh, "that would be the old quarto he fetched out of the Muniment Room. Perhaps he thought I'd come to steal it! What a mysterious-minded man he is. He seems to make good use of that oratory too. You never told me he was—shall I say?—a man of devotion."

The rector was silent for a while. He was a kindly, simple man and obviously did not relish discussing the eccentricities of a patron for whom he had so much regard.

"You know," he said at last, "it is very easy to misunderstand Dr. Propert. People say he is an oddity. Some—who would do well to take themselves to church a bit oftener—even whisper that he has become a religious maniac, and other nonsense. You, as a stranger, would find him perhaps a trifle erratic. But I know him well enough to make allowances. He has not always been like this, and he has not changed without a cause."

It was growing dark as the two men walked along under the beech avenue, and Courtleigh kept sympathetically silent till his friend resumed:

"You see, Dr. Propert scarcely saw Peryford till last year. He was born while his father, Sir Ronald, was busy with the Asia Commission. He spent his childhood in India before going to Oxford. There he met Faik (the man I mentioned before) and formed some sort of friendship with him. But the doctor's studies soon took him abroad again, first to Cairo and later to Peking where—as you know—he gained his name as an archaeologist. Being but distantly connected with the main branch of the Peryford family, he did not interest himself in its history, and certainly never looked to inherit the estate. But, as luck would have it, a succession of deaths (first Baron Peryford and his two sons and finally Lady Ann who died without issue) put the whole property, as they say, 'in Chancery.'

"This is where Faik with his legal knowledge comes on the scene again. As a friend of Propert's, he wrote urging him to press his claim at law before it became too late. The doctor, with characteristic nonchalance, put the matter in Faik's hands and bade him fight the case if he thought it worthwhile. The lawyer certainly did exert himself and actually secured the estate for his friend and client. Most men in Propert's shoes would have come back to see their inheritance, but the Doctor had just entered upon another project with some American explorers and was in no mood for returning to England then. So, to save himself trouble and also to reward his friend, he generously invited Faik to become his free tenant and reside at Peryford, looking after it in any way he thought best. That was five years ago.

"Then began the fatal renovations which led up to final quarrel. There was a huge but much-neglected library occupying half the east wing of the hall. To this was added a large batch of volumes belonging to Propert himself, books he had acquired in his travels and which he now decided to send home ready for when he should some day return. All these were in the charge of the rector—Mr. Laycock, my predecessor—who was quite a bibliographer.

"Now Faik, having a household of his own, soon formed a scheme for turning the old chapel, then ruinous, into a new library (that is, of course, the one we've just visited here in the park) and getting all the books down there together. Well, you've seen the place for yourself and can judge how much rebuilding and altering he did. I admit there was much to be said for the scheme. There was no reason (except to an architectural purist like yourself!) why some masonry from the priory ruins should not be incorporated into the restorations.

"I never understood the details but it was evident my predecessor took a dislike to Faik almost from the start. There was the vandalism to do with the priory remains; and also, of course, here was a consecrated building, however disused, suddenly being secularized. I think that grieved him. Whatever it was, he put his foot down about the whole plan though he was unable to stop its being carried out. It was a queer position for him, you see. So far as the books were concerned, Laycock was in charge; but he could not insist that they remain in the house if Faik wanted them out. There were valuable editions and unique specimens—a number of them uncatalogued—and after their removal to the new library there was talk of some volumes being missed: in fact the *Household Book* itself disappeared. In the end everything came to a head with the doctor's return to England. He supported my predecessor entirely; there was a violent quarrel with Faik (probably about the expenditure) and he was turned out. Propert came to reside here himself; poor Laycock died soon afterward and—here I am."

When the rector finished his story, it was some time before Courtleigh made any comment. "Did the doctor ever tell you the full extent of the charges Mr. Laycock made against Faik?" he asked at length.

"No. It's a matter he never likes referring to," answered Sanderton. "It was not merely financial. I fancy Laycock infected him with his own personal animus against the lawyer. It's plain he's still easily upset about the affair. 'We shall have to go warily,' he is often saying when we discuss any new arrangements for the library. Since coming here he's changed visibly."

"In what way?" pressed Courtleigh with some curiosity.

"Well, for one thing," resumed Sanderton, "he had his travel notes and research material put into that little reading-cabinet at the end of the gallery, and he works in there daily when at home. Of course, there's nothing surprising in that for, as you know, the final volume of his *Primitive Burial Rites* is not yet complete. But the doctor's got it firmly into his head that Faik's spies are often hanging about the place. It may seem fantastic but he certainly puts little limit to what that man would do, and declares there are several books here they would like to get their hands upon. That's why the choicest things are kept in the Muniment Room.

"But that's not all. The poor man was—and still is—constantly interrupting his studies by fancying he can hear the thieves actually in the place. I admit the library, like most old buildings, has its queer noises at times; but the doctor will not be persuaded it is only that. Anyway, he became very interested in the Puseyites (though he never mixes with them!) and got the idea all at once of putting in the oratory. The whole building had for a long time been the family chapel and, as he said, it seemed only fitting to have prayers in it again. I was pleased at this for I thought he intended restoring the library, at least partially, to its former use. I thought it would be a good thing to get the domestic staff down sometimes, and I gladly offered to read matins and evensong there daily."

The professor smiled at this bit of clerical zeal, but it was dark, and the other went on:

"But that was not what Dr. Propert wanted. His mind was set on a private oratory where he could slip in and say prayers alone before and after going to his books up in the cabinet. The place, as you saw, is rather quaint: he got various pieces of old church furniture to fit it up. But I've always felt that I was not very happy there. For one thing, it faces west; but for some perverse reason he would have it so. The consequence is I rarely go inside except to celebrate on certain saints' days about which the doctor is very particular."

After this lengthy recital the rector gave vent to a great sigh like a man much bewildered by half-knowledge.

"Well," said Courtleigh with grim cheerfulness, "you've tied yourself up to some very eccentric company. I shall feel quite guilty leaving you tomorrow! By the way, is anything known about this Faik's present activities and whereabouts?"

"Before leaving here," said Sanderton, "he bought a small property at Hengsward, beyond Malton, but they say he's mostly on the move. 'Away in London' is all the news I ever hear."

"Hm," grunted the professor, as they reached the rectory gate, "it's my opinion the less you see of that gentleman the better."

II

It was autumn before Courtleigh could make his second visit. During the long vacation he often thought of Peryford but was unable then to get away. One day, however, there came a letter from Sanderton reporting that Dr. Propert had unexpectedly become benevolently disposed toward Durham. The news was a complete surprise to Courtleigh who wrote eagerly to know what had led to such a turn of events. I will give the gist of the situation without quoting all the correspondence. Here it is.

Something has already been said about the doctor's ultra-Tractarian sympathies in matters of religion and of his zeal for ceremonies. It seems a tragic irony that this new access of piety should have expressed him to the ruin of his lifetime's greatest hope. For, along with his devotional bent, Propert was a notable scholar. He had indeed been a Fellow of Carpe Corpus, and it was an open secret that his valuable collection of books was to be bequeathed to that college. Furthermore, people with a knowledge of the probabilities considered it a foregone conclusion that Propert would be made Master at the next election.

The prospect of that honor was in fact the old man's most cherished ambition and accounted partly for his return to England. You may judge, therefore, what a blow it was to him when news came through that Cornwick, the other candidate, had been chosen instead. In due time it also transpired that the vote had only gone against him in consequence of certain malicious reports set forward by Faik—himself a Carpe Corpus man—that Propert had become a secret Papist.

It was without doubt a gross calumny which the unfortunate victim most strenuously answered, both directly and through the papers. But, as is usual in such cases, it was impossible to establish the author of the blow, and in any case the deed was done. After taking all possible legal advice the poor doctor had to realize that there could be no redress. But for ever afterward there would rankle in his mind, not so much the disappointment as the dastardly stab behind it.

Thus, with his declining years overshadowed by bitterness, he lived more than ever among his books in the reading-cabinet or in the oratory below, leaning upon the sympathetic offices of Mr. Sanderton, his chaplain.

Now this good man, being nephew of one of the Canons of Durham, had always entertained a lively concern for the new university then beginning to establish itself in the north. It was in this connection that his friendship with Professor Courtleigh had been ripened. The pair of them had drawn up a list of works which they considered the indispensable minimum for the use of the undergraduates; and Sanderton had sent along some of his own volumes as a gift. Only by chance did Dr. Propert make this discovery in conversation with his chaplain for it would have been abhorrent to Sanderton either to advertise his own donation or to suggest that another should follow his example. Yet, when the discovery was made, something of the bachelor cleric's devotion to so obscure a cause appealed to the old collector. Before long he himself—weaned by bitterness of any remaining love for his own college—began to take a growing interest in what he playfully called "our poor little Oxford of the north."

Mr. Sanderton, indeed, was half delighted and half startled to see how rapidly the fire of this fresh enthusiasm was devouring his patron's whole attention. Nothing could abate his eagerness. A slight seizure, which overtook the doctor in the summer, not only caused no diminution of interest but actually spurred him to an urgency of benevolent planning which took the little clergyman's breath away. Whispers reached Oxford that the Propert books were now likely to go to Durham, that the doctor was aging visibly, and that one of the professors from up north had even been invited to Peryford to select a number of the volumes to be transferred for use forthwith.

And so it came about that in October Courtleigh was down at Peryford Priory for the second time. Sanderton took him at once to meet the doctor, and the three of them had a thorough and very pleasant conference. It was agreed to draw up a legal instrument next day and make an inspection of the books at the same time. The following morning saw them busy in the library itself; and in the afternoon the doctor's solicitor came down from York to attend them there. It would have been a memorable day in any case but it was made more so by a strange intrusion.

For who should have the temerity to present himself again at Peryford but Faik! He came uninvited and without warning. Whether he deceived himself into believing that Propert was not aware of his infamous part in the college election, or whether he considered he could at last safely trade upon his old friend's good nature to accept him again, I cannot tell. Perhaps it was merely that he had the vulgarity to suppose that, armed with money and a direct proposal, he could carry off his purpose well enough.

Anyhow he had, knowingly or unknowingly, chosen a critical moment to reappear. The great library was a scene of unusual activity. The legal business had been concluded; and the doctor, assisted by Courtleigh, was superintending the labors of carpenter Hook and two old servingmen in the removal of some heavy tomes across to the Muniment Room, while Mr. Sanderton and the lawyer were in conversation by the gallery stairs, when the butler opened the door and ushered in the unwelcome visitor.

The air became electrified at once. The rector, who was nearest the door, made a stiff bow; Courtleigh and the solicitor looked up in mild surprise; but the doctor confronted his former friend with a withering stare.

"Good afternoon, Propert," cried the intruder with false geniality, "I'm sorry to surprise you like this. You seem busy!"

"Professor Courtleigh is here by my invitation on a little matter concerning some books. May I ask what your business is?" replied Propert coldly.

"Ah," said Faik in urbane tones, "I've heard some talk about your interest in Durham. But you have a duty to your own college, you know. I'm sure you've not forgotten that, despite that unfortunate little incident."

"Mr. Faik," repeated the doctor, "what is your business?"

Things were beginning to look ugly when, at a sign from the rector, Hook and the other men withdrew on tiptoe.

"If we must be so blunt," resumed Faik, more briskly now, "I've been commissioned by the Master and resident Fellows of Carpe Corpus to make an offer to purchase the whole collection of your books, Dr. Propert."

"I have no books to sell," answered the doctor curtly, and added with tremulous warmth, "the college might have had them as a gift—but for its readiness to listen to blackguards who slander honest men. I have decided, sir, to put my poor volumes at the disposal of a needier and, I hope, more grateful body."

"A most regrettable step," muttered Faik uncomfortably, "but there is still time to make a compromise. The college authorizes me to offer ten thousand pounds for the major part of the books, provided certain specified volumes are included."

The doctor was silent. Faik mistook the opportunity to press further: "Ten thousand pounds is a large sum. With it much might be done to benefit another institution," he urged, glancing suggestively toward the professor. "Nor would the terms preclude many useful volumes also going elsewhere."

He paused, looking more hopeful. Then the doctor said quietly, "Perhaps Mr. Bates will lead the way to the cabinet. I'd like you all to come, gentlemen."

They trooped upstairs after the lawyer and along the gallery to the little apartment at the end.

"And now," said the doctor, "will you, Mr. Bates, be so good as to read out for Mr. Faik's benefit the terms of my will which you witnessed earlier on—the portion, that is, relating to the books?"

The solicitor opened the dead-box again and, finding the place among the documents, read the relevant clauses and then repeated, ". . . and the residue of all books, manuscripts, incunabula, charters, tracts or pamphlets, contained in or appertaining to, the aforesaid Frater Library . . . I bequeath to the University of Durham . . ."

"I hope, Mr. Faik," said the doctor gravely after a pause, "you will now consider that your proposals are fully and decisively answered." It was a devastating blow, and Faik was evidently crestfallen. Yet he had not quite done, even then.

"This is a most lamentable decision, Dr. Propert," he said heavily, "but I will convey your answer to the college." He paused, strumming on one of the oak presses, then looked up to add, "I have but one more request or offer to make, and this time a personal one on my own account."

"There was," he continued, "in this library a certain *Household Book of Peryford Priory* which has always very much interested me. That it is valuable as a fifteenth-century record I am well aware. Nor do I ask it altogether as a favor. I am, I say as a collector, specially attracted by the volume. May I offer five hundred pounds for it now?"

Courtleigh and the rest looked quickly at the doctor.

"I have, sir," replied that veteran with just a hint of somber irony, "already heard from Mr. Sanderton's predecessor of your interest in this rather—let us call it—obscure book. But the fact is we have (without—at my request—going so far as to inspect its contents) very particularly disposed of the book in question only an hour ago."

He bent to open a cupboard at the side, and returned with an ancient calf-bound volume.

"As it is, its significance is largely wasted to be sure," he continued pensively as he weighed it in his hands, and cleared his throat to assume what might have been a mock tone of public speaking. "But in order to make its contents generally available, and fully intelligible—for let us be frank and say there are some apparently meaningless entries in it—I have asked Professor Courtleigh to undertake to bring out an annotated edition, and also to compose a preface embodying something of my personal biography. The whole thing, you see, will form a sort of memorial volume. For, I confess, I have lately entertained the vanity of acquainting the world how this little book has affected my own humble fortunes; and I fancy the disclosures may prove of some interest in academic circles. They certainly would go far to account for my change of intention toward my old college. On behalf of the authorities at Durham, Professor Courtleigh has very obligingly agreed to this—and, incidentally, we have also arranged that the bequest of my books come into effect immediately after the public issue of the memorial volume."

Faik was visibly disturbed. But the doctor, carrying the book with him and leading the way downstairs again, pursued the theme with benign malice, apparently addressing Faik:

"I am afraid any pleasure you or others could derive from the perusal of this publication may have to be postponed a little while as I do not wish it to appear in my lifetime. Probably you will not have long to wait; but until I am gone I wish the whole matter to remain dormant. When the time comes the Professor will find jotted down at the end of the *Household Book* a concise testimony of the facts he is to use—as well as some other curious matter which for a long time I was not able to understand and whose precise meaning I shall probably never comprehend fully—though (as you will in good time find from my comments there) I have made some headway with the clues. Yes, yes . . ."

Whatever these last remarks may have meant—and four faces were evidently arrested with intrigue—the doctor's voice trailed off at this point into silent musing. Then he pulled himself up sharp and in a different tone remarked,

"Tomorrow we will have the volume specially deposited and sealed, but for tonight I think it should be safe enough as it is in the Muniment Room."

By this time, he was again on the ground floor at the foot of the stone stairs at the other side of the library. In another minute he had gone up, placed the book somewhere within the Muniment Room and locked its heavy door.

"I don't think," he concluded simply as he rejoined the others, "we need detain ourselves here any longer, gentlemen."

The scene was over. Faik, tense with chagrin and alarm, departed abruptly as Propert, wearing a strange smile, stood meaningly at the outer door. As soon as the intruder had gone he insisted on locking it himself, then caught up with his friends who had set off for the hall, buzzing with excitement. The gong was sounding for dinner as they left the park and its much-disputed library under the gathering pall of night.

And a very memorable night it was, that 17th of October. A great gale was blowing and the trees about the old house were tossing wildly when Dr. Propert, his chaplain, and the professor withdrew after dinner to the smoking room.

Talk had turned again to Faik and his unexpected visit, and the doctor evinced a gleeful sense of elation at the way in which the deal with Durham had been culminated on a day which served to thwart his enemy so neatly. Certainly it was a rare thing for anyone to see the old benefactor so openly festive.

Perhaps, indeed, the excitement of the day had been too much for him. At any rate Mr. Sanderton could not but observe his patron's feverish mien and suggest an early bed. But the doctor brushed aside all solicitation, so set was he upon discussing with Courtleigh the business of publishing the memoirs that would one day vindicate him. More wine was ordered in, and the two guests settled down to hear what their host would disclose concerning Faik and his practices.

Courtleigh had been saying how mystified he was by the guarded words used by the doctor that afternoon in reference to the contents of the *Household Book* which, he observed with a whimsical shrug, neither Sanderton nor himself had yet seen.

THE PROPERT BEQUEST

Propert was silent awhile pondering the hint. Then he said, "Yes, I suppose it is time I let you both into the secret, especially after the transactions today. I had to be ambiguous in the presence of Faik, for—though I am certain he knew all about the jottings I referred to—I didn't want him to challenge me for proof. You see," he added with a wry inclination of the head, "you've got to be careful about accusing a man of certain things.

"The contents of the book," he continued, "the original contents, are normal enough; a diary of expenditure, inventories of gear and stores, cellarer's accounts and what not, such as you expect in a noble establishment of the fifteenth century. But there are later entries too; strange recipes—some of them quite barbarous—scraps of proverbs and weather lore. Again, not very surprising. Then, jotted in with this, a lot of rigmarole (some of it quite recently written) that I found totally meaningless at first. Lately, however, I have begun to see the purpose of it. I won't tell you my conclusions yet, but tomorrow we'll go down to the library again and you shall see it for yourselves."

His listeners could only remain mystified but deferential. "I ought to say," he added, "that it was Mr. Laycock's suspicions which first put me on the track. He was both a good man and a discerning man, though at first I thought his suggestion absurd. The whole thing is remarkably deep and complicated and, but for my dear friend (who had delved a good deal into some of the backwaters of profane learning), there is no knowing how far matters would have gone. And now, before anything public is done, I have arranged to give Faik an opportunity of, er, well, of proving his guilt!"

"But, I take it," interposed Courtleigh gently, "that Mr. Laycock had evidence enough. Certain books were missing?"

"Yes, yes," agreed the doctor. "It was not the number, though, but the kind of books that set him thinking. Moreover, quite apart from the volumes lost, there were some unusual volumes found."

"You mean atheism or blasphemy, I suppose?" ventured the rector in sad tones.

"Something of the sort," replied Propert with a certain restraint as he rose. "It is an unpleasant business to be handling, and it's as well to use every care. To begin with, I must bring down—no, I will not have it fetched—an old psalter that I keep for use in the oratory, but which I brought across with me tonight and put in my dressing room. No, even Perkins couldn't find it, thank you. I'll be back with it in a minute."

So saying, he shuffled stiffly out of the room while Sanderton looked worriedly toward his friend and shook his head.

"All this is very disturbing," he murmured. "I hate subversive writings but I think the doctor is magnifying Faik's mischief. Theft's a plain thing: why not stick to that and dispense with these scruples and precautions?"

"That's what I felt," said Courtleigh, "but I think he's on the track of something important. Faik may, or may not, be a criminal but I think he's the sort to go beyond mere burglary."

"What do you mean?" asked the rector with puzzled surprise.

"Blackmail? Pornography? Treason? Oh, I don't know," replied the professor with a shrug. "We'll soon see. When the doctor comes down I've one or two direct questions to ask him."

The doctor was, however, a long time. The two men had heard him open an upstairs door, but after that the house was silent save for the ticking of an antique clock. Sanderton went out to listen in the hall.

"Dr. Propert, are you there?" he called at length, ascending the stairs.

He entered the bedroom and there saw, in the light of his single candle, the old man collapsed over an oak chest by the window, with the curtains drawn back as if he had been staring out. As Sanderton raised and helped him to the bed, his lips faltered out what appeared to be part of a psalm; but he had scarcely got to the Gloria Patri when he died in his faithful cleric's arms.

Courtleigh and the butler were by this time upstairs in answer to Sanderton's cry. More lights were brought, but as Perkins moved to draw the curtains again, he exclaimed, "Lord spare us, Mr. Sanderton, there's someone across in the Chapel Library. I saw the big window light up, all colors like a lantern. One flash it was, sir, but it's all dark again now."

Courtleigh had seen it too. Whether it meant thieves or fire he did not know, but in any case it boded no good. Leaving Perkins to help Mr. Sanderton with his dead master, he ran downstairs, sent a boy to the lodge ordering the gardener to watch that no one passed the gate, while he himself tore across to the library with Hook the joiner to catch whomsoever might be there.

Someone certainly had been in since the doctor locked the place that afternoon. The outside door was open and stood slightly ajar. Snatching the lantern from Hook and bidding him stay there on guard, the resolute scholar, with his stick very grimly poised, went peering inside.

The place was deathly still as he made first for the Muniment Room and tried the strong oak door at the top of the steps. With a grunt of relief he found it quite secure. Next he searched the gallery and sent the shadows sweeping around alarmingly as the lantern's beams played through into the cabinet and down into the oratory below. But no sign of a trespasser could he find. In a few minutes Hook's voice from the door was growing less reverently subdued as the danger of encounter faded out. He was even becoming jocose when the professor gave up the search and rejoined him.

As luck would have it, though, a gust of wind swung the door hard back and sent the lantern crashing out of Courtleigh's hand.

"Devils of hell!" he muttered in a tone quite unlike himself when, as he fumbled for a match, a scurry of dead leaves swirled against his face.

"You don't think anybody did that so as to get past us, do you, sir?" asked the old servant, once more querulous.

"It was the wind, of course," retorted the professor rather shortly. "What makes you ask such silly questions?"

"Well, I just kind of thought I saw a figure—leastways a face—slide behind you, sir, as the lantern went out. But very like it was all my fancy, sir," mumbled the apologetic Hook.

"A face! What sort of a 'face'?" rapped Courtleigh with a challenging scorn as they walked back to the house in time to meet the other searchers also returning.

"See anybody at all?" he cried, hailing them by the steps. "Not a soul, sir," replied the stolid gardener, "'cept Lizzie what thinks she see Mr. Faik, bless yer life, slip behint a bush. Must be able to see double if yer ask me. All I say is—there's not a living soul in this 'ere park, barring present company, sir."

"Thank you, Jennings," replied the professor. "It seems to

have been a false alarm; or at any rate no damage has been done. We'd better all get off to bed, I think."

As the party filed into the house again, Hook could be heard muttering, "Faik! By Christmas, that was the face. I couldn't call it to mind. That was 'im all right—either 'im or the spelk of 'im."

Next day, as soon as the necessary arrangements for Dr. Propert's funeral had been put in hand, Mr. Sanderton and the professor stepped over to the library to make a thorough daylight investigation. The lock of the great door—the only way in or out—had not been forced for the key was in it. Either it had been stolen from the house, or the doctor must have forgotten it while in the very act of locking the place. Which it was, no one would ever know now. The door to the Muniment Room was still locked and bore no signs of violence. But when the rector unfastened it and went inside the moments reached a tempo of feverish anxiety. At first they dare not believe it, but a rapid search assured them both that the *Household Book* was gone. All the other volumes remained as on the day before; but, look where they would, the quaint old quarto upon which so much depended was nowhere to be found.

Courtleigh was almost broken-hearted. "That means goodbye to our bequest," he moaned with a bitter laugh. He paced about in silence for a while, then halted with a glint of comprehension. "Hook, that joiner fellow, was right!" he exclaimed. "Faik it must have been. Let me get down to the lawyer's, and we'll have him brought to justice no matter what the cost."

Sanderton was much inclined to the same impulse, but how even Faik could have got in and out of that room was beyond his surmising, for apart from the door there was no other means of access. Courtleigh was quite convinced the villain must have had another key. Yet the rector refused to see how he could ever have got one, as the lock was of recent make and of intricate design by the doctor's special order. Entry by a window was out of the question: the one small lancet with its leaded panes was still intact. In short, the mystery was not to be solved by any conjecture either of them could make.

Nor did time mend matters. Things looked more complicated than ever when it became evident that the search for Faik was futile. Besides the legal agents set on by Courtleigh, the man's own sister—Miss Hariett Faik of Hengsward—had also instituted widespread inquiries to find him. Even the police were completely baffled. As the weeks passed, and months, and no one had seen the missing person alive or dead since October 17th, the very newspapers ceased to interest themselves in the "mysterious disappearance of a retired barrister"; and Edgar Faik had to be presumed dead.

Of course, every effort was made by Durham authorities to secure the bequest. But no plea, however reasonable, could override the inability of the intended recipients to fulfill the conditions imposed in Dr. Propert's will. In the absence of the *Household Book* all negotiation was doomed to failure; and one of the finest private libraries in the country was left without a legal inheritor.

III

It was the second October after Propert's death and Courtleigh (just returned from a lengthy research tour in Sicily) had almost forgotten about Peryford when he received a letter from Sanderton to say that Sir Leslie Marlop, a retired Indian banker, was taking the priory on lease and coming to live there.

A local firm had refurnished the house, and most of the old servants were already back awaiting the arrival of their new master. The deserted place was coming into its own again. But the best news of the letter was Sanderton's joyful announcement that Sir Leslie knew about the unfulfilled bequest and was anxious to seek at least some means of loaning the books to Durham. To this end he would like Courtleigh to join him and the rector for lunch the following Tuesday at Peryford.

Term had just begun and the professor, after so long an absence, had little free time. But he determined, rather than disappoint Sir Leslie, to compress his engagements and get off to Peryford sometime on Tuesday. He replied to this effect and so it was arranged.

On the Saturday, however, Sanderton discovered something which made matters even more exciting. He had come across an announcement, previously overlooked, in an old *Yorkshire Post*: "Re: the Estate of Miss Hariett Faik, deceased." She had died, it seemed, in London and there was to be a sale of her properties and effects at Hengsward. What specially intrigued the rector was the item—"Miscellaneous books and papers of the late E. Faik, Esq., F.S.A."

There was not much time to be lost for the sale was to take place on Monday, the day before the proposed meeting with Sir Leslie. Sanderton decided he would have a look at those "miscellaneous books" at all costs, and wrote off to Courtleigh telling him of this latest bit of news and hoping to have something to report when they met on Tuesday. So, on the morning of the sale a hopeful-looking clergyman might have been seen among the crowd at the Black Bull at Hengsward. The auctioneer, though, began by apologizing for the withdrawal of certain lots, including the books, which a London firm had purchased by private treaty. Sanderton was crestfallen indeed; but having come, decided to stay on a little and see what other items were offered. Nor did he regret this when a bundle of old music, including some Tudor motets and madrigals, of Miss Faik's, was knocked down to him for half a guinea. Things were, in fact, sufficiently interesting to keep him till the bidding was adjourned for lunch. But a stroll among the remaining lots, as the attendance dispersed, convinced him there was no reason to be there when business was resumed. He had an invitation to lunch with an old parishioner who had just taken a farm in the Hengsward district and wanted to show him round.

The rector was leaving the inn-yard to look out for his farmer friend when his attention fell upon a dealer—from York or Harrogate perhaps—busy with a mass of unframed pictures and plates. The man was hastily sifting his purchases and casting aside most of them in disdain to a little old country fellow who was piling them up with grateful eagerness. As Sanderton drew nearer, the connoisseur made a final review of his prizes—a couple of mezzo-tints and some four or five engravings—slipped them into a portfolio, and was off.

"So you get the lion's leavings, eh Hook? Or should we call them windfalls?" the rector remarked, turning good-naturedly to the old joiner. "By the way, have you seen Mr. Elders at all this morning?"

"Why, good morning, sir!" exclaimed Hook as he turned around from tying up his newly-acquired collection. "Mr. Elders? I know him as was churchwarden at Peryford? No, rector, I 'aven't seen him about yet."

"He's half promised to meet me here—unless his wife's got worse, poor woman. I'll wait a while at any rate," said Mr. Sanderton, setting down his parcel of music on the bench. "And what brings you here today?"

"Sentimental reasons I suppose you'd call it, sir," replied the joiner. "I worked over here for Mr. Faik, you know, at one time."

"Indeed!" responded the rector. "I had an idea you'd always lived at Peryford. I know you helped us at the library last year, just before Dr. Propert died, but now I come to think of it I'd not seen you before that."

"Well, you see, I used to . . ." began Hook, but at that moment a trap flashed by the yard entrance.

"Excuse me. Was that Mr. Elders that just went past?" interrupted the rector suddenly starting up. "He may have been waiting for me inside and decided I'd not come."

Hook ran out to look and after shouting loudly down the High Street turned back nodding, "Yes, sir, it's him. He's just pulling up."

Mr. Sanderton seized his bundle hastily and trotted out to climb up alongside his old churchwarden. As the trap moved off he called out, "Thank you, Hook. Come round to the rectory sometime soon and we'll finish our little talk there."

What was done at Beckside Farm does not concern us much. Suffice it to say that Mrs. Elders had so far recovered as to provide a luncheon worthy of a churchwarden's wife; that Elders himself, having made good bargains at Malton market, was proud as punch to show the rector around; and that Sanderton saw every field and sty with a critical nod, inspected all the stock approvingly, spoke wisely about modern manures and former governments and (after assembling the full household in the parlor for prayers) waved farewell to them all at the lane end with a feeling that something of the land was sticking to him inside as well as to his boots.

Night had set in by the time he alighted from the train at Peryford. But he was not destined to get home just yet.

"Good evening, rector," cried a man loading trunks and boxes onto a drag in the station yard. "Can I take your bag along, sir, and would you care to ride back with me?"

"Why, it's Jennings!" exclaimed Mr. Sanderton. "This is fortunate indeed. Have you room for me? Thank you, thank you. How come you to be here so late as this?"

"Simple, sir," answered the cheerful groom as they jogged along. "It's like this. Sir Leslie arrived an hour ago and I was sent down for the luggage right away. He came a bit afore expected and was asking for you, sir."

"Hm," murmured the rector, "perhaps I had better see him before I go to the rectory. Yes, I think I ought."

Arrived at the house, he was ushered at once by Perkins into Sir Leslie's dressing room.

"Ah!" cried the new master of Peryford, shaking himself into a tightish pair of pantaloons. "How are you, Sanderton? I'd have sent across to the rectory but they said you were out. I'm a bit before my time but the fact is that Bates—my lawyer, you know—tells me there's a hitch over that idea of ours about the bequest. He's coming tomorrow and I wanted to see you first."

"I've been over to Faik's sale as it happens," explained the rector, "and I'm just on my way home. . . ."

"Well, look here," proposed the baronet eagerly. "Dinner's out of the question now. They're getting me some cold supper ready. I know you won't refuse to join me; then we can talk at length. You can spruce yourself up without going home. Yes . . . and I'll be down in a few minutes too."

The repast was concluded, and an engrossing talk had resulted in a tentative solution to the lawyer's difficulty, when conversation turned to Faik's sale.

"And the only bargain you got was a bundle of old music!" laughed Sir Leslie. "Well, well, I'm a bit of a musician myself. Let's see what you've picked up."

The parcel was opened and, to the rector's consternation and the other's unbounded amusement, it contained not musical scores but a very mixed selection of engravings and prints. Sanderton realized that he must have picked up Hook's bundle by mistake when he left the inn yard to hurry after Mr. Elders's trap. No doubt Hook would have his music.

"Why!" urged Sir Leslie, subsiding from jest to courtesy, "if Hook's in the village I'll get Perkins to send this stuff to him and get yours back. You needn't worry about that."

Without waiting for protests he rang and gave the order. Perkins said Hook was in the stables that very moment having been up to the rectory himself.

"I say," said Sanderton reflectively, "let's have him in. He was telling me he worked for Faik at one time. I'd like to ask him a few things."

He had been glancing idly through the gratuitous portfolio when he noticed a familiar name at the foot of one of the prints—"Peryford Park and Chapel."

It was a thing of no merit but arrested the clergyman's eye because he had never before seen a view of what the chapel was like previous to its being restored and made into a library. To his surprise, there were numerous other pictures of the same place—pen sketches, prints, watercolors and so on. In every one there appeared the chapel from one point of view or another. But what set him thinking was that, whereas the library as he knew it had a plain gable at its eastern end, all these drawings depicted it as flanked with turrets.

"This looks interesting," commented Marlop, glancing over his shoulder. "Ha! Here's the fellow to tell us all about it. Well, Hook (that's your name?), you've been picture dealing, I see. What are you going to do with 'em?"

"Maybe sell them, sir. All depends. Either road am not bothered," replied the local virtuoso awkwardly. "You see, sir, I'm interested, as you might say, in old things hereabouts."

"Oh! Perhaps you'd better sit down and tell us all about yourself," said Sir Leslie encouragingly.

"I used to work here on Peryford estate as carpenter till Mr. Faik took me to Hengsward and set me on. Not that I wouldn't go back to oblige Dr. Propert which was away then: I told him so. But Mr. Faik paid very generous, and I did hope in them days to get set up on my own—and be independent like for old age, sir," began Hook.

The host nodded slightly as he poured out some whisky.

"Ah," continued Hook, sighing, "he made some alterations, did Mr. Faik, and not much to Dr. Propert's liking as it turned out. But yet I will say this, sir, Mr. Faik must'a been partial to the old chapel for look how he bought up every picture of it far and near as he might lay 'is 'ands upon. I warrant there's scarce a painting o' Peryford anywhere in England but was in 'is persession when he died. That's what makes me think some o' these 'ere might be valuable, sir."

"But," objected Sir Leslie, ignoring the last suggestion, "I understand that Mr. Faik almost entirely rebuilt the chapel when it became a library. Why should he make such drastic alterations if he valued the original building? This east end with the turrets, for instance, bears no resemblance to the place as it is now."

"Now you've beat me, sir," replied Hook. "All I can say is—there's summat queer about the edifice. Take them turrets now: it's my belief they was 'aunted and best done away with."

"What makes you say that?" inquired the baronet with mild interest, handing him a glass.

"Only what I've 'eard, sir, and putting two and two together, as you might say. (Thank you, sir.) When them alterations was in and Mr. Faik he comes to me and says 'Hook, I don't like that east end and I've got an idea to improve it. I'm having a bigger window put in to give more light.' You see, sir, there was some tracery for an old rose window, as they call it, among them priory ruins in the grounds, and he told me he'd got a firm from away to fix in some glass sent special from Boyhemia or some foreign place. Well, sir, that was the beginning of all the trouble. The rector, Mr. Laycock—afore Mr. Sanderton came—objected to Mr. Faik's 'remodeling scheme' as they called it, and wrote off to Dr. Propert. Then there was quarrels between my men off the estate and the foreign chaps from London measuring and ordering. In the end, sir, Mr. Faik had all the gable, window and all, covered up with a tarpaulin sheet, sacked the local men, and sent me off to work at his place there in 'Engsward.

"When next I was past Peryford—that is for Mop Fair at the back-end—I see the chapel all completed and these Italian 'craftsmen' (what's wrong with ordinary workmen, I don't know) all cleared back to London. The turrets is gone, and the gable all altered just as you see it now, but to keep up the old appearance like they'd trained the ivy and stuff back to cover the new stonework. Aye, and to cap all, my cousin (as was housekeeper to Mr. Laycock afore he died, sir) she tells me Mr. Faik is busy with all sorts o' science professors and whatnot (a queer sample by all accounts) having meetings in the new library every month."

Sanderton looked pointedly at Sir Leslie. "And you, had you any hand in the alterations?" he said.

"O yes, sir. That's the funny part. Me and the under-joiner, Tom Cass, and two lads had very near done all the woodwork when this 'ere plan for pulling out the east end come up. Gallery was finished and I had all but fixed the walls with shelves when we was packed off. When the new window was in, some of Mr. Faik's men filled in the sides of it with some old paneling (as you may still see, sir, at the gallery end and in that Monument Room)."

"You mean the Muniment Room! Yes, I have seen it— some old Tudor work, nearly black," nodded Sir Leslie. "But I thought you said the place was haunted or queer in some way?"

"I'm coming to that, sir," continued the old carpenter. "Changes came very quick. Poor Mr. Laycock died, sir, as you know. Then one day Dr. Propert came back from China or somewhere—it was afore Mr. Sanderton's time—and there was 'ard words by all accounts, and Mr. Faik left pretty sharp. It was plain the old doctor was grieved about the alterations. Not that he could ever 'a seen the chapel as it was, for he had never lived at Peryford, but he had heard plenty from Mr. Laycock.

"Well, all I know is, one Friday when I was mending a wagon in the yard over there, who should come in but Dr. Propert on that roan hunter of his. He'd been told about me, doubtless, and what he wanted was to know why I'd gone to 'Engsward, seeing as our family was always on the Peryford estate. I told 'im, sir, what I've told you. 'Well,' he says, 'you've made your bed and I'm not sure but you'll have it to lie on. Anyway I want you now to come over to the priory with me and bring some keys and locksmith's gear with you.'

"So I got ready and he took me to the library, and round through the bushes at the back, to the left 'and corner outside . . ."

"Yes," interposed Sanderton, "the northeast corner, you mean?"

"That will be so, sir," continued the joiner. "The doctor

went straight to it. 'Now, Hook,' he says, 'get that axe and clear this ivy back.' I did as he said, and there was a little door in the wall; and I soon had it unlocked. 'The turrets may be gone,' says the doctor, 'but the turret stairs are still here at any rate. Give me that lantern, and stay here and see that nobody comes prying round.'

"With that, sir, he went up and I 'eard 'im tramping round and round up them winding steps inside the wall. I had not noticed before, but there were one or two window slits higher up among the ivy, and I saw them light up as he climbed to the top. After that I waited a longish time, and no sign of the doctor at all. I was just going to shout up after 'im when he came round the corner outside, behind me, and I got quite a start.

" 'Don't be alarmed, Hook,' he says, 'there's a way through to the gallery inside. That's what I suspected. When one sees lights in the night, it may be ghosts—or, it may be burglars, eh? Come along inside with me. No, not that way—it's rather stuffy and unpleasant. We'll "enter by the door" as the Bible says.'

"So along we went to the main door into the library and up to the gallery, right to the far end. We went quite close to the east window and I saw at once how the doctor had got through: one of the panels was evidently a door, for it stood open as he had left it, and I could see a spiral stairs inside, leading down.

"Well, sir, to cut a long story short, Dr. Propert got me to bar up that bottom door outside, so as nobody could get in or out again. I was to have fixed the panel door up in the gallery too, but he got the idea of locking it instead. I thought perhaps it might lead up to the roof and be useful in case of fire. But that was not the idea, sir. The doctor ordered a special little safety latch and I had to place it neatly on the inside. (In fact I was doing it that day when Professor Courtleigh came the first time to look round.)

"I often wondered what the doctor's game was, and I think it was a trap, for you could set it so as anyone could push it open from the gallery side (that is if they knowed about the panel!) and get into that stair. But if you was inside when it springed to—well, you'd be catched like a rat in a cage! But that was the doctor all over. A very egsentric man, sir, if I may say so. Well, he took the little key when I'd finished the job, and then he looks at me very stern, and says, 'Now, Hook, you've left my service and I'm not sure whether I can find room to have you back. I'll give you a trial; and if you can keep your own counsel about this little discovery of ours, I'll not forget you later on.'

"I didn't know what he might mean, sir, but when he died, not so long after, there was fifty pound for me in the will. I've not told a soul about this panel, but you're an educated man and a gentleman—and the rector, too, sir—and I see no 'arm as can be done now as the doctor's dead?"

Sir Leslie nodded his head reassuringly. "You need have no fear, Hook. But there's one thing I should like to know. I gather that the stair of the northeast turret is still there. But what about the one on the other side of the window—I mean where the Muniment Room is? Didn't you explore that too?"

"No, sir," answered the old man. "There was a doorway outside, like the other, but it was already built up, so no one could have got in there."

"Thank you," said Sir Leslie, bringing the interview to a close. "This is very interesting. There's a friend of the rector's—Professor Courtleigh, in fact—coming to see us tomorrow about the library. After what you've said, I should like to be able to show him this panel. So perhaps you can come round again in the morning?"

As Hook took his leave the rector returned him his parcel. "Look after these pictures of yours. I think I know a purchaser for them," he said, adding with a grin, "and thanks for bringing back my old scores!"

His pleasantry gave place to something quite serious, though, as soon as the carpenter had gone. "That's a rare story!" he said gloomily. "Something sinister about all this. Here's Faik with his expensive alterations and secret conclaves—and for what purpose? What is behind it all?"

"Well," said Sir Leslie with a shrug, "there're all the symptoms of Black Magic! In India, you know . . ."

"Yes, but seriously," interrupted the rector with a wry smile, "would anyone in England, any educated person, fool about with that nonsense?"

"I'm not so sure," answered the other, composed. "This country had plenty of it in the past and, as for education, well, it's sometimes the scholar versed in antiquity who's most susceptible to this kind of thing. As a matter of fact, I came across an instance of what I mean just before you arrived. When I lifted the lid of the window seat in my dressing room (thinking it a good place to put my bootjacks in), I found a curious sort of prayer-book inside. You shall see it," he promised, ringing for Perkins.

When the book came Sanderton recognized it. "Why," he said, "it's an old psalter of Dr. Propert's: he used to have it in the oratory. I know it by that braided bookmark and crucifix. He mentioned bringing it over with him the night he died. In fact he collapsed while upstairs fetching it. I often wondered where it had disappeared to."

"I suppose you've never perused its contents?" suggested Sir Leslie. "No? Well, have a look at it now. I take it to be a Jacobean psalter bound up with certain eighteenth-century additions to form a private manual of devotions."

As he handed it to the rector the little book sprang open at a well-thumbed page entitled:

AN OFFICE FOR DELIVERANCE FROM THE EVIL ONE.

Ps. xxvii, 5—*For in the time of trouble He shall hide me in His pavilion.*

Several collects ensued, then an old metrical version of Psalm 91, introduced by rubric in italics, thus:

Divers portions of Holy Writ are commended for ejaculatory usage, and in especiall certain verses of the Psalms xxxi, xxxv, xxxviii, cxlii, and the like. Or, let him that is distress'd sing or chant the following to himself aloud, duly making the sign of the Cross—

Ps. xci: It shall not come nigh thee.

> Whoso doeth reach the secret Shade
>   Of God's most holy Place
> Shall pluck his Soule that was afraid
>   From its most deadly case.
>
> Whenas that Horror draweth nigh
>   At Noon with shadow fell,

The Lord upon thine instant cry
  Shall stay the powers of hell.

The Hunter's visage here in vaine
  Shall peer into thy Bower
And o'er thy blood its nightly bane
  May have no mortal power.

"Good heavens," gasped Sanderton. "I begin to see why the doctor fled to the oratory so much, and why he furnished it in the first place. It's almost unbelievable. He must have been deluded. Surely there's nothing in all this?"

"Don't be too sure," warned Sir Leslie. "Neither Faik nor Propert were fools. Anyway, we'll talk it over with Courtleigh and be careful to act together in this. The danger with these things comes by tampering with them unawares."

While the rector lingered at the hall conversing with Sir Leslie, Professor Courtleigh was in fact up at the rectory awaiting his return. By a stroke of fate he had arrived before his time.

That morning when Sanderton was getting ready to set out for Hengsward, the Professor had received two letters in his rooms at Durham. The first was his friend's hurried note giving news of the sale and regretting that since it was such short notice he would have to go alone. "I should like you to have come a day earlier and gone with me to bid for those books of Faik's," ran the message, "but I know how difficult it is for you to come, even on Tuesday."

The second letter was from the secretary to say the examiners' meeting, called for that day, had to be unexpectedly postponed. On receiving this, Courtleigh pondered the irony which could cause last-minute situations like that. Here he was, after all, comparatively at a loose end. When he came to think of it, this Peryford visit might well prove to be more important than anything else he could be doing for his university just then. He had another matter too which would take him to York. With a sudden resolution he reached down the railway time-table.

"I'll be there for lunch at any rate," he thought as the train went moving south, "and we shall be able to go on to Hengsward together in the afternoon. It will be a pleasant surprise for Nat." He had somehow had it in his head that the sale began at 2:30 or so. Not till he arrived at Peryford Rectory and found that Sanderton had gone off hours before, on the only possible train that way, did he realize how irritating it can be to follow an impulse without going into the practical details.

Mrs. Willerby, poor lady, housekeeper at the rectory, thought out all the ways of bringing the two friends together but it turned out to be as impossible to get word to the rector as it was to get a train till nearly tea-time. Unfortunately, too, Sanderton had left word that he hoped to call after the sale on a friend near Malton but would be back at Peryford in the evening in time for dinner. "But, sir, you'll surely stay for lunch, and I'll stack up a good fire in the study and it's all cozy and private."

Courtleigh had no mind to be "all cozy and private" for seven or eight hours. He had business in York and there was plenty of time to do that and still be back to meet Sanderton on his return. After a slight snack, therefore, he was strolling leisurely through the park while the stable boy caught the cob and got ready the rector's gig.

And then it was he could not forbear having another peep at the fateful library. It was unlocked—probably left ready for the decorators—so he went inside. Certainly it was dingy and neglected beyond words. Dust lay thick upon the furniture everywhere, and shaggy cobwebs hung from the roof timbers and festooned the corners of every alcove and recess. Most of the books had been removed of course, but some miscellaneous volumes remained up in the gallery. Courtleigh, in idle vein, reached down a few of these, but the place was so imbued with melancholy that he soon gave up and went below again.

He was crossing the center of the floor when he noticed that the matting, which ran full length there, had got pulled on one side. Was that an old brass he could detect beneath it? Throwing the matting back, he discovered a large square flagstone of white marble bearing a circular pattern inlaid in black. It was divided out in sectors and marked off somewhat like the chart of a mariner's compass; but in place of the cardinal points and sub-points were curious hieroglyphics around the edge. The main spaces were quite blank, and it was a puzzle to Courtleigh to think what the purpose of it all could be.

As he was stooping over it, he again sensed—for in that position he could not see—the swoop of something above. It darkened the atmosphere for one quick second, and his ears pricked up at that faint, uneasy pattering sound once more.

That old fear, experienced at his first visit, was upon him again. He had a guilty feeling of being watched. He looked up and got a shock to see Dr. Propert observing him from the gallery with a most intent and frightening look. Another moment and he knew it could not have been so. Nevertheless he decided to retreat before morbid thoughts took any further hold upon him. So he wisely left the place and went around to the stables where the gig was just about ready.

He had an excellent time in York. He saw his man—a fellow antiquary—enjoyed yet another visit to the minster, had a meal at a curious little inn nearby, and left himself but little daylight for returning. The cob, it seemed, knew its own way to Peryford and the lamp-lit ride had almost lulled the professor to sleep by the time they got to the rectory. To his disappointment, though, Sanderton had not yet returned. Mrs. Willerby was almost distracted with anxiety but rallied a little at the guest's reassurances and set about serving dinner for him. Had she but known it, her master was not a mile away dining with Sir Leslie.

Alone at the rectory things were getting dull for Courtleigh. After vainly trying to keep himself interested in a bookseller's catalog, he finally informed the housekeeper he would not wait up any longer but would see the rector in the morning. He then retired for the night.

Now it was the professor's regular routine when undressing to take two special sedative pills which his doctor had ordered on account of his nerves. Without them he was subject to insomnia followed by most dreadful nightmares. You may judge of his annoyance, therefore, when he felt in the accustomed pocket for the little box and found it gone. He went downstairs again but it was not there. Could he have lost it on the road or while in the town? It seemed unlikely. Then he remembered—"This afternoon when I was in the library I took off my jacket in the gallery to shake the dust from it. My matchbox fell out and I picked it up. No doubt the box of pills fell out too and I never noticed. Yes, that will be it..."

He was not very keen to turn out again now, and tried for some time to settle down and forget it. But the thing went round and round in his mind and gave him no peace. It was no use denying it: he dare not face the night without that sleeping dose. So, after some reluctance, he put on his overcoat, opened the front door quietly, and sallied forth across the park.

There was almost a full moon, that orb casting about the whole prospect of lawns and trees a magic atmosphere of still expectancy, like an opera stage the moment before the eloping heroine steals across. The library itself, in the soft night air, stood out with toyland boldness, a pinnacled casket of silver steeped slantwise in pools of indigo shade. As he traversed the open moonlight toward the shadowed doorway, Courtleigh felt strangely conspicuous, and almost pathetic, like an insect crawling across the lens of a great telescope. In a dreamy surmise he brought his own Cassandra to the scene. What if a human speck entering that slumbering panorama should constitute a sort of outrage? But he knew he had to go and, putting aside poetics, was soon stepping to the heavy door.

Inside the library the gloom was so mottled with pale light that Courtleigh had no difficulty finding his way into the gallery. And there to be sure, at the far end against the banister, was the little box he was looking for. As he was picking it up, though, his foot tripped against the leg of one of the reading tables; and in regaining his balance he steadied himself against the wainscoted wall. To his surprise the woodwork gave back a little as his hand pressed upon its carved surface. Then the moonlight came flooding through most powerfully into the building, and showed a telltale crevice along one of the panels.

It was time, in all reason, for a professor of classical antiquities to be in bed. But Courtleigh was very human, and you will not be surprised that, at the thought of having discovered a secret panel, curiosity got the better of him. He determined at any rate to have one peep inside that little opening while he was there. But the door, after coming ajar some three or four inches, had somehow jammed. Hardening with impatience, Courtleigh got his shoulder to it and gave a quick thrust. Back it went and landed him staggering inside. There was a smart slam: and things went suddenly dark.

He got to his feet and struck a match—only to note that he was trapped. What on the other side might have seemed a panel of innocent thickness now showed itself to the captive as a stout oak door with a great iron spring but no visible lock or fastening of any kind. When every attempt to lever it around the edges with his penknife proved futile, he had nothing left but to look for another way out.

He tried the downward direction first, hoping to come out somewhere on the ground level. But the steps were getting soft and flaky and he had to be careful. There was also a suffocating thickness about the air as he neared the bottom and peered down, holding the lighted match in front of him.

Now what could that be? A heap of debris down there started to remind him of . . . but then the step crumbled under his foot, and the light fell from his hand. Instinctively he sprang back to the step above. It was giving too, like shale, and the flakes rattling around had strewn him from head to foot before he managed to again reach firm footholds at the top. As he brushed himself and collected his thoughts he heaved a sigh of relief to find himself safe once more. He felt as if there was something at the bottom he was glad he had not discovered. And, whatever it was, he had come within an ace of being entombed with it.

He decided to explore things higher up. Ascending past his starting point, he had hopes of coming to an exit on the roof; for once in the open air he might climb down some buttress or at least call out for help. But his hopes on this score were also dashed. A few yards up and this time the stair was sealed by a blank wall of masonry.

Courtleigh was by now almost ready to despair. But, striking another match, he was relieved to discover a narrow door set back a little to the side by his right hand. It was not fast and he pulled it open with new expectancy. By a miracle he did not break his neck, for the passage was no more and he gasped to find himself on the verge of a sheer drop, looking into the moonlit library.

There, below him on the right, it lay like the auditorium of some deserted theater viewed from a scaffolding high up in the wings. Close by him on the left loomed the upper part of the great east window, the gigantic wheel of tracery sweeping overhead and foreshortened so as to seem toppling down upon the beholder. He was, in fact, standing in a niche, or panelled recess, within the framework of the window. What purpose such an outlet could have remained a puzzle. If it was intended to allow the window to be inspected and repaired from time to time there would still have to be some scaffolding to take workmen to the window face. But the thing which concerned Courtleigh was the prospect of his own escape. Could he scramble down the mullions into the well of the library? It looked so perilous that he thought better of it.

While craning his neck to take the situation in, his hand had found a convenient little rail fastened in the wall. His weight upon it seemed to loosen it a bit. Another look and he noticed it was really a lever of some sort, and as he pulled it farther his eyes almost dropped out of his head to see a line of what looked like ornamental masonry slide out horizontally from the window. In a few moments there had appeared a narrow footway, battlemented at the edge, stretching right across to the other side of the window. It was about a foot wide and had slid out like a shelf in an old-fashioned desk.

As his astonishment subsided, Courtleigh guessed that a certain ogee-headed panel at the far side would be a door like the one by which he was standing. Trying the proffered bridge with his foot, hesitating somewhat to trust his weight to it, he at last decided to make the crossing. He sidled forth slowly, steadied himself by grasping the curved stonework of the window, and reached the other side only after an agony of carefulness.

Yes, it was a door as he had hoped. He lost little time in pushing it open, but saw that any upward way was sealed, and found descent the only course open to him. This second stairway spiraled around till it brought him to another wooden barrier, and his heart beat wildly at the sight of a metal catch. In a moment he was through this panel and inside the Muniment Room, sighing with renewed hope.

He groped about the presses with a lighted match and found the door which led into the library. Of course, it was locked. He sat for a while quite beaten. Only one other possibility remained: without much hope, he looked into the little stair again to see if there was any way to the ground floor. No luck: it was built up. As he leaned against the wall considering things, he suddenly realized that he had at least discovered a possible solution to the mystery of the *Household Book*. If Faik had known about the panels into these two stairways and the transom bridge along the window, what could be easier for him than to get from the gallery across into the Muniment Room and steal the book! No wonder the ordinary door had shown no signs of violence. But if the man had entered, he must have got out as well. "Of course," thought Courtleigh, "he had probably known about the spring catch behind the panel in the gallery and taken precautions not to be trapped inside as I have been, like a fool. And yet . . . and yet . . . neither Faik nor the book had been heard of since that fatal October night two years ago. *What if the man had not got out?"*

A panicky feeling of claustrophobia came over him as he pictured his own fate, burrowing like a trapped fox within walled passages each ending in a cul-de-sac. And then there came into his mind what might be lying down in the pit of the other stair where the steps had given way . . . Putting such thoughts aside, he determined to again get up to the window level where he could at least see into the library. He reached the top of the stair and saw the moonlit window, but the gangway across was no longer there. Still, there must also be a lever at this side to bring it out again. Ah! there it was. Pulling at it, Courtleigh breathed more easily to see the transom shelf emerge once more, and he could not but wonder at the ingenuity of it all. While pondering the situation, he found yet another handle! The curiosity was too much. Stiff as it was, he pressed hard upon it and managed to make it turn.

The whole building began to shudder. It could hardly be a ventilator arrangement; the vibration was too violent for that. He looked up and was amazed to see the rose window beginning to rock gently to and fro. Behind the crude Victorian Gothic glass which filled the spans between the spokes of tracery, some other glass could now be seen. Courtleigh worked with all his might and the huge translucent disc began to go slowly around like windmill sails.

Nor had he need to strain himself in looking up to observe results. The moonlight was casting the circular pattern upon the library floor below. To his further surprise he also noted that this reflection fell exactly on the circle marked upon the stone slab he had uncovered that afternoon. At last he began to see its purpose. He realized he had stumbled upon the work of the eccentric Faik. This would be something to tell Sanderton about in the morning!

As the disc slowly revolved, a flux of strange tints and shapes came into play on the dial below. It was like watching the tinctures which flow from certain crystals as they sink dissolving in a bowl of water. But soon the forms became less blurred as the two cycles of design within the window began to coincide. When this occurred the handle stopped with a click, and an upward glance told the professor that the disc was stationary again.

But the colored patch upon the floor still drew his full attention. And what a fascinating sight it was! The vacant divisions of the dial were now peopled with fantastic forms; some suggesting a mystical significance, like the signs of the zodiac in an old almanac; others of frighteningly grotesque and evil creatures of the night. Each in its appointed place was motionless, frozen into liquid clarity.

All Courtleigh's fear was now swallowed up in wonderment. Then, even as he gazed into the lighted dial, its placidity was broken. A fresh shape had appeared, this time a moving shadow hovering furtively in the arena of signs. It was a wiry silhouette, as of a blackened lobster, running hither and thither among the symbols with fierce agility like a witch doctor in a tribal dance.

He felt himself going giddy as he stared at this devilish marionette. He must have jerked the lever with his hand for without warning a ratchet crackled rapidly overhead; the lights on the floor whirled into rainbow confusion, and in a few seconds the heavy disc of glass was back in its first position. The sudden motion disturbed the dust and cobwebs up above as well. Quite a shower of particles were filtering through the moonbeams, and a roundish clump of soft debris came bowling down onto the transom.

This sordid finish to the uncanny vision brought the watcher to his senses. For a second or two he felt vaguely puzzled, then once more that strange uneasiness came over him; he sensed he was being watched. He almost felt something stalking him, and found himself trying to catch it in the corner of his eye. With an effort he roused himself: action was what he needed. It was time to be getting out of that place and back to his warm bed again. "There's nothing for it," he told himself, "but to scramble down these mullions into the library. But . . . I'm a bit past the age for a thirty-foot drop."

He was groping cautiously along the transom footway when he noticed an obstruction in his path. It was in the shadow and all he could make out was a basketlike mass frayed out at the edge like the twigs of a besom. He raised his foot to go across it, but as he started the stride, something in that dark mass began to twitch. He was going to crouch down and look at it, and suddenly recoiled with a gasp of horror.

At that very moment the moonlight failed and left him in pitch darkness. With heart beating madly, he quickly edged backward from the thing. Then the light reappeared and nothing was there. He tried to believe he was imagining things; but was soon undeceived. A tiny pattering sound on the glass above caused him to look up just as the horrid form came at him, from behind this time, tacking in a nimble detour across the rose window like some gigantic spider running out along its web.

With a cry of terror the trapped man rushed madly the other way, quite heedless of his precarious path. And now he saw the footway narrowing as the transom shelf again slid in. In another moment his foot had caught the parapet and sent him headlong over.

To the library floor was a considerable drop, but Courtleigh fell obliquely, tearing his jacket on the battlemented stonework of the transom, and so swung inwards against the double mullions below. He clutched out wildly and managed to grasp one of these upright shafts. It did not stop his fall but slowed him down enough so he could slither with one foot against the horizontal bar of the second transom lower down. Instinct alone dictated what to do. With a mighty thrust upon his lucky foothold, he lunged out sideways and cast himself towards the gallery not far below.

It was this desperate leap that saved him. The agile fiend had been within a foot of him upon the mullions. But, by a marvel, he had cleared the wooden balusters and landed sprawling against a case of books. He was now at the east end of the gallery panting for a moment's respite, knowing full well he dare not linger. He quickly scrambled up, heedless of bruises, staggering forward among the moonlit reading-tables toward the stair-head. Still going tiptoe, he was just preparing to descend and quit the place when he was again confronted by the hideous creature coming crabwise up the steps to intercept him.

Back he swung in flight along the gallery, but this time he took the other way, making for the reading-cabinet at the end. He floundered in exhausted and slammed the screen door after him. Once in, he knew how futile this move was; there was no way out. Already the hideous face was looking through the open woodwork at him. With nightmare fascination he watched it craning its gaunt head about as though blind, then squeeze between the carved foliage, straining its quivering legs against the sides. By some uncanny sense it came straight for him as he stood transfixed against the balustrade. It fastened on him without haste and though he raised his arms to beat it off, they fell limply down again and left him to his fate. A fiery glow suffused all vision now as he felt the bristling tendons on his chest and saw the ghastly proboscis nosing up for his throat...

A rapid tinkling of melodious bells mingled below with a heavy thud. But Courtleigh did not hear them. Nor did he hear that fearsome screech that scalded the night air. Mortal consciousness had given out, and his inert body—with the demon fast clawed upon it, had hurtled backwards over the gallery rail.

That unearthly wail had carried right across the park and pierced every ear at the hall. The whole household woke into commotion as at an earthquake. There was a barking of dogs, lights appeared in distant corridors, doors flung open while figures with sticks and shotguns ran out from every quarter. From upstairs windows night-capped heads appeared, calling to know what was amiss.

It was amidst this hue and cry that Sir Leslie (beslippered and holding a pistol) accompanied by Mr. Sanderton (pulling his priest's cloak round his shoulders) appeared upon the terrace.

"By jingo!" ejaculated Marlop, "the library's on fire! Perkins, Jennings, and you other men come with me. The rest get buckets and whatever you can, and down to the lake with them."

THE PROPERT BEQUEST

"I think it's chiefly the east end that's going," panted Sanderton as they headed across the grass. "It's to be hoped we can get it stopped before the rest gets hold."

Without more words they burst through the great door and were nearly choked with smoke. But masking their mouths and noses, they pressed forward and found the fire buckets by the wall. The seat of the conflagration was the end nearest the great window, but flames were spreading right along the gallery. Sir Leslie and two of the men were soon up there with axes to cut away the burning beams and banisters. Others got to work with a relay of buckets while Sanderton, assisted by the tremulous Hook, was shoving blindly at the screen door to get into the oratory. All inside was a pit of smoke but he determined to rescue what he could of the antique altar furnishings.

Hook, treading gingerly, entered first; but had not gone above a pace or two before he took fright. The rector pushed past him impatiently to see what was wrong. A current of air had cleared away the smoke sufficiently to show a prostrate figure on the floor. Whether dead or alive, the man could not be left there. Having got him dragged into the open, Sanderton held up a lantern and recognized, with a shock of dismay, the features of his Durham friend.

The fire was nothing to him now. He left Sir Leslie and the rest to deal with it as they could, and with two men to help him, he moved the unconscious professor across to the house and up to bed. Not till he had gotten Dr. Green over from the village and received the blessed verdict that Courtleigh was out of mortal danger, did the old bookworm give any real thought to the fate of the library.

"He's terribly bruised," said the doctor as they left the patient sleeping soundly, "and has had a nasty shock. There are some queer scratches about the chest but I don't find any bones broken. I'll have another look at him when he comes round. And now, hadn't we better see about this awful fire?"

By the time they reached the scene, however, the amateur fire brigade had gotten things well under control. The place was still smoldering but it was felt safe for most of the helpers to get off home again.

"Well," cried Sir Leslie, grimy but triumphant, as they trooped back, "thank God that's over. I'll never say another word against ornamental lakes! Hey, Sanderton, what's this about finding a man unconscious in the oratory? Professor Courtleigh! What? How the devil did *he* come to be there?"

They had to wait till next day to answer that. The rector, not much helped by Mrs. Willerby's contributions to things, went across to the hall again straight after breakfast.

"How is Courtleigh now?" he inquired as Sir Leslie showed him into the morning room to talk things over. "Has a sleep done him good?"

"I've just been up," replied the other, "and he's much better. A day in bed and thinking things steady for a bit, and he'll be all right, I think. But he's very talkative. In fact he's told me the queerest tale about how he got into the library yesterday. A thorough nightmare story it is, I assure you. So far as I can judge, the poor fellow's been sleepwalking. I'd better tell you what he said."

Sanderton listened to the story very intently. "My word," he said when he had heard it, "he must have had a frightful fall from the cabinet into the oratory! It's a mercy that pile of hassocks was there, or he'd have broken his neck: as it was, he hit the Sanctus bell."

"Good for him!" commented Marlop grimly. "That would be enough to send any orthodox ghost packing!"

"Good old Courtleigh, he certainly had the sense to fall in the right place; let us put it that way," smiled the cleric. "But this story about being pursued is a bit strange. I suppose you're right: sleepwalking's the most reasonable explanation."

"Not much doubt, I reckon," nodded Sir Leslie, "but Courtleigh needs reassuring about it. Says he would like to think it all a dream but somehow he feels that it really happened. He's particularly anxious to know if that revolving window and those passages exist. And also whether his speculation about Faik was correct. I told him we'd be going across to see what the fire had left, then we can set his mind at rest. If you're willing, we'll go now. I'd like, in any case, to see this turret that Hook sealed up."

The rector, by this time prepared for almost anything, accompanied Sir Leslie to the scene of the fire. There was, however, not much to be examined. The window had completely collapsed and, though some twisted ironwork showed among the debris, it was impossible to reconstruct much from that. The stonework flanking the space where the window had been was still intact, and the door at the base of the first turret—being at the far side—was quite unburnt. As soon as Hook arrived with the tools Sir Leslie directed him to force it open.

Jennings assisted and it was not a many minutes' job. As the last shove flung it open there came forth a terrible stench of foul air, and the men paused outside to let it clear.

"Hm. A pair o' moldy shoes!" commented Jennings, looking in with his arms akimbo.

"Aye, and an ancient book lying open agen that . . . Lord 'a mercy it's . . ." began Hook and suddenly stopped.

Sir Leslie brushed past him and stepped inside. "Looks like a bird's nest," he was saying as he bent forward. All at once he sprang clear as if stung. "Keep back, man!" he cried to Sanderton who had that moment pressed in to have a look.

What happened next was hard to tell. They saw the rector recoil, as a man does when a rat springs at his throat, then cross himself rapidly. There was a rumble of collapsing masonry up in the stair as he slowly stepped backwards with his hand to his brow like one dazed.

"Courtleigh was right," he gasped, leaning by the wall as the rumbling ceased and all became quiet again.

The disturbance had jolted the whole turret, but when the dust began to clear Sir Leslie advanced again, very cautiously this time, to look inside; and the rest peered over his shoulder. And there they saw, perched on what appeared to be a bundle of rags, a black form shriveled up. It might have been the charred skeleton of a small ape but the face was a mere leperlike mask, frightful to look upon.

Seizing a spade, and averting his glance with a shudder, Sir Leslie darted in upon the instant to strike it down. But it was quite dead, and crumbled at the first touch, leaving only a pile of feathery ashes. Instinct, however, made him stamp even that to powder.

While they still stared, scarce believing what their eyes had seen, the real meaning of those moldy rags and shoes also appeared. The book had tumbled from the step and disclosed five digit bones protruding from a sleeve, while in the shadow—no longer hidden by that charred form—lay a human skull, Faik's.

When the first shock of ghastliness had passed, Sanderton picked up the book and came out into the light to examine it.

Then, looking up after a brief scrutiny to meet Sir Leslie's inquiring glance, he gave a little sigh and nodded simply: "The bequest is safe at last. This is the *Household Book*, the cause of all our cares."

The other almost snatched it from him and stood turning the pages over with wrapt attention. He paused some time over the final entry, scribbled in pencil—

Erubescant impii, et deducantur in infernum: multa fiant labia dolosa quae loquuntur adversus justum iniquitatem.

"That looks like Propert's hand," commented a voice over his shoulder. It was Courtleigh, pale but eager, who had hobbled down unnoticed to join them.

"So you had to be in at the kill!" remonstrated Sir Leslie, as he and Sanderton turned in surprise upon the professor. Then, reverting to the book, he scowled at the pencilling again. "What's this mean?" he demanded. "My Latin's a bit rusty."

"A quotation from Psalm 31, I think," answered the rector slowly. " 'Let the ungodly be put to confusion, and be put to silence in the grave. Let the lying lips be put to silence which cruelly, disdainfully and despitefully speak against the righteous.' "

"That man had a grim sense of poetic justice," muttered the baronet gravely, handing the Propert bequest to the now-thoughtful Courtleigh.

ON CALL

Dennis Etchison

One of those lovable stupid questions that fantasy writers are forever being asked is, "Where do you get your ideas?" A trade secret, of course. Occasionally, however, an author will experience some particularly vivid dream (or, if you will, nightmare) and will incorporate this into a story. Such is the case with Dennis Etchison's disturbing Kafkaesque nightmare, "On Call."

Born March 30, 1943 in Stockton, California, Etchison currently lives in Los Angeles—a congenial location for a writer with an avid interest in movies and television. Although he has been writing professionally since 1961, Etchison has only recently begun to receive the recognition he deserves. This is primarily due to the fact that Etchison works almost exclusively in the short story field, and that most of his work is published outside the few science-fiction and fantasy magazines with which the majority of fandom is familiar. "On Call" appeared in a monthly fanzine devoted to news of the fantasy genre, *Fantasy Newsletter*; others of his stories from 1980 appeared in *Mike Shayne's Mystery Magazine*, *Adelina*, *Dark Forces*, and *New Terrors 1*. In addition, Etchison has written the novelization of the film *The Fog*, as well as several as-yet-unproduced screenplays. His horror novel, *The Shudder*, is awaiting publication, and a collection of his short fiction would be most welcome. While his downbeat, intensely introspective style is not to every taste (for some it succeeds *too* well), Dennis Etchison may well be the finest writer of psychological horror this genre has seen.

"*Read it now*," called the blind newspaper vendor. "*Many are dying and many are dead!*"

Wintner geared down and rounded the corner, trying to spot an opening. He glided past a photo shop, a dry cleaners and laundromat, a stationers, a multi-leveled parking structure that covered half the block and, at the next corner, the florist's stall. He felt a fleeting regret that from this lane he was unable to catch even a glimpse of the young woman who worked there; most days he noticed her on his way back from the freeway, her face moving in among the flowers there, and the cheerfulness of the sight, the very rightness of it, seemed to shorten the distance of his commuting and make his burden somehow easier to bear. But today was Saturday, anyway, he remembered. He kept going.

He would have to drive round again.

He could, of course, find a parking place easily enough in the municipal structure—but then Laurie never liked having to walk all that way from the clinic entrance.

How long would his wife be this time? Ten minutes? More like twenty, he thought, if she's running true to form. Or thirty. *I only have to find out about the x rays*, she had said. *It won't take long.*

God, he hoped so. He knew what happened to time when her mind got hold of it.

He circled the block once more, just as a black Mustang slid into a vacant space in front of the clinic office. He groaned and set his teeth. He had lost track of how many times he had gone around. He turned his wrist to check his watch, but couldn't remember how long it was since he had dropped her off.

He neared the corner.

Already it was turning late in the day. He noticed now that the buildings had begun to resemble oblong boxes, row upon row of them set on end, as shadows filled the doorways and slanted down from the rooftops. He slowed to a crawl and saw that his car was actually pacing one of the pedestrians, a stoop-shouldered old man who was stepping laboriously along the sidewalk that fronted the clinic. Wintner shuddered without yet understanding why and eased up on the block.

There was a taxi zone at the traffic light. He slipped into neutral and rolled in close to the curb. He cut the ignition, adjusted the rear-view mirror so that he could see her when she came out, and sat listening to the ticking down of the engine as it tried to cool.

A meter maid cruised past his open window. She shook her helmet and motioned for him to move on. He nodded. When she came by a second time—forty minutes later—he started the car and crossed the intersection and drove until he found a place to park on the next block.

"I'm sorry," said the nurse, "but I can't find a Mrs. *Wintner*—is that the name? I don't see her down here in the book."

"She only stopped in to find out about her tests." He offered a smile, got a good look at the nurse and withdrew it. "It must have been about an hour ago."

"Well, just a sec. I'll ask the other girl."

Girl, he repeated to himself in wonderment. Only the very young—and the middle-aged, like these—call themselves that. How many more years will they be able to get away with it? Until their faces crack and turn to dust?

Wintner scanned the waiting room. Even, monotonous walls, a reading rack haphazardly stocked with plastic-bound magazines, a planter stuck full of dingy artificial flowers. An endless dose of taped music issued forth from a concealed speaker; reflexively he identified the selection as the theme from the movie *Doctor Zhivago*.

A second nurse appeared from behind the frosted partition.

"Sir?" she said in a precise, controlled tone. Like a librarian, he thought.

She waited for him to approach her.

"Your wife's probably with one of the doctors. He may have wanted to go over the results with her. Why don't you find a seat for a little while longer? I'm sure she'll be out any minute."

There was a cool authority to her voice. It must come with the territory, he thought. Or maybe she had been a librarian once, a long time ago. He could have pressed her, but why bother? She was undoubtedly right. Besides, he was hot and tired and—he let it pass.

He faced the waiting room. No. He shook his head. He

certainly did not need to rub shoulders with a roomful of poor, sick bastards, not right now. He avoided looking at them. A permanent rain check on that one, he thought, sighed, and headed back out, past a rosy woman and her two apple-faced children.

There was a hofbrau on the other side of the street, barely identifiable by a fringe of old-world lettering. He took a seat at the bar, keeping an eye on the front of the clinic building.

He ordered a schooner of Lowenbrau Dark and stared past the beef jerky and pickled eggs until the stein was empty.

Still no sign of Laurie.

He started on another Lowenbrau and, surprisingly, began to feel the effects. It hit him then: he hadn't taken time yet to eat today. It seemed that he had spent every minute on the run, placing calls, shuffling his schedule so that he would get her here before the clinic closed ...

As he reapproached the office, he couldn't help noticing how dirty it really was. The paint appeared to peel off the door even as he reached for it; the stucco was beginning to crumble from around the foundation, falling away into piles of pulverized dust like insect droppings. There was an official-looking notice tacked to the door, something about National Suicide Week. He didn't take time to read it.

A new, younger nurse glanced up. He spread his hands on the counter.

"And how are you feeling today?" she asked. Her eyes flicked over him, reading his features as she reached for a form.

"I feel fine," he began. "It's my wife. I know this sounds crazy but—"

He told her what had happened. When he finished she said, "I'll see."

He watched as another white figure materialized behind the opaque glass. He heard the first nurse recapping the story.

She concluded, "I thought maybe he should see Dr. . . ." He didn't catch the name.

The other nurse, the fourth one he had seen today, looked him up and down. He was beginning to feel like a man caught without papers in a nudist camp.

She moved her head briskly from side to side. He could almost hear a mental *click* as she came to a decision.

"No," she said, "I don't quite think so." Then, to him: "Maybe she's incognito."

"What?"

"I say, she may be incognito, do you think so?"

"That's what I'd say," said the other nurse. "Try that."

"Incognito?" he repeated. He seemed to have missed something. He replayed the word several times in his mind until it lost meaning.

"You could at least check," said the first nurse, returning to her chair, as the senior nurse disappeared behind the partition.

He felt like laughing. He held out his hands helplessly, turning around to share the joke with anyone who might have been listening.

But no one paid any attention. Actually, he thought, maybe I should have waited here from the very beginning. Maybe I missed her, after all. Who knows?

Shaking his head, he returned to the door. He passed the same woman with the two children. What kind of place is this? he wondered. Those kids don't look like there's anything the matter with them. Plenty of color in their cheeks. What in hell are they doing here?

She was not at the car.

The sky was darkening rapidly. The street took on a grim, vaguely menacing facade as shadows lengthened over the dim, slick edge of curbing below the disturbing asymmetry of the architecture. Old cornices and abutments and rainpipes jutted like broken teeth too close to the glass panes, rendering the buildings awkward, topheavy, ready to topple; each step he took seemed to threaten to pull everything down around him.

He stopped by the hofbrau, trying to get his bearings. He felt like someone waiting for a train, one that might not even stop at this station.

He saw only a few scattered pedestrians out on the pavement. Even the traffic here had thinned until it was nearly invisible, though he was aware of an almost physical wall of sound from another part of the city. He turned toward the windows of the restaurant and squinted inside.

The faces grouped at the bar were old. All of them. It might have been an illusion caused by the unwashed glass, but he didn't think so.

One face in particular was oddly familiar.

Suddenly he was sure. Yes, he had seen the same man in the waiting room, seated calmly with the others, reading a magazine or—no. He had been staring at the floor. Wintner remembered. The people in the room. They had all been staring at the floor. Waiting.

Only it was not quite the same man. Wintner seemed to remember him as younger, healthier.

He caught his own reflection in the coated glass. And took a breath. He was oddly relieved.

His own face, at least, was more or less as he remembered it.

As he crossed the street to the clinic he checked the shops on either side. They were seedy, rundown. Most of them were already closed for the night. Not one was the kind Laurie would have gone into, anyway.

He thought he saw a figure shuffling away from his line of sight. It was the only movement on the sidewalk now. He could not make out who it was. It could have been one of the shopkeepers locking up and heading home, but for a second he almost recognized the gait.

The doorknob practically came off in his hand.

An elderly couple brushed past him on their way out, smelling of lilac and formaldehyde. He could see two new nurses, both younger than the others he had spoken to. As he neared the counter they stopped talking. He almost heard what they were saying.

"Did you have an appointment?" said the first one. She glanced worriedly at the clock which hummed high and white on the wall. "Most of the doctors have gone, I'm afraid."

"Listen," he said, and he began. He told her. Then he said, "I want to talk to whoever's in charge. Then I want her, or you, or someone to check the examination rooms, the offices, the bathrooms, for God's sake. I want to know if my wife's still in this building, and I want to know now."

"Just a moment, sir."

His fingers tapped the sterile counter.

As he stood there, a door to an inner office swung open and the woman with the two children came out. A nurse held the door for them. They needed it. The woman moved so slowly she seemed at death's door; the children were pale as ghosts.

He nodded automatically as they passed. The old woman raised her tired eyes, noted his face and muttered something unintelligible.

"This way, please."

At first he didn't know the nurse was talking to him. Then he saw that the white door was being held open like a protective wing. For him.

"You found her," he said, his muscles relaxing.

The nurse cleared her throat but said nothing.

He followed her. The hallway was as immaculate as her starched uniform. He heard the swishing of her white stockings as she led him to a room at the end of the corridor.

"The doctor on call will help you," she said.

"Just a—"

She shut the door behind him.

The office was comfortably appointed in leathers and dark woods. There was another door on the other side. He tried an overstuffed chair, but only got up again to pace the carpet. Books were everywhere, and entombed among them within the walls were various artifacts that appeared to be the taxidermied remains of small animals of unknown species.

He went over to the desk.

A sheaf of notes tucked under the border of a thick blotter. An open notebook filled with indecipherable scratchings. Behind the desk, an assortment of framed certificates from foundations around the country, including one from the Menninger Clinic in Topeka.

So that was it. He was a head man—some kind of doctor for the monkeys of the mind.

Is that what they think I need?

He took a step back. His shoulder touched one of the bookcases. He turned.

A row of glass vials sealed in resin, each larger than the last. They contained embalmed extractions of some strangely familiar organisms floating in various stages of growth. His eyes followed the sequence. Near the end of the line the vials became bottles, then jars.

What have they done with her? he thought.

A thump sounded at the far wall, from behind the door to

the other side. Without thinking, he closed his fingers around one of the glass specimens.

The door clicked and started to whisper open.

His body jerked as his feet moved backward too fast. He fumbled for the door to the hall, found the knob and stumbled out.

There was movement behind him but he did not look back. He heard the nurses' crepe soles squeaking across the reception room floor. He heard their nervous, practiced, too-young voices, saw their grasping hands in a blur as he ran past. He saw the vinyl curling around the aging magazines, smelled the waft of preserved death in the air. He smelled the chemicals on their skin, felt the cold, smeared door and the sudden rush of night air on his chest. He tasted the darkness and the clot of fear in his throat.

As he ran, voices struggled to be heard within him.

The nurses. What had they been saying when he came in? It had sounded like—like—

We live by death, he thought they had said.

And the newspaper vendor. Wasn't there something more the blind man had been shouting?

None of the dead have been identified, he thought it was.

And the old woman. What had she been trying to tell him?

We are the dead, she had said. *We are the dead.*

He wound down to a fast walk. He could almost see the ancient man who had been shuffling along the sidewalk earlier, away from the clinic. A man who had once, not too long ago, perhaps not too long ago at all been so much more than he was now.

He found himself at the corner, next to the flower stall. It was dark, empty except for the sickly-sweet scented wreaths and arrangements waiting in the shadows.

He shuddered and crossed the street swiftly, mechanically, trying to make it to the car.

He passed the hofbrau.

The faces were inside. They were grouped around the dark wood bar, all of them old beyond belief now and sick unto death, staring into their glasses, waiting. They reminded him of faces he had seen before.

Then he saw the flower girl.

He pushed his way inside.

She was standing there. Her voice alone was almost cheerful as she began to move among them, asking questions, giving advice, making arrangements. He noticed for the first time that she was armless on one side, her pink stump smooth and rounded under the opening in her summer dress.

How long has she been that way? he wondered. Or does it work the other way for her, too? He thought crazily, *Was she born with even less?*

He stood shivering, watching her animated form and the vase of wilted flowers at the end of the dark, polished bar. After a minute she became aware that she was being watched.

Slowly he held out his hand to her.

"I brought you something," he heard himself saying, still uncertain, trying to think of the right words as he handed her the bottle. "I—I thought you should see it. God damn you."

She turned in painstaking slow motion, her muscles stopping and starting, stopping and starting with each part of the movement, until at last her eyes met his.

"What?" she said.

There was a pause that seemed to go on forever. Then someone offered up a sound that was somewhere between a laugh and a deathrattle, and the black fear was on him.

THE CATACOMB

Peter Shilston

Rosemary Pardoe has to date published two excellent chapbooks devoted to M. R. James, featuring articles relating to the work of the famed English writer along with new fiction written after the style of this master of the ghost story. Peter Shilston has had stories in both of these as well as in other amateur publications. While the reprinting here of "The Catacomb" may mark his first professional appearance as a writer of fiction, Shilston has over seventy articles to his credit on the subject of women's gymnastics, in which sport he works both as a coach and as a correspondent for various British and American magazines.

Born in 1946, Shilston, who lives in Stoke-on-Trent, is a Cambridge history graduate and earns his living as a teacher of history. He became interested in fantasy at age eleven when he began reading J. R. R. Tolkien, followed by M. R. James and Jorge Luis Borges. "The Catacomb," Shilston explains, "was actually based on a visit to Sicily two years ago. The town and cathedral represent Cefalu (the site, coincidentally, of Aleister Crowley's famous 'abbey'); the catacomb itself is the Capuchin cemetery in Palermo." I shouldn't consult my guidebooks for this cathedral, however.

I am retailing this story as it was told to me. Imagine if you can, a coach making a tour of the island of Sicily in the middle of August, carrying a couple of dozen English package holiday-makers on the usual lightning inspection of places of interest—Palermo in two days, Agrigento in another two, Syracuse meriting only one, a trip by chairlift up Mount Etna, and then home. The sort of people one finds on such tours are invariably the same: a number of schoolteachers, earnest retired couples, parents who have inappropriately brought children and are beginning to wonder why they didn't save themselves trouble by going to the beach instead, and a handful of single unattached people. Furthermore, their behavior is always the same: some spend all their time grumbling at the quality of the hotels and food, the young men wonder why there are no available attractive young ladies on the tour, the children get bored, and the schoolteachers carry guidebooks and maps around everywhere and take enormous numbers of photographs. Others seem to show no interest in the historical sites at all, and spend all their time either sitting in the nearest cafe or buying various unpleasant souvenirs.

This particular coach party was a typical one, I think. Among its members was a certain Mr. Pearsall; a quiet, solitary, middle-aged man of vaguely scholarly appearance. He had enjoyed the tour, and had been duly impressed by the Greek temples of Agrigento and the mosaics in the great cathedral at Monreale, but he had not managed to make close friends of any of the other passengers, and now that the holiday had only a couple of days left to run, he was looking forward to getting back home again. Consequently he was mildly irritated when old Mrs. Tavistock in the back of the coach started to complain of stomach pains. She had been something of a moaner throughout the tour, but now she was looking genuinely ill, with the result that Giuliano the courier had to ask the driver to stop in the next town, so that a doctor could be brought.

The next town turned out to be a nondescript settlement nestling beneath an enormous cliff, with little apart from this huge overshadowing presence to distinguish it from any one of fifty other small towns that they had already passed through on their tour. Here Giuliano went in search of a medical man, leaving his charges dozing, idly reading their books or making desultory conversation. It was mid-afternoon and the sun was blazing fiercely. All sensible Sicilians were indoors having a siesta. Shutters were down on every window, and not a soul was visible in the street.

After a while, Giuliano returned, and regretted to inform them that they would have to wait at least an hour for Mrs. Tavistock to receive attention before they could proceed. In the meantime they could get out and stretch their legs, though it was unlikely that they would find anywhere open. The coach would sound its horn to call them back when it was time to go. Here he engaged in an animated conversation in Italian with Umberto, the driver, who made many emphatic gestures, the upshot of which was some more uncouraging information. The local people, said Giuliano, kept themselves very much to themselves, and there were really no facilities for tourists at all. No coaches normally stopped there, and there was little point in trying to explore the town; really it had nothing to offer. He expressed his regret again and had a few more words with Umberto. Mr. Pearsall's command of Italian was not great, but he seemed to detect the phrase, "can't come to much harm if they're all together."

Mr. Pearsall, however, did not intend to stay with the others as they stood around on the pavement in a pointless fashion. He had glimpsed a church down a side street as they drove into the town. It had looked old and surprisingly large for such an insignificant place, and he thought it might just be worth an exploratory visit. The "harm" Giuliano had mentioned (assuming he had understood him right), he took to mean thieves. They had been warned to beware of bag-snatchers in the major cities, but it was hardly likely that gangs of muggers would bother to patrol a town where no tourists ever stopped. The streets seemed absolutely deserted. Besides, Mr. Pearsall was still quite fit, and imagined he could hold his own against the average thief; or at the very worst, run fast enough to get away. So, taking his camera, he imparted his intended destination to a fellow passenger (who showed not the slightest inclination to accompany him) and set out at a brisk pace.

The side streets of the town were very narrow and ran steeply up the hill toward the great beetling overhang of the cliff. Some of them had steps in them. Mr. Pearsall wondered how claustrophobic it would be to live beneath that great black shadow, and also speculated whether the town was ever damaged by rockfalls. After a couple of turns into dead ends, he found himself in a little gravel-strewn square, as devoid of people as the rest of the town, facing the church itself. A glance at the sun told him that he was approaching it from the west end; the southeastern corner of it almost touched the base of the cliff. Because it had exactly the same color and texture as that towering mass, the church gave the slightly disturbing impression of having been carved by the hand of a giant in a single piece out of the living rock.

His first sensation, Mr. Pearsall tells us, was of great age and general dilapidation. The church looked far older than the Doric temples at Agrigento which he had admired earlier in the week, though his intellect told him this could not possibly be the case. He supposed it must be a Norman building, though possibly on an older foundation; Arabic or even Roman. The style was typical enough, though rather ill-proportioned. Two squat, heavy towers, with hardly any windows (and those very small) flanked a portico of three large pointed arches. What little decoration there had ever been was now barely discernible. There seemed at one time to have been fresco paintings inside the portico, but now the plaster was badly cracked and in some places fallen away entirely. Only a few dim outlines of human figures—presumably saints—could be discovered. There was a large wooden door, decayed and worm-eaten, with panels carved in what had once been ornate abstract patterns. Moorish influence, said Mr. Pearsall to himself, and tried the door. It was locked.

This was predictable under the circumstances, but still annoying. Mr. Pearsall retreated to the square to take a picture, and then looked at his watch. A mere fifteen minutes had passed since he left the coach, and he still had plenty of time to kill. The day was hotter than ever, and if there was any shops in this godforsaken place, they were resolutely shut. He decided to stroll round the outside of the church, for sheer lack of anything else to do. Besides, he would be in the shade for part of his walk, and it would be cooler. Without any great enthusiasm, he set out. He was a mild-tempered man, but if there was one thing that caused him irritation, it was suddenly finding himself with nothing whatsoever to do when he had expected to be occupied.

Along the south side of the church, the shuttered houses ran so close that the street was more like a tunnel. He had not gone far when he noticed a small side door. It should cause us no great surprise that he tried to open it, and much to his gratification, found it was not locked. Surprised at his good fortune, and congratulating himself on his persistence, he went inside.

At first there was nothing to be seen, so dark was the interior after the savagery of the afternoon glare outside. But soon Mr. Pearsall's eyes had grown accustomed to the gloom, and he was able to look around him. He knew at once that his walk had been worthwhile. In his tidy fashion, he began to classify what he could see. A long, high nave with aisles on either side; clearly another Norman church; with the pointed arches learned from the Arabs. But unlike some of the others he had seen on his visit, this church had not been revamped later on in the Baroque period. There was not a Corinthian pilaster to be seen. The capitals of the columns seemed to be a mass of grotesque carvings, but were so thick with grime that he could not distinguish them clearly. Indeed, the whole interior was very dirty; the pews were thick with dust and the candles so discolored that they looked as if they had not been lit in years. Clearly they were expecting no visitors, for there was not a guidebook or a postcard visible anywhere.

Then Mr. Pearsall saw the mosaics. He had already been initiated into the marvels which the Normans had bequeathed to Sicily in this field, in such staggering compilations as the cathedral of Monreale and the Palatine Chapel in Palermo; but even so, the examples of the art on display at this out-of-the-way place quite took his breath away. Here some nameless craftsman of the twelfth century had taken the Byzantine style and interpreted it with a vigor and a liveliness that were all his own. A veritable poor man's bible of astonishing power covered the walls. Mr. Pearsall quite forgot the passing of time as he followed the treasures on display. Here was the creation of the world in a sequence of seven pictures, and there were Adam and Eve tempted by the serpent and expelled from Paradise. More scenes followed; Cain murdering Abel, the building of the Ark, the drunkenness of Noah, the Tower of Babel, Abraham and the destruction of the Cities of the Plain, the sacrifice of Isaac; on and on, each one more startling than the last.

How odd, thought Mr. Pearsall, as he moved from scene to scene full of wonder and admiration, that the inhabitants of this town should discourage tourists! Here they had some of the finest mosaics on the island, if not in the whole of Italy, and yet they were left to decay out of sight in a locked and dirty church. Why, with just a little initiative and energy from the town's authorities, visitors would surely come flocking to see such marvels. Did they object to the very idea of tourists? Surely there were enough prospective cafe owners and postcard dealers in the place to insist that something was done! And why was the church not mentioned in any of the guidebooks which he had read so assiduously before starting on his tour? Such were the musings that passed through Mr. Pearsall's mind, but after a while, he began to have doubts.

It became noticeable that, though the artist had great natural vigor, it was the portrayal of evil which called forth his finest efforts. The serpent in the Garden of Eden, for instance, was given a human face that bore a sinister and seductive leer. In the story of Cain and Abel, there was no doubt that it was Cain who was intended as the hero; for Abel as he lay helpless on the ground was a mere hapless simpleton, whereas his murderer, standing over him with a spade raised to cleave his skull, was full of savage power. King Nimrod's soldiers at Babel looked like mindless automata. The picture of Saul and the Witch of Endor was situated in the darkest corner of the church, perhaps deliberately, and was covered with cobwebs. After examining it closely, Mr. Pearsall was almost glad of this, for inside the witch's cave were certain unpleasant nonhuman shapes that were perhaps well left unseen.

"Perhaps the artist was a Manichaean," mused Mr. Pearsall, "a Cathar or an Albigensian (or are they the same thing? Have I got the dates right?), more convinced of the existence of evil than of good. Perhaps his mosaics were condemned as heretical. But in that case, why weren't they destroyed, instead of just closing the church down? Now I wonder what he's made of the New Testament!"

These mosaics were even more unsettling. Mr. Pearsall could not find an Annunciation, or even a Nativity, but there was a quite horribly realistic Massacre of the Innocents, in which a number of ingenious and disgusting means had been devised of slaughtering the children, while King Herod sat on his throne overlooking the carnage and laughed. The portrayal of Judas receiving his thirty pieces of silver from Caiaphas would have stood as one of the artistic masterpieces of all time, were it not so exceedingly unpleasant. And so it progressed; through various nasty portrayals of people possessed by devils; through the stories of Simon Magus and Ananias, both of whom once again were the most vivid characterizations in their particular scenes; right up to a terrifyingly powerful portrayal of the Four Horsemen of the Apocalypse.

By this time, not only was Mr. Pearsall distinctly upset by the mosaics, but he was feeling increasingly ill at ease. At first the church had been completely silent, but as time went on it seemed full of little noises he could not locate. His footsteps echoed round and round in a long diminuendo, but they seemed to be answered by odd rustlings and creakings. No doubt these were the normal sounds of rodent life, or of aged woodwork at the start of its death throes; but when, like Mr. Pearsall, one is alone in an ancient church in the middle of a strange town where not a single human inhabitant has yet shown his face, and when furthermore one is surrounded by the most disturbing illustrations of Biblical evil, such rational explanations carry distinctly less force. Once or twice he held his breath and stood perfectly still, to see if the noises continued. Not only that, he also increasingly felt that he was being watched. Probably it was only the faces in the mosaic that caused this, but on more than one occasion he thought he saw a movement right in the corner of his field of vision, and whirled around in alarm only to find nothing.

Finally he came to a Virgin Mary who was quite devoid of the usual serenity, but instead had the voluptuousness of a vampire. So appalling was her expression that he thought for a while she must be a portrayal of the Scarlet Whore of Babylon, but no, she had the posture and the usual clothing of the Virgin, and there in her arms was the Christ-child, a hideous infant with an oily and sanctimonious grin which put Mr. Pearsall in mind of a satiated appetite for something perverse. He shuddered and was filled with a sensation of such acute distaste that for a moment he quite forgot the noises.

All this time, he had avoided looking at the east end, intending to keep till last his viewing of what was always the glory of the Sicilian churches; the great figure of Christ in the apse above the altar. Now he could keep from it no longer, and turned his gaze in that direction.

It was indeed a masterpiece, in spite of the dirt and the cobwebs that encrusted it. As usual, Christ's head and shoulders were portrayed, robed in red and blue, the right arm extended in blessing, the left holding an open book lettered in Greek. The treatment of the material by the unknown artist was marvelous, but the expression on Christ's face was uniquely horrible; a malignant sneer of contempt. The eyes were very piercing. Mr. Pearsall could not read Greek, but he suspected that the words written on the open page of the book were hardly a normal scriptural text. And the right hand—was that the usual gesture of blessing? Or was it the first and last fingers held up—the gesture known as the devil's horns?

"This is a blasphemous church," said Mr. Pearsall to himself. "The mosaics may be very fine, but they are also very horrible. Some bishop, perhaps even the Pope, condemned them and had the church closed down. Even the townspeople don't like to talk about them, because they are still a very religious people, and they don't let tourists in. Just as well, these pictures are enough to give anyone nightmares! Well; I'm glad I've seen them, but it's not a pleasant place to visit on your own, and I can't say I'll be sorry to leave." He glanced at his watch, and was almost relieved to find that his hour had practically expired; it gave him an excuse to leave without exploring the rest of the church. With a brisk walk that an unsympathetic observer might have thought perilously close to a panic-stricken run, he turned away toward the south door by which he had entered. But now it was locked.

For some time Mr. Pearsall struggled in a quiet futile fashion, shaking the door, twisting the iron ring this way and that, searching for a catch, but he was entirely unable to shift it. He thumped the door with the palm of his hand and kicked it, and a great ringing boom echoed round the church like a salvo of cannonfire, and to this day he swears that from somewhere there came a kind of sinister chuckle in answer.

With a considerable effort, he pulled himself together. "This is stupid," he told himself. "There is probably some custodian who forgot to lock the church up before his siesta, and only realized his mistake when he woke up. But he must be a very careless or stupid man, or he would have checked to see if anyone had gone inside." All the same, he did not want to knock again and risk that dreadful echo, so he decided to search for another door that might be open. Logic suggested there should be one on the north side, perhaps opening to a cloister or something similar. Crossing the nave with a certain trepidation (and carefully avoiding a glance at the blasphemous figure of Christ, though he imagined he could sense the cruel eyes bearing on him with an almost tangible force), he went in search.

Sure enough, there was a door in the corner of the north aisle, and it was not locked, though it seemed a long time since it had been opened. A strong thrust was needed to shift it, and it groaned horribly as it swung inward, dislodging a shower of dirt. A peculiar musty smell seeped into the air. Mr. Pearsall found himself peering at a flight of worn stone steps running downward into the darkness.

Now this did not look like the way out at all; indeed, the smell suggested that the lower chamber, whatever it was, was completely sealed from the outer air, and had been so for a very long time. It was a most unpromising route for one wishing to leave the building, and to this day Mr. Pearsall has never been able to give a satisfactory explanation of why he decided to descend those steps. He was already late, and after the unsettling effect of the mosaics, most of his exploratory zeal had evaporated, but nonetheless he could not resist the lure of the doorway. He wondered afterwards whether he was in full control of his movements anymore. The whole place bore a distinctly sinister air, but still he had to push the door fully open and take his first tentative steps into the darkness.

The stairs were long and curiously dank in spite of the dryness of the climate. Soon all trace of the light of the main body of the church (which had itself seemed so gloomy when he had first entered) had been lost, and he was obliged to take his cigarette lighter from his pocket and proceed by its flickering illumination. He turned a corner beneath a glowering archway of uncut stone, descended a ramp, and gasped at what he saw.

It was a catacomb. A long corridor opened before him, with side passages running from it. Perhaps the whole area beneath the nave was covered. And it was inhabited. A long double line of human forms stood along each passage. All ages and classes had their representatives here; men and women and infants, monks and warriors, learned scholars and ladies of fashion. They were dressed in clothes that must once have been their finest, furs and silks and embroidered gowns, now sadly moldering and decayed, but bearing still a glimmer of their former glories. And they had faces, for clearly much ingenuity had been expended to preserve the bodies, though with mixed degrees of success. There was a girl-child whose clothing looked at least two hundred years old, but who from her skin and hair might just have fallen asleep; but beyond her a man in priestly robes had lost his nose and his cheeks, and his eyes had decayed to blank milky globules; and further on the soldier in the chased steel breastplate, who was perhaps a mercenary from the Renaissance period, had lost his flesh entirely, and now grinned mindlessly with a naked skull.

Poor Mr. Pearsall! The effect would have been quite nasty enough under bright electric lights and surrounded by his fellow tourists; but here, on his own, locked in, and after already being alarmed and upset by those hideous mosaics, and furthermore with just a single weak flame to protect him from the darkness, the shock was overwhelming. Quite why he did not turn and bolt he has never managed to explain. He takes refuge in mysterious talk of "feeling a call" which dragged him onwards. Certainly it is irrefutable that he walked on down the passage, through the grisly ranks of the dead, horror mounting within him, but quite unable to save himself.

All the bodies had been there a very long time. Mr. Pearsall's knowledge of the history of costume was not great, but he was fairly certain that none of the garments worn could be placed any later than the middle eighteenth century, and the majority seemed to be medieval. What was left of his rational mind told him that similar catacombs were not unknown elsewhere, but such a piece of information seemed extraordinarily useless. As he walked onward, he appeared to be moving back steadily in time toward the early middle ages. Very few of the faces had any flesh on them by this time; some were left almost naked, with their clothing in flimsy rags, and others had simply fallen and lay in heaps on the floor. But still he had to go onward until he reached the end.

He had lost all sense of direction by now, but suspected he was moving beneath the altar, beneath the Christ of the devil's horns blessing and the malevolent glance. And here was the center of this labyrinth of death; a great throne of gilded wood, much rotted, where sat a body clad in the gorgeous robes and mitre of a bishop. This much Mr. Pearsall took in at a distance; but as he drew near, he would not look at the figure directly. He tried to force his eyes to look only at the slippers; he was sure he would lose his reason if he looked higher, but he could not fight as a force stronger than his mind raised his head gradually higher; the gold-embroidered cope, the skeletal hands with the episcopal ring loosely enclosing a bony finger, the crozier propped up in the other hand, the bones of the face bare of all flesh, the grinning yellow teeth, the eyes . . . the eyes! Not decayed at all, but alive, piercing, glaring! My God! The same eyes as Christ in the mosaic!

The lighter fell from Mr. Pearsall's nerveless grasp and he plunged into darkness. It was a lighter of cylindrical shape, and he heard it roll tinkling away out of his reach. For a few seconds he scrabbled uselessly on the floor for it, then realized how pointless such a search was. He would have to find his way out in total darkness. How far was it? How many turns had he taken? He waved his arms in front and to either side, walked a few paces, touched stone, turned, walked more until he met another obstacle, turned again . . . it was at this stage that he began to hear noises again; a horrible dry rustling, which he would have loved to think was a rat. It came from behind him. He moved quicker, and walked slap into one of the bodies. His face buried itself in the rotting fabric and he felt the lifeless arms slump across his shoulders. His nerve snapped entirely and he screamed; a muffled noise quickly extinguished. He ran at random, hit another body, and ran again, and struck again. Corpses were collapsing all around him, but still there was a rustling and a padding and a dry, gravelly cackling behind him, and it too was moving; not fast, but soon it would reach him if he could not find the stairs. He fell and cut his hands, and screamed again, but not from pain. He lost count of how many times he smashed into obstacles, until, bruised and bleeding, he could go no further, and cowered back against the stone wall. The rustling was quite close now. Light; he must have light! He had lost his cigarette lighter, he had no matches. Frantically his hands searched his pockets for a miracle. Of course! He had flashcubes for his camera! With trembling fingers he pulled one out and fiddled for what seemed an eternity to fit it into place. He pressed the shutter-button and nothing happened. A dud! He turned it around and tried once more. Still nothing. The rustling was only inches away. Think, man, think! He had forgotten to wind on the film, so of course nothing would happen. Pull round the winding lever and try again . . . just time . . .

In the blinding instantaneous moment he saw; not more than a yard from his face; the golden robe, the mitre, the skull, and the eyes, the terrible eyes . . .

He must have fainted. When he awoke, it was bright daylight and he was lying on the back seat of the coach. Giuliano was leaning over him. The courier had been told where Mr. Pearsall had gone, and when he failed to return on time, Giuliano and Umberto had gone to the church to find him. Entering by the south door (which they emphatically denied was locked) they heard his screams from the crypt and saw the flash. They found him without much difficulty; he was within a few yards of the steps.

Giuliano was more relieved than annoyed, but he chided Mr. Pearsall for disturbing the bodies in the catacomb. Banging into them in the dark was careless and destructive, but as for deliberately dragging one body all that way from its resting place . . . and it being the body of a bishop too! . . .

Mr. Pearsall did not have the strength to argue.

BLACK MAN WITH A HORN

T. E. D. Klein

"Black Man With a Horn" marks a return to *The Year's Best Horror Stories* by T. E. D. Klein, who had earlier appeared in DAW's *Series II* and *Series III*. His few appearances here are certainly not a reflection on the quality of his writing: rather, Klein is an author who prefers to work in the novelette-novella length, meticulously creating his stories at the rate of about one every other year or three. This past year saw a positive outpouring of his work, with the publication of this novelette and a novella, "Children of the Kingdom," in Kirby McCauley's *Dark Forces*.

Klein is a native New Yorker, born there in 1947 and now living in Manhattan. Previously he taught high school in Maine, worked in Paramount Pictures' story department, and he is currently editor of the new *Twilight Zone Magazine*. In addition to his fiction, Klein has written articles for the *New York Times*, as well as the story notes for Kirby McCauley's horror anthology, *Beyond Midnight*. He holds degrees from Brown and Columbia, but it was during the four years he lived in Providence while attending the former university that Klein became interested in the writing of H. P. Lovecraft. Much as M. R. James influenced subsequent writers of supernatural fiction in Britain, Lovecraft inspired successive generations of writers to continue his "Cthulhu Mythos." As a rule such continuations or pastiches have been awful beyond belief. "Black Man With a Horn" offers both proof that this need not be the case, as well as a bitter comment upon fandom's obsessive dead-hero worship.

BLACK MAN WITH A HORN

> The Black [words obscured by postmark] was fascinating—I must get a snap shot of him.
> —H. P. LOVECRAFT, POSTCARD TO
> E. HOFFMANN PRICE, 7/23/1934

There is something inherently comforting about the first-person past tense. It conjures up visions of some deskbound narrator puffing contemplatively upon a pipe amid the safety of his study, lost in tranquil recollection, seasoned but essentially unscathed by whatever experience he's about to relate. It's a tense that says, "I am here to tell the tale. I lived through it."

The description, in my own case, is perfectly accurate—as far as it goes. I am indeed seated in a kind of study: a small den, actually, but lined with bookshelves on one side, below a view of Manhattan painted many years ago, from memory, by my sister. My desk is a folding bridge table that once belonged to her. Before me the electric typewriter, though somewhat precariously supported, hums soothingly, and from the window behind me comes the familiar drone of the old air conditioner, waging its lonely battle against the tropic night. Beyond it, in the darkness outside, the small night-noises are doubtless just as reassuring: wind in the palm trees, the mindless chant of crickets, the muffled chatter of a neighbor's TV, an occasional car bound for the highway, shifting gears as it speeds past the house . . .

House, in truth, may be too grand a word: the place is a green stucco bungalow just a single story tall, third in a row of nine set several hundred yards from the highway. Its only distinguishing features are the sundial in the front yard, brought here from my sister's former home, and the jagged little picket fence, now rather overgrown with weeds, which she had erected despite the protests of neighbors.

It's hardly the most romantic of settings, but under normal circumstances it might make an adequate background for meditations in the past tense. "I'm still here," the writer says, adjusting to the tone. (I've even stuck the requisite pipe in mouth, stuffed with a plug of latakia.) "It's over now," he says. "I lived through it."

A comforting premise, perhaps. Only, in this case, it doesn't happen to be true. Whether the experience is really "over now" no one can say; and if, as I suspect, the final chapter has yet to be enacted, then the notion of my "living through it" will seem a pathetic conceit.

Yet I can't say I find the thought of my own death particularly disturbing. I get so tired, sometimes, of this little room, with its cheap wicker furniture, the dull outdated books, the night pressing in from outside . . . And of that sundial out there in the yard, with its idiotic message. *"Grow old along with me . . ."*

I have done so, and my life seems hardly to have mattered in the scheme of things. Surely its end cannot matter much either.

Ah, Howard, you would have understood.

> That, boy, was what I call a travel-experience!
> —LOVECRAFT, 3/12/1930

If, while I set it down, this tale acquires an ending, it promises to be an unhappy one. But the beginning is nothing of the kind; you may find it rather humorous, in fact—full of comic pratfalls, wet trouser cuffs, and a dropped vomit-bag.

"I steeled myself to *endure* it," the old lady to my right was saying. "I don't mind telling you I was exceedingly frightened. I held on to the arms of the seat and just *gritted my teeth*. And then, you know, right after the captain warned us about that *turbulence*, when the tail lifted and fell, flip-flop, flip-flop, *well*—" she flashed her dentures at me and patted my wrist, "—I don't mind telling you, there was simply nothing for it but to *heave*."

Where had the old girl picked up such expressions? And was she trying to pick me up as well? Her hand clamped wetly round my wrist. "I *do* hope you'll let me pay for the dry cleaning."

"Madam," I said, "think nothing of it. The suit was already stained."

"Such a nice man!" She cocked her head coyly at me, still gripping my wrist. Though their whites had long since turned the color of old piano keys, her eyes were not unattractive. But her breath repelled me. Slipping my paperback into a pocket, I rang for the stewardess.

The earlier mishap had occurred several hours before. In clambering aboard the plane at Heathrow, surrounded by what appeared to be an aboriginal rugby club (all dressed alike, navy blazers with bone buttons), I'd been shoved from behind and had stumbled against a black cardboard hatbox in which some Chinaman was storing his dinner; it was jutting into the aisle near the first-class seats. Something inside sloshed over my ankles—duck sauce, soup perhaps—and left a sticky yellow puddle on the floor. I turned in time to see a tall, beefy Caucasian with an Air Malay bag and a beard so thick and black he looked like some heavy from the silent era. His manner was equally suited to the role, for after shouldering me aside (with shoulders broad as my valises), he pushed his way down the crowded passage, head bobbing near the ceiling like a gas balloon, and suddenly disappeared from sight at the rear of the plane. In his wake I caught the smell of treacle, and was instantly reminded of my childhood: birthday hats, Callard and Bowser gift packs, and after-dinner bellyaches.

"So very sorry." A bloated little Charlie Chan looked fearfully at this departing apparition, then doubled over to scoop his dinner beneath the seat, fiddling with the ribbon.

"Think nothing of it," I said.

I was feeling kindly toward everyone that day. Flying was still a novelty. My friend Howard, of course (as I'd reminded audiences earlier in the week), used to say he'd "hate to see aëroplanes come into common commercial use, since they merely add to the goddam useless speeding up of an already overspeeded life." He had dismissed them as "devices for the amusement of a gentleman"—but then, he'd only been up once, in the twenties, and for only as long as $3.50 would bring. What could he have known of whistling engines, the wicked joys of dining at thirty thousand feet, the chance to look out a window and find that the earth is, after all, quite round? All this he had missed; he was dead and therefore to be pitied.

Yet even in death he had triumphed over me . . .

It gave me something to think about as the stewardess helped me to my feet, clucking in professional concern at the mess on my lap—though more likely she was thinking of the wiping up that awaited her once I'd vacated the seat. "Why do they make those bags so *slippery?*" my elderly neighbor asked plaintively. "And all over this nice man's suit. You really should do something about it." The plane dropped and settled; she rolled her yellowing eyes. "It could happen again."

The stewardess steered me down the aisle toward a restroom at the middle of the plane. To my left a cadaverous young woman wrinkled her nose and smiled at the man next to her. I attempted to disguise my defeat by looking bitter—"Someone else has done this deed!"—but doubt I succeeded. The stewardess's arm supporting mine was superfluous but comfortable; I leaned on her more heavily with each step. There are, as I'd long suspected, precious few advantages in being seventy-six and looking it—yet among them is this: though one is excused from the frustration of flirting with a stewardess, one gets to lean on her arm. I turned toward her to say something funny, but paused; her face was blank as a clock's.

"I'll wait out here for you," she said, and pulled open the smooth white door.

"That will hardly be necessary." I straightened up. "But could you—do you think you might find me another seat? I have nothing against that lady, you understand, but I don't want to see any more of her lunch."

Inside the restroom the whine of the engines seemed louder, as if the pink plastic walls were all that separated me from the jet stream and its arctic winds. Occasionally the air we passed through must have grown choppy, for the plane rattled and heaved like a sled over rough ice. If I opened the john I half expected to see the earth miles below us, a frozen gray Atlantic fanged with icebergs. England was already a thousand miles away.

With one hand on the door handle for support, I wiped off my trousers with a perfumed paper towel from a foil envelope, and stuffed several more into my pocket. My cuffs still bore a residue of Chinese goo. This, it seemed, was the source of the treacle smell; I dabbed ineffectually at it. Surveying myself in the mirror—a bald, harmless-looking old baggage with stooped shoulders and a damp suit (so different from the self-confident young fellow in the photo captioned "HPL and disciple")—I slid open the bolt and emerged, a medley of scents. The stewardess had found an empty seat for me at the back of the plane.

It was only as I made to sit down that I noticed who occupied the adjoining seat: he was leaning away from me, asleep with his head resting against the window, but I recognized the beard.

"Uh, stewardess—?" I turned, but saw only her uniformed back retreating up the aisle. After a moment's uncertainty I inched myself into the seat, making as little noise as possible. I had, I reminded myself, every right to be here.

Adjusting the recliner position (to the annoyance of the black behind me), I settled back and reached for the paperback in my pocket. They'd finally gotten around to reprinting one of my earlier tales, and already I'd found four typos. But then, what could one expect? The front cover, with its crude cartoon skull, said it all: "*Goosepimples*: Thirteen Cosmic Chillers in the Lovecraft Tradition."

So this is what I was reduced to—a lifetime's work shrugged off by some blurb-writer as "worthy of the Master himself," the creations of my brain dismissed as mere pastiche. And the tales themselves, once singled out for such elaborate praise, were now simply—as if this were commendation enough—"Lovecraftian." Ah, Howard, your triumph was complete the moment your name became an adjective.

I'd suspected it for years, of course, but only with the past week's conference had I been forced to acknowledge the fact that what mattered to the present generation was not my own body of work, but rather my association with Lovecraft. And even this was demeaned: after years of friendship and support, to be labeled—simply because I'd been younger—a mere "disciple." It seemed too cruel a joke.

Every joke must have a punchline. This one's was still in my pocket, printed in italics on the folded yellow conference schedule. I didn't need to look at it again: there I was, characterized for all time as "a member of the Lovecraft circle, New York educator, and author of the celebrated collection *Beyond the Garve*."

That was it. the crowning indignity: to be immortalized by a misprint! You'd have appreciated this, Howard. I can almost hear you chuckling from—where else?—beyond the *garve* . . .

Meanwhile, from the seat next to me came the rasping sounds of a constricted throat; my neighbor must have been caught in a dream. I put down my book and studied him. He looked older than he had at first—perhaps sixty or more. His hands were roughened, powerful looking; on one of them was a ring with a curious silver cross. The glistening black beard that covered the lower half of his face was so thick as to be nearly opaque; its very darkness seemed unnatural, for above it the hair was streaked with gray.

I looked more closely, to where beard joined face. Was that a bit of gauze I saw, below the hair? My heart gave a little jump. Leaning forward for a closer look, I peered at the skin to the side of his nose; though burned from long exposure to the sun, it had an odd pallor. My gaze continued upward along the weathered cheeks toward the dark hollows of his eyes.

They opened.

For a moment they stared into mine without apparent comprehension, glassy and bloodshot. In the next instant they were bulging from his head and quivering like hooked fish. His lips opened, and a tiny voice croaked, *"Not here."*

We sat in silence, neither of us moving. I was too surprised, too embarrassed, to answer. In the window beyond his head the sky looked bright and clear, but I could feel the plane buffeted by unseen blasts, its wingtips bouncing furiously.

"Don't do it to me here," he whispered at last, shrinking back into his seat.

Was the man a lunatic? Dangerous, perhaps? Somewhere in my future I saw spinning headlines: "Jetliner Terrorized . . . Retired NYC Teacher Victim . . ." My uncertainty must have shown, for I saw him lick his lips and glance past my head. Hope, and a trace of cunning, swept his face. He grinned up at me. "Sorry, nothing to worry about. Whew! Must have been having a nightmare." Like an athlete after a particularly tough race he shook his massive head, already regaining command of the situation. His voice had a hint of Tennessee drawl. "Boy"—he gave what should have been a hearty laugh—"I'd better lay off the Kickapoo juice!"

I smiled to put him at his ease, though there was nothing about him to suggest that he'd been drinking. "That's an expression I haven't heard in years."

"Oh, yeah?" he said, with little interest. "Well, I've been away." His fingers drummed nervously—impatiently?—on the arm of his chair.

"Malaya?"

He sat up, and the color left his face. "How did you know?"

I nodded toward the green flight-bag at his feet. "I saw you carrying that when you came aboard. You, uh—you seemed to be in a little bit of a hurry, to say the least. In fact, I'm afraid you almost knocked me down."

"Hey." His voice was controlled now, his gaze level and assured. "Hey, I'm really sorry about that, old fella. The fact is, I thought someone might be following me."

Oddly enough, I believed him; he looked sincere—or as sincere as anyone can be behind a phony black beard. "You're in disguise, aren't you?" I asked.

"You mean the whiskers? They're just something I picked up in Singapore. Shucks, I knew they wouldn't fool anyone for long, at least not a friend. But an enemy, well . . . maybe." He made no move to take them off.

"You're—let me guess—you're in the service, right?" The foreign service, I meant; frankly, I took him for an aging spy.

"In the service?" He looked significantly to the left and right, then dropped his voice. "Well, yeah, you might say that. In *His* service." He pointed toward the roof of the plane.

"You mean—?"

He nodded. "I'm a missionary. Or was until yesterday."

> Missionaries are infernal nuisances who ought to be kept at home.
> —LOVECRAFT, 9/12/1925

Have you ever seen a man in fear of his life? I had, though not since my early twenties. After a summer of idleness I'd at last found temporary employment in the office of what turned out to be a rather shady businessman—I suppose today you'd call him a small-time racketeer—who, having somehow offended "the mob," was convinced he'd be dead by Christmas. He had been wrong, though; he'd been able to enjoy that and many other Christmases with his family, and it wasn't till years later that he was found in his bathtub, face down in six inches of water. I don't remember much about him, except how hard it had been to engage him in conversation; he never seemed to be listening.

Yet talking with the man who sat next to me on the plane

was all too easy; he had nothing of the other's distracted air, the vague replies and preoccupied gaze. On the contrary, he was alert and highly interested in all that was said to him. Except for his initial panic, in fact, there was little to suggest he was a hunted man.

Yet so he claimed to be. Later events would, of course, settle all such questions, but at the time I had no way to judge if he was telling the truth, or if his story was as phony as his beard.

If I believed him, it was almost entirely due to his manner, not the substance of what he said. No, he didn't claim to have made off with the Eye of Klesh; he was more original than that. Nor had he violated some witch doctor's only daughter. But some of the things he told me about the region in which he'd worked—a state called Negri Sembilan, south of Kuala Lumpur—seemed frankly incredible: houses invaded by trees, government-built roads that simply disappeared, a nearby colleague returning from a ten-day vacation to find his lawn overgrown with ropy things they'd had to burn twice to destroy. He claimed there were tiny red spiders that jumped as high as a man's shoulder—"there was a girl in the village gone half-deaf because one of the nasty little things crawled in her ear and swelled so big it plugged up the hole"—and places where mosquitoes were so thick they suffocated cattle. He described a land of steaming mangrove swamps and rubber plantations as large as feudal kingdoms, a land so humid that wallpaper bubbled on the hot nights and bibles sprouted mildew.

As we sat together on the plane, sealed within an air-cooled world of plastic and pastel, none of these things seemed possible; with the frozen blue of the sky just beyond my reach, the stewardesses walking briskly past me in their blue-and-gold uniforms, the passengers to my left sipping Cokes or sleeping or leafing through *In-Flite*, I found myself believing less than half of what he said, attributing the rest to sheer exaggeration and a Southern regard for tall tales. Only when I'd been home a week and paid a visit to my niece in Brooklyn did I revise my estimate upward, for glancing through her son's geography text I came upon this passage: "Along the [Malayan] peninsula, insects swarm in abundance; probably more varieties exist here than anywhere else on earth. There is some good hardwood timber, and camphor and ebony trees are found in profusion. Many orchid varieties thrive, some of extraordinary size." The book alluded to the area's "rich mixture of races and languages," its "extreme humidity" and "colorful native fauna," and added: "Its jungles are so impenetrable that even the wild beasts must keep to well-worn paths."

But perhaps the strangest aspect of this region was that, despite its dangers and discomforts, my companion claimed to have loved it. "They've got a mountain in the center of the peninsula—" He mentioned an unpronounceable name and shook his head. "Most beautiful thing you ever saw. And there's some really pretty country down along the coast, you'd swear it was some kind of South Sea island. Comfortable, too. Oh, it's damp all right, especially in the interior where the new mission was supposed to be—but the temperature never even hits a hundred. Try saying that for New York City."

I nodded. "Remarkable."

"And the *people*," he went on, "why, I believe they're just the friendliest people on earth. You know, I'd heard a lot of bad things about the Moslems—that's what most of them are, part of the Sunni sect—but I'm telling you, they treated us with real neighborliness . . . just so long as we made the teachings *available*, so to speak, and didn't interfere with their affairs. And we didn't. We didn't have to. What we provided, you see, was a hospital—well, a clinic, at least, two RNs and a doctor who came twice a month—and a small library with books and films. And not just theology, either. All subjects. We were right outside the village, they'd have to pass us on their way to the river, and when they thought none of the *lontoks* were looking they'd just come in and look around."

"None of the what?"

"Priests, sort of. There were a lot of them. But they didn't interfere with us, we didn't interfere with them. I don't know that we made all that many converts, actually, but I've got nothing bad to say about those people."

He paused, rubbing his eyes; he suddenly looked his age. "Things were going fine," he said. "And then they told me to establish a second mission, farther in the interior."

He stopped once more, as if weighing whether to continue. A squat little Chinese woman was plodding slowly up the aisle, holding on to the chairs on each side for balance. I felt her hand brush past my ear as she went by. My companion watched her with a certain unease, waiting till she'd passed. When he spoke again his voice had thickened noticeably.

"I've been all over the world—a lot of places Americans can't even go to these days—and I've always felt that, wherever I was, God was surely watching. But once I started getting up into those hills, well . . ." He shook his head. "I was pretty much on my own, you see. They were going to send most of the staff out later, after I'd got set up. All I had with me was one of our grounds keepers, two bearers, and a guide who doubled as interpreter. Locals, all of them." He frowned. "The grounds keeper, at least, was a Christian."

"You needed an interpreter?"

The question seemed to distract him. "For the new mission, yes. My Malay stood me well enough in the lowlands, but in the interior they used dozens of local dialects. I would have been lost up there. Where I was going they spoke something which our people back in the village called *agon di-gatuan*—'the Old Language.' I never really got to understand much of it." He stared down at his hands. "I wasn't there long enough."

"Trouble with the natives, I suppose."

He didn't answer right away. Finally he nodded. "I truly believe they must be the nastiest people who ever lived," he said with great deliberation. "I sometimes wonder how God could have created them." He stared out the window, at the hills of cloud below us. "They called themselves the Chauchas, near as I could make out. Some French colonial influence, maybe, but they looked Asiatic to me, with just a touch of black. Little people. Harmless looking." He gave a small shudder. "But they were nothing like what they seemed. You couldn't get to the bottom of them. They'd been living way up in those hills I don't know how many centuries, and whatever it is they were doing, they weren't going to let a stranger in on it. They called themselves Moslems, just like the lowlanders, but I'm sure there must have been a few bush-gods mixed in. I thought they were primitive, at first. I mean, some of their rituals—you wouldn't believe it. But now I think they weren't primitive at all. They just kept those rituals because they enjoyed them!" He tried to smile; it just accentuated the lines in his face.

"Oh, they seemed friendly enough in the beginning," he said. "You could approach them, do a bit of trading, watch them breed their animals. You could even talk to them about Salvation. And they'd just keep smiling, smiling all the time. As if they really *liked* you."

I could hear the disappointment in his voice, and something else.

"You know," he confided, suddenly leaning closer, "down in the lowlands, in the pastures, there's an animal, a kind of snail, the Malays kill on sight. A little yellow thing, but it scares them silly: they believe that if it passes over the shadow of their cattle, it'll suck out the cattle's life-force. They used to call it a 'Chaucha snail.' Now I know why."

"Why?" I asked.

He looked around the plane, and seemed to sigh. "You understand, at this stage we were still living in tents. We had yet to build anything. Well, the weather got bad, the mosquitoes got worse, and after the grounds keeper disappeared the others took off. I think the guide persuaded them to go. Of course, this left me—"

"Wait. You say your grounds keeper disappeared?"

"Yes, before the first week was out. It was late afternoon. We'd been pacing out one of the fields less than a hundred yards from the tents, and I was pushing through the long grass thinking he was behind me, and I turned around and he wasn't."

He was speaking all in a rush now. I had visions out of 1940s movies, frightened natives sneaking off with the supplies, and I wondered how much of this was true.

"So with the others gone, too," he said, "I had no way of communicating with the Chauchas, except through a kind of pidgin language, a mixture of Malay and their tongue. But I knew what was going on. All that week they kept laughing about something. Openly. And I got the impression that they were somehow responsible. I mean, for the man's disappearance. You understand? He'd been the one I trusted." His expression was pained. "A week later, when they showed him to me, he was still alive. But he couldn't speak. I think they wanted it that way. You see, they'd—they'd *grown* something in him." He shuddered.

Just at that moment, from directly behind us came an inhumanly high-pitched caterwauling that pierced the air like a siren, rising above the whine of the engines. It came with heart-stopping suddenness, and we both went rigid. I saw my companion's mouth gape as if to echo the scream. So much for the past; we'd become two old men gone all white and clutching at themselves. It was really quite comical. A full minute must have passed before I could bring myself to turn around.

By this time the stewardess had arrived and was dabbing at the place where the man behind me, dozing, had dropped his cigarette on his lap. The surrounding passengers, whites especially, were casting angry glances at him, and I thought I smelled burnt flesh. He was at last helped to his feet by the stewardess and one of his teammates, the latter chuckling uneasily.

Minor as it was, the accident had derailed our conversation and unnerved my companion; it was as if he'd retreated into his beard. He would talk no further, except to ask me ordinary and rather trivial questions about food prices and accommodations. He said he was bound for Florida, looking forward to a summer of, as he put it, "R and R," apparently financed by his sect. I asked him, a bit forlornly, what had happened in the end to the grounds keeper; he said that he had died. Drinks were served; the North American continent swung toward us from the south, first a finger of ice, soon a jagged line of green. I found myself giving the man my sister's address—Indian Creek was just outside Miami, where he'd be staying—and immediately regretted doing so. What did I know of him, after all? He told me his name was Ambrose Mortimer. "It means 'Dead Sea,'" he said. "From the Crusades."

When I persisted in bringing up the subject of the mission, he waved me off. "I can't call myself a missionary anymore," he said. "Yesterday, when I left the country, I gave up that right." He attempted a smile. "Honest, I'm just a civilian now."

"What makes you think they're after you?" I asked.

The smile vanished. "I'm not so sure they are," he said, not very convincingly. "I may just be getting paranoid in my old age. But I could swear that in New Delhi, and again at Heathrow, I heard someone singing—singing a certain song. Once it was in the men's room, on the other side of a partition; once it was behind me on line. And it was a song I recognized. It's in the Old Language." He shrugged. "I don't even know what the words mean."

"Why would anyone be singing? I mean, if they were following you?"

"That's just it. I don't know." He shook his head. "But I think—I think it's part of the ritual."

"What sort of ritual?"

"I don't know," he said again. He looked quite pained, and I resolved to bring this inquisition to an end. The ventilators had not yet dissipated the smell of charred cloth and flesh.

"But you'd heard the song before," I said. "You told me you recognized it."

"Yeah." He turned away and stared at the approaching clouds. We were passing over Maine. Suddenly the earth seemed a very small place. "I'd heard some of the Chaucha women singing it," he said at last. "It was a sort of farming song. It's supposed to make things grow."

Ahead of us loomed the saffron yellow smog that covers Manhattan like a dome. The "No Smoking" light winked silently on the console above us.

"I was hoping I wouldn't have to change planes," my companion said presently. "But the Miami flight doesn't leave for an hour and a half. I guess I'll get off and walk around a bit, stretch my legs. I wonder how long customs'll take." He seemed to be talking more to himself than to me. Once more I regretted my impulsiveness in giving him Maude's address. I was half tempted to make up some contagious disease for her, or a jealous husband. But then, quite likely he'd never call on her anyway; he hadn't even bothered to write down the name. And if he did pay a call—well, I told myself, perhaps he'd unwind when he realized he was safe among friends. He might even turn out to be good company; after all, he and my sister were practically the same age.

As the plane gave up the struggle and sank deeper into the warm encircling air, passengers shut books and magazines, organized their belongings, made last hurried forays to the bathroom to pat cold water on their faces. I wiped my spectacles and smoothed back what remained of my hair. My companion was staring out the window, the green Air Malay bag in his lap, his hands folded on it as if in prayer. We were already becoming strangers.

"Please return seat backs to the upright position," ordered

a disembodied voice. Out beyond the window, past the head now turned completely away from me, the ground rose to meet us and we bumped along the pavement, jets roaring in reverse. Already stewardesses were rushing up and down the aisles pulling coats and jackets from the overhead bins; executive types, ignoring instructions, were scrambling to their feet and thrashing into raincoats. Outside I could see uniformed figures moving back and forth in what promised to be a warm gray drizzle. "Well," I said lamely, "we made it." I got to my feet.

He turned and flashed me a sickly grin. "Good-bye," he said. "This really has been a pleasure." He reached for my hand.

"And do try to relax and enjoy yourself in Miami," I said, looking for a break in the crowd that shuffled past me down the aisle. "That's the important thing—just to relax."

"I know that." He nodded gravely. "I know that. God bless you." I found my slot and slipped into line. From behind me he added, "And I won't forget to look up your sister." My heart sank, but as I moved toward the door I turned to shout a last farewell. The old lady with the eyes was two people in front of me, but she didn't so much as smile.

One trouble with last farewells is that they occasionally prove redundant. Some forty minutes later, having passed like a morsel of food through a series of white plastic tubes, corridors, and customs lines, I found myself in one of the airport gift shops, whiling away the hour till my niece came to collect me; and there, once again, I saw the missionary.

He did not see me. He was standing before one of the racks of paperbacks—the so-called "Classics" section, haunt of the public domain—and with a preoccupied air he was glancing up and down the rows, barely pausing long enough to read the titles. Like me, he was obviously just killing time.

For some reason—call it embarrassment, a certain reluctance to spoil what had been a successful good-bye—I refrained from hailing him. Instead, stepping back into the rear aisle, I took refuge behind a rack of gothics, which I pretended to study while in fact studying him.

Moments later he looked up from the books and ambled over to a bin of cellophane-wrapped records, idly pressing the beard back into place below his right sideburn. Without warning he turned and surveyed the store; I ducked my head toward the gothics and enjoyed a vision normally reserved for the multifaceted eyes of an insect: women, dozens of them, fleeing an equal number of tiny mansions.

At last, with a shrug of his huge shoulders, he began flipping through the albums in the bin, snapping each one forward in an impatient staccato. Soon, the assortment scanned, he moved to the bin on the left and started on that.

Suddenly he gave a little cry, and I saw him shrink back. He stood immobile for a moment, staring down at something in the bin; then he whirled and walked quickly from the store, pushing past a family about to enter.

"Late for his plane," I said to the astonished salesgirl, and strolled over to the albums. One of them lay faceup in the pile—a jazz record featuring John Coltrane on saxophone. Confused, I turned to look for my erstwhile companion, but he had vanished in the crowd hurrying past the doorway.

Something about the album had apparently set him off; I studied it more carefully. Coltrane stood silhouetted against a tropical sunset, his features obscured, head tilted back, saxophone blaring silently beneath the crimson sky. The pose was dramatic but trite, and I could see in it no special significance: it looked like any other black man with a horn.

> New York eclipses all other cities in the spontaneous cordiality and generosity of its inhabitants—at least, such inhabitants as I have encountered.
> —LOVECRAFT, 9/29/1922

How quickly you changed your mind! You arrived to find a gold Dunsanian city of arches and domes and fantastic spires . . . or so you told us. Yet when you fled two years later you could see only "alien hordes."

What was it that so spoiled the dream? Was it that impossible marriage? Those foreign faces on the subway? Or was it merely the theft of your new summer suit? I believed then, Howard, and I believe it still, that the nightmare was all your own; though you returned to New England like a man reemerging into sunlight, there was, I assure you, a very good life to be found amid the shade. I remained—and survived.

I almost wish I were back there now, instead of in this ugly little bungalow, with its air conditioner and its rotting wicker furniture and the humid night dripping down its windows.

I almost wish I were back on the steps of the natural history museum where, that momentous August afternoon, I stood perspiring in the shadow of Teddy Roosevelt's horse, watching matrons stroll past Central Park with dogs or children in tow and fanning myself ineffectually with the postcard I'd just received from Maude. I was waiting for my niece to drive by and leave off her son, whom I planned to take round the museum; he'd wanted to see the life-size mockup of the blue whale and, just upstairs, the dinosaurs...

I remember that Ellen and her boy were more than twenty minutes late. I remember too, Howard, that I was thinking of you that afternoon, and with some amusement: much as you disliked New York in the twenties, you'd have reeled in horror at what it's become today. Even from the steps of the museum I could see a curb piled high with refuse and a park whose length you might have walked without once hearing English spoken; dark skins crowded out the white, and mambo music echoed from across the street.

I remember all these things because, as it turned out, this was a special day: the day I saw, for the second time, the black man and his baleful horn.

My niece arrived late, as usual; she had for me the usual apology and the usual argument. "How can you still live over here?" she asked, depositing Terry on the sidewalk. "I mean, just look at those people." She nodded toward a park bench around which blacks and Latins congregated like figures in a group portrait.

"Brooklyn is so much better?" I countered, as tradition dictated.

"Of course," she said. "In the Heights, anyway. I don't understand it—why this pathological hatred of moving? You might at least try the East Side. You can certainly afford it." Terry watched us impassively, lounging against the fender. I think he sided with me over his mother, but he was too wise to show it.

"Ellen," I said, "let's face it. I'm just too old to start hanging around singles bars. Over on the East Side they read nothing but best-sellers, and they hate anyone past sixty. I'm better off where I grew up—at least I know where the cheap restaurants are." It was, in fact, a thorny problem: forced to choose between whites whom I despised and blacks whom I feared, I somehow preferred the fear.

To mollify Ellen I read aloud her mother's postcard. It was the prestamped kind that bore no picture. "I'm still getting used to the cane," Maude had written, her penmanship as flawless as when she'd won the school medallion. "Livia has gone back to Vermont for the summer, so the card games are suspended & I'm hard into Pearl Buck. Your friend Rev. Mortimer dropped by & we had a nice chat. What amusing stories! Thanks again for the subscription to *McCall's*; I'll send Ellen my old copies. Look forward to seeing you all after the hurricane season."

Terry was eager to confront the dinosaurs; he was, in fact, getting a little old for me to superintend, and was halfway up the steps before I'd arranged with Ellen where to meet us afterward. With school out the museum was almost as crowded as on weekends, the halls' echo turning shouts and laughter into animal cries. We oriented ourselves on the floor plan in the main lobby—YOU ARE HERE read a large green dot, below which someone had scrawled *"Too bad for you"*—and trooped toward the Hall of Reptiles, Terry impatiently leading the way. "I saw that in school." He pointed toward a redwood diorama. "That too"—the Grand Canyon. He was, I believe, about to enter seventh grade, and until now had been little given to talk; he looked younger than the other children.

We passed toucans and marmosets and the new Urban Ecology wing ("concrete and cockroaches," sneered Terry), and duly stood before the brontosaurus, something of a disappointment: "I forgot it was just the skeleton," he said. Behind us a group of black boys giggled and moved toward us; I hurried my nephew past the assembled bones and through the most crowded doorway, dedicated, ironically, to Man in Africa. "This is the boring part," said Terry, unmoved by masks and spears. The pace was beginning to tire me. We passed through another doorway—Man in Asia—and moved quickly past the Chinese statuary. "I saw that in school." He nodded at a stumpy figure in a glass case, wrapped in ceremonial robes. Something about it was familiar to me, too; I paused to stare at it. The outer robe, slightly tattered, was spun of some shiny green material and displayed tall, twisted-looking trees on one side, a kind of stylized river on the other. Across the front ran five yellow-brown shapes in loincloth and headdress, presumably fleeing toward the robe's frayed edges; behind them stood a larger one, all black. In its mouth was a pendulous horn. The figure was crudely woven—little more than a stick figure, in fact—but it bore an unsettling resemblance, in both pose and proportion, to the one on the album cover.

Terry returned to my side, curious to see what I'd found. "Tribal garment," he read, peering at the white plastic notice below the case. "Malay Peninsula, Federation of Malaysia, early nineteenth century." He fell silent.

"Is that all it says?"

"Yep. They don't even have which tribe it's from." He reflected a moment. "Not that I really care."

"Well, I do," I said. "I wonder who'd know."

Obviously I'd have to seek advice at the information counter in the main lobby downstairs. Terry ran on ahead, while I followed even more slowly than before; the thought of a mystery evidently appealed to him, even one so tenuous and unexciting as this.

A bored-looking young college girl listened to the beginning of my query and handed me a pamphlet from below the counter. "You can't see anyone till September," she said, already beginning to turn away. "They're all on vacation."

I squinted at the tiny print on the first page: "Asia, our largest continent, has justly been called the cradle of civilization, but it may also be a birthplace of man himself." Obviously the pamphlet had been written before the current campaigns against sexism. I checked the date on the back: "Winter 1958." This would be of no help. Yet on page four my eye fell on the reference I sought:

> ... The model next to it wears a green silk ceremonial robe from Negri Sembilan, most rugged of the Malayan provinces. Note central motif of native man blowing ceremonial horn, and the graceful curve of his instrument; the figure is believed to be a representation of "Death's Herald," possibly warning villagers of approaching calamity. Gift of an anonymous donor, the robe is probably Tcho-tcho in origin, and dates from the early 19th century.

"What's the matter, uncle? Are you sick?" Terry gripped my shoulder and stared up at me, looking worried; my behavior had obviously confirmed his worst fears about old people. "What's it say in there?"

I gave him the pamphlet and staggered to a bench near the wall. I wanted time to think. The Tcho-Tcho People, I knew, had figured in a number of tales by Lovecraft and his disciples—Howard himself had called them "the wholly abominable Tcho-Tchos"—but I couldn't remember much about them except that they were said to worship one of his imaginary deities. For some reason I associated them with Burma ...

But whatever their attributes, I'd been certain of one thing: the Tcho-Tchos were completely fictitious.

Obviously I'd been wrong. Barring the unlikely possibility that the pamphlet itself was a hoax, I was forced to conclude that the malign beings of the stories were in fact based upon an actual race inhabiting the Southeast Asian subcontinent—a race whose name the missionary had mistranslated as "the Chauchas."

It was a rather troublesome discovery. I had hoped to turn some of Mortimer's recollections, authentic or not, into fiction; he'd unwittingly given me the material for three or four good plots. Yet I'd now discovered that my friend Howard had beaten me to it, and that I was put in the uncomfortable position of living out another man's horror stories.

> Epistolary expression is with me largely replacing conversation.
>
> —LOVECRAFT, 12/23/1917

I hadn't expected my second encounter with the black horn-player. A month later I got an even bigger surprise: I saw the missionary again.

Or at any rate, his picture. It was in a clipping my sister had sent me from the *Miami Herald*, over which she had written in ballpoint pen, *"Just saw this in the paper—how awful!!"*

I didn't recognize the face; the photo was obviously an old one, the reproduction poor, and the man was clean-shaven. But the words below it told me it was him.

CLERGYMAN MISSING IN STORM

(Wed.) The Rev. Ambrose B. Mortimer, 56, a lay pastor of the Church of Christ, Knoxville, Tenn., has been reported missing in the wake of Monday's hurricane. Spokesmen for the order say Mortimer had recently retired after serving nineteen years as a missionary, most recently in Malaysia. After moving to Miami in July, he had been a resident of 311 Pompano Canal Road.

Here the piece ended, with an abruptness that seemed all too appropriate to its subject. Whether Ambrose Mortimer still lived I didn't know, but I felt certain now that, having fled one peninsula, he had strayed onto another just as dangerous, a finger thrust into the void. And the void had swallowed him up.

So, anyway, ran my thoughts. I have often been prey to depressions of a similar nature, and subscribe to a fatalistic philosophy I'd shared with my friend Howard: a philosophy one of his less sympathetic biographers has dubbed "futilitarianism."

Yet pessimistic as I was, I was not about to let the matter rest. Mortimer may well have been lost in the storm; he may even have set off somewhere on his own. But if, in fact, some lunatic religious sect had done away with him for having pried too closely into its affairs, there were things I could do about it. I wrote to the Miami police that very day.

"Gentlemen," I began. "Having learned of the recent disappearance of the Reverend Ambrose Mortimer, I think I can provide information which may prove of use to investigators."

There is no need to quote the rest of the letter here. Suffice it to say that I recounted my conversation with the missing man, emphasizing the fears he'd expressed for his life: pursuit and "ritual murder" at the hands of a Malayan tribe called the Tcho-Tcho. The letter was, in short, a rather elaborate way of crying "foul play." I sent it care of my sister, asking that she forward it to the correct address.

The police department's reply came with unexpected speed. As with all such correspondence, it was more curt than courteous. "Dear Sir," wrote a Detective Sergeant A. Linahan, "in the matter of Rev. Mortimer we had already been apprised of the threats on his life. To date a preliminary search of the

Pompano Canal has produced no findings, but dredging operations are expected to continue as part of our routine investigation. Thanking you for your concern—"

Below his signature, however, the sergeant had added a short postscript in his own hand. Its tone was somewhat more personal; perhaps typewriters intimidated him. "You may be interested to know," it said, "that we've recently learned a man carrying a Malaysian passport occupied rooms at a North Miami hotel for most of the summer, but checked out two weeks before your friend disappeared. I'm not at liberty to say more, but please be assured we are tracking down several leads at the moment. Our investigators are working full-time on the matter, and we hope to bring it to a speedy conclusion."

Linahan's letter arrived on September twenty-first. Before the week was out I had one from my sister, along with another clipping from the *Herald*; and since, like some old Victorian novel, this chapter seems to have taken an epistolary form, I will end it with extracts from these two items.

The newspaper story was headed WANTED FOR QUESTIONING. Like the Mortimer piece, it was little more than a photo with an extended caption.

> (Thurs.) A Malaysian citizen is being sought for questioning in connection with the disappearance of an American clergyman, Miami police say. Records indicate that the Malaysian, Mr. D. A. Djaktu-tchow, had occupied furnished rooms at the Barkleigh Hotella, 2401 Culebra Ave., possibly with an unnamed companion. He is believed still in the greater Miami area, but since August 22 his movements cannot be traced. State Dept. officials report Djaktu-tchow's visa expired August 31; charges are pending.
>
> The clergyman, Rev. Ambrose B. Mortimer, has been missing since September 6.

The photo above the article was evidently a recent one, no doubt reproduced from the visa in question. I recognized the smiling moon-wide face, although it took me a moment to place him as the man whose dinner I'd stumbled over on the plane. Without the moustache, he looked less like Charlie Chan.

The accompanying letter filled in a few details. "I called up the *Herald*," my sister wrote, "but they couldn't tell me any more than was in the article. Just the same, finding that out took me half an hour, since the stupid woman at the switchboard kept putting me through to the wrong person. I guess you're right—anything that prints color pictures on page one shouldn't call itself a newspaper.

"This afternoon I called up the police department, but they weren't very helpful either. I suppose you just can't expect to find out much over the phone, though I still rely on it. Finally I got an Officer Linahan, who told me he's just replied to that letter of yours. Have you heard from him yet? The man was very evasive. He was trying to be nice, but I could tell he was impatient to get off. He did give me the full name of the man they're looking for—Djaktu Abdul Djaktu-tchow, isn't that marvelous?—and he told me they have some more material on him which they can't release right now. I argued and pleaded (you know how persuasive I can be!) and finally, because I claimed I'd been a close friend of Rev. Mortimer's, I wheedled something out of him which he swore he'd deny if I told anyone but you. Apparently the poor man must have been deathly ill, maybe even tubercular—I intended to get a patch test next week, just to play safe, and I recommend that you get one too—because it seems that, in the reverend's bedroom, they found something *very* odd: pieces of lung tissue. Human lung tissue."

> I, too, was a detective in youth.
> —LOVECRAFT, 2/17/1931

Do amateur detectives still exist? I mean, outside the novels? I doubt it. Who, after all, has the time for such games today? Not I, unfortunately; though for more than a decade I'd been nominally retired, my days were quite full with the unromantic activities that occupy everyone this side of the paperbacks: letters, luncheon dates, visits to my niece and to my doctor; books (not enough) and television (too much) and perhaps a Golden Agers' matinee (though I have largely stopped going to films, finding myself increasingly out of sympathy with their heroes). I also spent Halloween week in Atlantic City, and most of another attempting to interest a rather overpolite young publisher in reprinting some of my early work.

All this, of course, is intended as a sort of apologia for my having put off further inquiries into poor Mortimer's case till mid-November. The truth is, the matter almost slipped my mind; only in novels do people not have better things to do.

It was Maude who reawakened my interest. She had been avidly scanning the papers—in vain—for further reports on the man's disappearance; I believe she had even phoned Sergeant Linahan a second time, but had learned nothing new. Now she wrote me with a tiny fragment of information, heard at thirdhand: one of her bridge partners had had it on the authority of "a friend in the police force" that the search for Mr. Djaktu was being widened to include his presumed companion—"a Negro child," or so my sister reported. Although there was every possibility that this information was false, or that it concerned an entirely different case, I could tell she regarded it as very sinister indeed.

Perhaps that was why the following afternoon found me struggling once more up the steps of the natural history museum—as much to satisfy Maude as myself. Her allusion to a Negro, coming after the curious discovery in Mortimer's bedroom, had recalled to mind the figure on the Malayan robe, and I had been troubled all night by the fantasy of a black man—a man much like the beggar I'd just seen huddled against Roosevelt's statue—coughing his lungs out into a sort of twisted horn.

I had encountered few other people on the streets that afternoon, as it was unseasonably cold for a city that's often mild till January; I wore a muffler, and my gray tweed overcoat flapped round my heels. Inside, however, the place, like all American buildings, was overheated; I was soon the same as I made my way up the demoralizingly long staircase to the second floor.

The corridors were silent and empty, but for the morose figure of a guard seated before one of the alcoves, head down as if in mourning, and, from above me, the hiss of the steam radiators near the marble ceiling. Slowly, and rather enjoying the sense of privilege that comes from having a museum to oneself, I retraced my earlier route past the immense skeletons of dinosaurs ("These great creatures once trod the earth where you now walk") and down to the Hall of Primitive Man, where two Puerto Rican youths, obviously playing hooky, stood by the African wing gazing worshipfully at a

Masai warrior in full battle gear. In the section devoted to Asia I paused to get my bearings, looking in vain for the squat figure in the robe. The glass case was empty. Over its plaque was taped a printed notice: "Temporarily removed for restoration."

This was no doubt the first time in forty years that the display had been taken down, and of course I'd picked just this occasion to look for it. So much for luck. I headed for the nearest staircase, at the far end of the wing. From behind me the clank of metal echoed down the hall, followed by the angry voice of the guard. Perhaps that Masai spear had proved too great a temptation.

In the main lobby I was issued a written pass to enter the north wing, where the staff offices were located. "You want the workrooms on basement level," said the woman at the information counter; the summer's bored coed had become a friendly old lady who eyed me with some interest. "Just ask the guard at the bottom of the stairs, past the cafeteria. I do hope you find what you're looking for."

Carefully keeping the pink slip she'd handed me visible for anyone who might demand it, I descended. As I turned onto the stairwell I was confronted with a kind of vision: a blond, Scandinavian-looking family were coming up the stairs toward me, the four upturned faces almost interchangeable, parents and two little girls with the pursed lips and timidly hopeful eyes of the tourist, while just behind them, apparently unheard, capered a grinning black youth, practically walking on the father's heels. In my present state of mind the scene appeared particularly disturbing—the boy's expression was certainly one of mockery—and I wondered if the guard who stood before the cafeteria had noticed. If he had, however, he gave no sign; he glanced without curiosity at my pass and pointed toward a fire door at the end of the hall.

The offices in the lower level were surprisingly shabby—the walls here were not marble but faded green plaster—and the entire corridor had a "buried" feeling to it, no doubt because the only outside light came from ground-level window gratings high overhead. I had been told to ask for one of the research associates, a Mr. Richmond; his office was part of a suite broken up by pegboard dividers. The door was open, and he got up from his desk as soon as I entered; I suspect that, in view of my age and gray tweed overcoat, he may have taken me for someone important.

A plump young man with sandy-colored beard, he looked like an out-of-shape surfer, but his sunniness dissolved when I mentioned my interest in the green silk robe. "And I suppose you're the man who complained about it upstairs, am I right?"

I assured him that I was not.

"Well, someone sure did," he said, still eyeing me resentfully; on the wall behind him an Indian war-mask did the same. "Some damn tourist, maybe, in town for a day and out to make trouble. Threatened to call the Malaysian Embassy. If you put up a fuss those people upstairs get scared it'll wind up in the *Times*."

I understood his allusion; the previous year the museum had gained considerable notoriety for having conducted some really appalling—and, to my mind, quite pointless—experiments on cats. Most of the public had, until then, been unaware that the building housed several working laboratories.

"Anyway," he continued, "the robe's down in the shop, and we're stuck with patching up the damn thing. It'll probably be down there for the next six months before we get to it. We're so understaffed right now it isn't funny." He glanced at his watch. "Come on, I'll show you. Then I've got to go upstairs."

I followed him down a narrow corridor that branched off to either side. At one point he said, "On your right, the infamous zoology lab." I kept my eyes straight ahead. As we passed the next doorway I smelled a familiar odor. "It makes me think of treacle," I said.

"You're not so far wrong." He spoke without looking back. "The stuff's mostly molasses. Pure nutrient. They use it for growing microorganisms."

I hurried to keep up with him. "And for other things?"

He shrugged. "I don't know, mister. It's not my field."

We came to a door barred by a black wire grille. "Here's one of the shops," he said, fitting a key into the lock. The door swung open on a long unlit room smelling of wood shavings and glue. "You sit down over here," he said, leading me to a small anteroom and switching on the light. "I'll be back in a second." I stared at the object closest to me, a large ebony chest, ornately carved. Its hinges had been removed.

Richmond returned with the robe draped over his arm. "See?" he said, dangling it before me. "It's really not in such bad condition, is it?" I realized he still thought of me as the man who'd complained.

On the field of rippling green fled the small brown shapes, still pursued by some unseen doom. In the center stood the black man, black horn to his lips, man and horn a single line of unbroken black.

"Are the Tcho-Tchos a superstitious people?" I asked.

"They *were*," he said pointedly. "Superstitious and not very pleasant. They're extinct as dinosaurs now. Supposedly wiped out by the Japanese or something."

"That's rather odd," I said. "A friend of mine claims to have met up with them earlier this year."

Richmond was smoothing out the robe; the branches of the snake-trees snapped futilely at the brown shapes. "I suppose it's possible," he said, after a pause. "But I haven't read anything about them since grad school. They're certainly not listed in the textbooks anymore. I've looked, and there's nothing on them. This robe's over a hundred years old."

I pointed to the figure in the center. "What can you tell me about this fellow?"

"Death's Herald," he said, as if it were a quiz. "At least that's what the literature says. Supposed to warn of some approaching calamity."

I nodded without looking up; he was merely repeating what I'd read in the pamphlet. "But isn't it strange," I said, "that these others are in such a panic? See? They aren't even waiting around to listen."

"Would you?" He snorted impatiently.

"But if the black one's just a messenger of some sort, why's he so much *bigger* than the others?"

Richmond began folding the cloth. "Look, mister," he said, "I don't pretend to be an expert on every tribe in Asia. But if a character's important, they'd sometimes make him larger. Anyway, that's what the Mayans did. But listen, I've really got to get this put away now. I've got a meeting to go to."

While he was gone I sat thinking about what I'd just seen. The small brown shapes, crude as they were, had expressed a terror no mere messenger could inspire. And that great black figure standing triumphant in the center, horn twisting from its mouth—that was no messenger either, I was sure of it. That was no Death's Herald. That was Death itself.

I returned to my apartment just in time to hear the telephone ringing, but by the time I'd let myself in it had stopped. I sat down in the living room with a mug of coffee and a book which had lain untouched on the shelf for the last thirty years: *Jungle Ways*, by that old humbug, William Seabrook. I'd met him back in the twenties and had found him likable enough, if rather untrustworthy. His book described dozens of unlikely characters, including "a cannibal chief who had got himself jailed and famous because he had eaten his young wife, a handsome, lazy wench called Blito, along with a dozen of her girl friends," but I discovered no mention of a black horn-player.

I had just finished my coffee when the phone rang again. It was my sister.

"I just wanted to let you know that there's another man missing," she said breathlessly; I couldn't tell if she was frightened or merely excited. "A busboy at the San Marino. Remember? I took you there."

The San Marino was an inexpensive little luncheonette on Indian Creek, several blocks from my sister's house. She and her friends ate there several times a week.

"It happened last night," she went on. "I just heard about it at my card game. They say he went outside with a bucket of fish heads to dump in the creek, and he never came back."

"That's very interesting, but . . ." I thought for a moment; it was highly unusual for her to call me like this. "But really, Maude, couldn't he have simply run off? I mean, what makes you think there's any connection—"

"Because I took Ambrose there, too!" she cried. "Three or four times. That was where we used to meet."

Apparently Maude had been considerably better acquainted with the Reverend Mortimer than her letters would have led one to believe. But I wasn't interested in pursuing that line right now. "This busboy," I asked, "was he someone you knew?"

"Of course," she said. "I know everyone in there. His name was Carlos. A quiet boy, very courteous. I'm sure he must have waited on us dozens of times."

I had seldom heard my sister so upset, but for the present

there seemed no way of calming her fears. Before hanging up she made me promise to move up the month's visit I'd expected to pay her over Christmas; I assured her I would try to make it down for Thanksgiving, then only a week away, if I could find a flight that wasn't filled.

"Do try," she said—and, were this a tale from the old pulps, she would have added: "If anyone can get to the bottom of this, you can." In truth, however, both Maude and I were aware that I had just celebrated my seventy-seventh birthday and that, of the two of us, I was by far the more timid; so that what she actually said was, "Looking after you will help take my mind off things."

> I couldn't live a week without a private library.
> —LOVECRAFT, 2/25/1929

That's what I thought, too, until recently. After a lifetime of collecting I'd acquired thousands upon thousands of volumes, never parting with a one; it was this cumbersome private library, in fact, that helped keep me anchored to the same West Side apartment for nearly half a century.

Yet here I sit, with no company save a few gardening manuals and a shelf of antiquated best-sellers—nothing to dream on, nothing I'd want to hold in my hand. Still, I've survived here a week, a month, almost a season. The truth is, Howard, you'd be surprised what you can live without. As for the books I've left in Manhattan, I just hope someone takes care of them when I'm gone.

But I was by no means so resigned that November when, having successfully reserved seats on an earlier flight, I found myself with less than a week in New York. I spent all my remaining time in the library—the public one on Forty-second Street, with the lions in front and with no book of mine on its shelves. Its two reading rooms were the haunt of men my age and older, retired men with days to fill, poor men just warming their bones; some leafed through newspapers, others dozed in their seats. None of them, I'm sure, shared my sense of urgency: there were things I hoped to find out before I left, things for which Miami would be useless.

I was no stranger to this building. Long ago, during one of Howard's visits, I had undertaken some genealogical researches here in the hope of finding ancestors more impressive than his, and as a young man I had occasionally attempted to support myself, like the denizens of Gissing's *New Grub Street*, by writing articles compiled from the work of others. But by now I was out of practice: how, after all, does one find references to an obscure Southeast Asian tribal myth without reading everything published on that part of the world?

Initially that's exactly what I tried; I looked through every book I could find with "Malaya" in its title. I read about rainbow gods and phallic altars and something called "the *tatai*," a sort of unwanted companion; I came across wedding rites and The Death of Thorns and a certain cave inhabited by millions of snails. But I found no mention of the Tcho-Tcho, and nothing on their gods.

This in itself was surprising. We are living in a day when there are no more secrets, when my twelve-year-old nephew can buy his own grimoire and books with titles like *The Encyclopedia of Ancient and Forbidden Knowledge* are remaindered at every discount store. Though my friends from the twenties would have hated to admit it, the notion of stumbling across some moldering old "black book" in the attic of a deserted house—some lexicon of spells and chants and hidden lore—is merely a quaint fantasy. If the *Necronomicon* actually existed, it would be out in Bantam paperback with a preface by Lin Carter.

It's appropriate, then, that when I finally came upon a reference to what I sought, it was in that most unromantic of forms, a mimeographed film-script.

"Transcript" would perhaps be closer to the truth, for it was based upon a film shot in 1937 and that was now presumably crumbling in some forgotten vault. I discovered the item inside one of those brown cardboard packets, held together with ribbons, which libraries use to protect books whose bindings have worn away. The book itself, *Malay Memories*, by a Reverend Morton, had proved a disappointment despite the author's rather suggestive name. The transcript lay beneath it, apparently slipped there by mistake, but though it appeared unpromising—only ninety-six pages long, badly typed, and held together by a single rusty staple—it more than repaid the reading. There was no title page, nor do I think there'd ever been one; the first page simply identified the film as "Documentary—Malaya Today," and noted that it had been financed, in part, by a U.S. government grant. The filmmaker or makers were not listed.

I soon saw why the government may have been willing to lend the venture some support, for there were a great many scenes in which the proprietors of rubber plantations expressed the sort of opinions Americans might want to hear. To an unidentified interviewer's query, "What other signs of prosperity do you see around you?" a planter named Mr. Pierce had obligingly replied, "Why, look at the living standard—better schools for the natives and a new lorry for me. It's from Detroit, you know. May even have my own rubber in it."

> INT: And how about the Japanese? Are they one of today's better markets?
> PIERCE: Oh, see, they buy our crop all right, but we don't really trust 'em, understand? (Smiles) We don't like 'em half so much as the Yanks.

The final section of the transcript was considerably more interesting, however; it recorded a number of brief scenes that must never have appeared in the finished film. I quote one of them in its entirety:

PLAYROOM, CHURCH SCHOOL—LATE AFTERNOON.
(DELETED)

> INT: This Malay youth has sketched a picture of a demon he calls Shoo Goron. (To Boy) I wonder if you can tell me something about the instrument he's blowing out of. It looks like the Jewish *shofar*, or ram's horn. (Again to Boy) That's all right. No need to be frightened.
> BOY: He no blow out. Blow in.
> INT: I see—he draws air in through the horn, is that right?
> BOY: No horn. Is no horn. (Weeps) Is *him*.

Miami did not produce much of an impression ...
—LOVECRAFT, 7/19/1931

Waiting in the airport lounge with Ellen and her boy, my bags already checked and my seat number assigned, I fell prey to the sort of anxiety that had made me miserable in youth: it was a sense that time was running out; and what caused it now, I think, was the hour that remained before my flight was due to leave. It was too long a time to sit making small talk with Terry, whose mind was patently on other things; yet it was too short to accomplish the task which I'd suddenly realized had been left undone.

But perhaps my nephew would serve. "Terry," I said, "how'd you like to do me a favor?" He looked up eagerly; I suppose children his age love to be of use. "Remember the building we passed on the way here? The International Arrivals building?"

"Sure," he said. "Right next door."

"Yes, but it's a lot farther away than it looks. Do you think you'd be able to get there and back in the next hour and find something out for me?"

"Sure." He was already out of his seat.

"It just occurs to me that there's an Air Malay reservations desk in that building, and I wonder if you could ask someone there—"

My niece interrupted me. "Oh, no he won't," she said firmly. "First of all, I won't have him running across that highway on some silly errand—" she ignored her son's protests, "—and secondly, I don't want him involved in this game you've got going with Mother."

The upshot of it was that Ellen went herself, leaving Terry and me to our small talk. She took with her a slip of paper upon which I'd written "Shoo Goron," a name she regarded with sour skepticism. I wasn't sure she would return before my departure (Terry, I could see, was growing increasingly uneasy), but she was back before the second boarding call.

"She says you spelled it wrong," Ellen announced.

"Who's she?"

"Just one of the flight attendants," said Ellen. "A young girl, in her early twenties. None of the others were Malayan. At first she didn't recognize the name, until she read it out loud a few times. Apparently it's some kind of fish, am I right? Like a suckerfish, only bigger. Anyway, that's what she said. Her mother used to scare her with it when she was bad."

Obviously Ellen—or, more likely, the other woman—had misunderstood. "Sort of a bogeyman figure?" I asked. "Well, I suppose that's possible. But a fish, you say?"

Ellen nodded. "I don't think she knew that much about it, though. She acted a little embarrassed, in fact. Like I'd asked her something dirty." From across the room a loudspeaker issued the final call for passengers. Ellen helped me to my feet, still talking. "She said she was just a Malay, from somewhere on the coast—Malacca? I forget—and that it's a shame I didn't drop by three or four months ago, because her summer replacement was part Chocha—Chocho?—something like that."

The line was growing shorter now. I wished the two of them a safe Thanksgiving and shuffled toward the plane.

Below me the clouds had formed a landscape of rolling hills. I could see every ridge, every washed-out shrub, and in the darker places, the eyes of animals.

Some of the valleys were split by jagged black lines that looked like rivers seen on a map. The water, at least, was real enough: here the cloudbank had cracked and parted, revealing the dark sea beneath.

Throughout the ride I'd been conscious of lost opportunity, a sense that my destination offered a kind of final chance. With Howard gone these forty years I still lived out my life in his shadow; certainly his tales had overshadowed my own. Now I found myself trapped within one of them. Here, miles above the earth, I felt great gods warring; below, the war was already lost.

The very passengers around me seemed participants in a masque: the oily little steward who smelled of something odd; the child who stared and wouldn't look away; the man asleep beside me, mouth slack, who'd chuckled and handed me a page ripped from his "in-flight" magazine: NOVEMBER PUZZLE PAGE, with an eye staring in astonishment from a swarm of dots. "Connect the dots and see what you'll be *least* thankful for this Thanksgiving!" Below it, half buried amid *"B'nai B'rith to Host Song Fest"* and advertisements for beach clubs, a bit of local color found me in a susceptible mood:

> Have Fins, Will Travel
> (Courtesy *Miami Herald*) If your hubby comes home and swears he's just seen a school of fish walk across the yard, don't sniff his breath for booze. He may be telling the truth! According to U. of Miami zoologists, catfish will be migrating in record numbers this fall and South Florida residents can expect to see hundreds of the whiskered critters crawling overland, miles from water. Though usually no bigger than your pussycat, most breeds can survive without...

Here the piece came to a ragged end where my companion had torn it from the magazine. He stirred in his sleep, lips moving; I turned and put my head against the window, where the limb of Florida was swinging into view, veined with dozens of canals. The plane shuddered and slid toward it.

Maude was already at the gate, a black porter beside her with an empty cart. While we waited by a hatchway in the basement for my luggage to be disgorged, she told me the sequel to the San Marino incident: the boy's body found washed up on a distant beach, lungs in mouth and throat. "Inside out," she said. "Can you imagine? It's been on the radio all morning. With tapes of some ghastly doctor talking about smoker's cough and the way people drown. I couldn't even listen after a while." The porter heaved my bags onto the cart and we followed him to the taxi stand, Maude using her cane to gesticulate. If I hadn't seen how aged she'd become I'd have thought the excitement was agreeing with her.

We had the driver make a detour westward along Pompano Canal Road, where we paused at number 311, one of nine shabby green cabins that formed a court round a small and very dirty wading pool; in a cement pot beside the pool drooped a solitary half-dead palm, as if in some travesty of an oasis. This, then, had been Ambrose Mortimer's final home. My sister was very silent, and I believed her when she said she'd never been here before. Across the street glistened the oily waters of the canal.

The taxi turned east. We passed interminable rows of hotels, motels, condominiums, shopping centers as big as Central Park, souvenir shops with billboards bigger than themselves, baskets of seashells and wriggly plastic auto toys out front. Men and women our age and younger sat on canvas beach chairs in their yards, blinking at the traffic. The sexes had merged; some of the older women were nearly as bald as I was, and men wore clothes the color of coral, lime, and peach. They walked very slowly as they crossed the street or moved along the sidewalk; cars moved almost as slowly, and it was forty minutes before we reached Maude's house, with its pastel orange shutters and the retired druggist and his wife living upstairs. Here, too, a kind of languor was upon the block, one into which I knew, with just a memory of regret, I would soon be settling. Life was slowing to a halt, and once the taxi had roared away the only things that stirred were the geraniums in Maude's window box, trembling slightly in a breeze I couldn't even feel.

A dry spell. Mornings in my sister's air-conditioned parlor, luncheons with her friends in air-conditioned coffee shops. Inadvertent afternoon naps, from which I'd waken with headaches. Evening walks, to watch the sunsets, the fireflies, the TV screens flashing behind neighbors' blinds. By night, a few faint cloudy stars; by day, tiny lizards skittering over the hot pavement, or boldly sunning themselves on the flagstones. The smell of oil paints in my sister's closet, and the insistent buzz of mosquitoes in her garden. Her sundial, a gift from Ellen, with Terry's message painted on the rim. Lunch at the San Marino and a brief, halfhearted look at the dock in back, now something of a tourist attraction. An afternoon at a branch library in Hialeah, searching through its shelves of travel books, an old man dozing at the table across from me, a child laboriously copying her school report from the encyclopedia. Thanksgiving dinner, with its half-hour's phone call to Ellen and the boy and the prospect of turkey for the rest of the week. More friends to visit, and another day at the library.

Later, driven by boredom and the ghost of an impulse, I phoned the Barkleigh Hotella in North Miami and booked a room there for two nights. I don't remember the days I settled for, because that sort of thing no longer had much meaning, but I know it was for midweek; "we're deep in the season," the proprietress informed me, and the hotel would be filled each weekend till long past New Year's.

My sister refused to accompany me out to Culebra Avenue; she saw no attraction in visiting the place once occupied by a fugitive Malaysian, nor did she share my pulp-novel fantasy that, by actually living there myself, I might uncover some clue unknown to police. ("Thanks to the celebrated author of *Beyond the Garve* . . .") I went alone, by cab, taking with me half a dozen volumes from the branch library. Beyond the reading, I had no other plans.

The Barkleigh was a pink adobe building two stories tall, surmounted by an ancient neon sign on which the dust lay thick in the early afternoon sunlight. Similar establishments lined the block on both sides, each more depressing than the last. There was no elevator here and, as I learned to my disappointment, no rooms available on the first floor; the staircase looked like it was going to be an effort.

In the office downstairs I inquired, as casually as I could, which room the notorious Mr. Djaktu had occupied; I'd hoped, in fact, to be assigned it, or one nearby. But I was doomed to disappointment. The preoccupied little Cuban behind the counter had been hired only six weeks before and claimed to know nothing of the matter; in halting English he explained that the proprietress, a Mrs. Zimmerman, had just left for New Jersey to visit relatives and would not be back till Christmas. Obviously I could forget about gossip.

By this point I was half tempted to cancel my visit, and I confess that what kept me there was not so much a sense of honor as the desire for two days' separation from Maude, who, having been on her own for nearly a decade, was rather difficult to live with.

I followed the Cuban upstairs, watching my suitcase bump rhythmically against his legs, and was led down the hall to a room facing the rear. The place smelled vaguely of salt air and hair oil; the sagging bed had served many a desperate holiday. A small cement terrace overlooked the yard and a vacant lot behind it, the latter so overgrown with weeds and the grass in the yard so long unmown that it was difficult to tell where one began and the other ended. A clump of palms rose somewhere in the middle of this no-man's-land, impossibly tall and thin, with only a few stiffened leaves to grace the tops. On the ground below them lay several rotting coconuts.

This was my view the first night when I returned after dining at a nearby restaurant. I felt unusually tired and soon went inside to sleep. The night being cool, there was no need for the air conditioner; as I lay in the huge bed I could hear people stirring in the adjoining room, the hiss of a bus moving down the avenue, and the rustle of palm leaves in the wind.

I spent part of the next morning composing a letter to Mrs. Zimmerman, to be held for her return. After the long walk to a coffee shop for lunch, I napped. After dinner I did the same. With the TV turned on for company, a garrulous blur at the other side of the room, I went through the pile of books on my night-table, final cullings from the bottom of the travel shelf; most of them hadn't been taken out since the thirties. I found nothing of interest in any of them, at least upon first inspection, but before turning out the light I noticed that one, the reminiscences of a Colonel E. G. Paterson, was provided with an index. Though I looked in vain for the demon Shoo Goron, I found reference to it under a variant spelling.

The author, no doubt long deceased, had spent most of his life in the Orient. His interest in Southeast Asia was slight, and the passage in question consequently brief:

> . . . Despite the richness and variety of their folklore, however, they have nothing akin to the Malay *shugoran*, a kind of bogey-man used to frighten naughty children. The traveller hears many conflicting descriptions of it, some bordering on the obscene. (*Oran*, of course, is Malay for 'man,' while *shug*, which here connotes 'sniffing' or 'questing,' means literally, 'elephant's trunk.') I well recall the hide which hung over the bar at the Traders' Club in Singapore, and which, according to tradition, represented the infant of this fabulous creature; its wings were black, like the skin of a Hottentot. Shortly after the War a regimental surgeon was passing through on his way back to Gibraltar and, after due examination, pronounced it the dried-out skin of a rather large catfish. He was never asked back.

I kept my light on until I was ready to fall asleep, listening to the wind rattle the palm leaves and whine up and down the row of terraces. As I switched off the light I half expected to see a shadowy shape at the window, but I saw, as the poet says, nothing but the night.

The next morning I packed my bag and left, aware that my stay in the hotel had proved fruitless. I returned to my sister's house to find her in agitated conversation with the druggist from upstairs; she was in a terrible state and said she'd been trying to reach me all morning. She had awakened to find the flower box by her bedroom window overturned and the shrubbery beneath it trampled. Down the side of the house ran two immense slash marks several yards apart, starting at the roof and continuing straight to the ground.

> My gawd, how the years fly. Stolidly middle-aged—when only yesterday I was young and eager and awed by the mystery of an unfolding world.
> —LOVECRAFT, 8/20/1926

There is little more to report. Here the tale degenerates into an unsifted collection of items which may or may not be related: pieces of a puzzle for those who fancy themselves puzzle fans, a random swarm of dots, and in the center, a wide unwinking eye.

Of course, my sister left the house on Indian Creek that very day and took rooms for herself in a downtown Miami hotel. Subsequently she moved inland to live with a friend in a green stucco bungalow several miles from the Everglades, third in a row of nine just off the main highway. I am seated in its den as I write this. After the friend died my sister lived on here alone, making the forty-mile bus trip to Miami only on special occasions: theater with a group of friends, one or two shopping trips a year. She had everything else she needed right here in town.

I returned to New York, caught a chill, and finished out the winter in a hospital bed, visited rather less often than I might have wished by my niece and her boy. Of course, the drive in from Brooklyn is nothing to scoff at.

One recovers far more slowly when one has reached my age; it's a painful truth we all learn if we live long enough. Howard's life was short, but in the end I think he understood. At thirty-five he could deride as madness a friend's "hankering after youth," yet ten years later he'd learned to mourn the loss of his own. "The years tell on one!" he'd written. "You young fellows don't know how lucky you are!"

Age is indeed the great mystery. How else could Terry

have emblazoned his grandmother's sundial with that saccharine nonsense?

> *Grow old along with me;*
> *The best is yet to be.*

True, the motto is traditional to sundials—but that young fool hadn't even kept to the rhyme. With diabolical imprecision he had written, *"The best is yet to come"*—a line to make me gnash my teeth, if I had any left to gnash.

I spent most of the spring indoors, cooking myself wretched little meals and working ineffectually on a literary project that had occupied my thoughts. It was discouraging to find that I wrote so slowly now, and changed so much. My sister only reinforced the mood when, sending me a rather salacious story she'd found in the *Enquirer*—about the "thing like a vacuum cleaner" that snaked through a Swedish sailor's porthole and "'made his face all purple'"—she wrote at the top, *"See? Right out of Lovecraft."*

It was not long after this that I received, to my surprise, a letter from Mrs. Zimmerman, bearing profuse apologies for having misplaced my inquiry until it turned up again during "spring cleaning." (It is hard to imagine any sort of cleaning at the Barkleigh Hotella, spring or otherwise, but even this late reply was welcome.) "I am sorry that the minister who disappeared was a friend of yours," she wrote. "I'm sure he must have been a fine gentleman.

"You asked me for 'the particulars,' but from your note you seem to know the whole story. There is really nothing I can tell you that I did not tell the police, though I do not think they ever released all of it to the papers. Our records show that our guest Mr. Djaktu arrived here nearly a year ago, at the end of June, and left the last week of August owing me a week's rent plus various damages which I no longer have much hope of recovering, though I have written the Malaysian Embassy about it.

"In other respects he was a proper boarder, paid regularly, and in fact hardly ever left his room except to walk in the back yard from time to time, or stop at the grocer's. (We have found it impossible to discourage eating in rooms.) My only complaint is that in the middle of the summer he may have had a small colored child living with him without our knowledge, until one of the maids heard him singing to it as she passed his room. She did not recognize the language, but said she thought it might be Hebrew. (The poor woman, now sadly taken from us, was barely able to read.) When she next made up the room, she told me that Mr. Djaktu claimed the child was 'his,' and that she left because she caught a glimpse of it watching her from the bathroom. She said it was naked. I did not speak of this at the time, as I do not feel it is my place to pass judgment on the morals of my guests. Anyway, we never saw the child again, and we made sure the room was completely sanitary for our next guests. Believe me, we have received nothing but good comments on our facilities. We think they are excellent and hope you agree, and I also hope you will be our guest again the next time you come to Florida."

Unfortunately, the next time I came to Florida was for my sister's funeral late that winter. I know now, as I did not know then, that she had been in ill health for most of the previous year, but I cannot help thinking that the so-called "incidents"—the senseless acts of vandalism directed against lone women in the South Florida area, culminating in several reported attacks by an unidentified prowler—may have hastened her death.

When I arrived here with Ellen to take care of my sister's affairs and arrange for the funeral, I intended to remain a week or two at most, seeing to the transfer of the property. Yet somehow I lingered, long after Ellen had gone. Perhaps it was the thought of that New York winter, grown harsher with each passing year; I just couldn't find the strength to go back. Nor, in the end, could I bring myself to sell this house; if I am trapped here, it's a trap I'm resigned to. Besides, moving has never much agreed with me; when I grow tired of this little room—and I do—I can think of nowhere else to go. I've seen all the world I want to see. This simple place is now my home—and I feel certain it will be my last. The calendar on the wall tells me it's been almost three months since I moved in. I know that somewhere in its remaining pages you will find the date of my death.

The past week has seen a new outbreak of the "incidents." Last night's was the most dramatic by far. I can recite it almost word for word from the morning news. Shortly before midnight Mrs. Florence Cavanaugh, a housewife living at 24

Alyssum Terrace, South Princeton, was about to close the curtains in her front room when she saw, peering through the window at her, what she described as "a large Negro man wearing a gas mask or scuba outfit." Mrs. Cavanaugh, who was dressed only in her nightgown, fell back from the window and screamed for her husband, asleep in the next room, but by the time he arrived the Negro had made good his escape.

Local police favor the "scuba" theory, since near the window they've discovered footprints that may have been made by a heavy man in swim fins. But they haven't been able to explain why anyone would wear underwater gear so many miles from water.

The report usually concludes with the news that "Mr. and Mrs. Cavanaugh could not be reached for comment."

The reason I have taken such an interest in the case—sufficient, anyway, to memorize the above details—is that I know the Cavanaughs rather well. They are my next-door neighbors.

Call it an aging writer's ego, if you like, but somehow I can't help thinking that last evening's visit was meant for me. These little green bungalows all look alike in the dark.

Well, there's still a little night left outside—time enough to rectify the error. I'm not going anywhere.

I think, in fact, it will be a rather appropriate end for a man of my pursuits—to be absorbed into the denouement of another man's tale.

Grow old along with me;
The best is yet to come.

Tell me, Howard: how long before it's my turn to see the black face pressed to my window?

THE KING

William Relling, Jr.

William Relling, Jr. is one of the newer writers to break into the fantasy genre, with recent sales to *Cavalier, Dude, Whispers,* and various small press publications—as well as an article for a now-defunct science magazine called *Probe,* "which despite the title was on a different shelf from *Cavalier.*" Born March 14, 1954 in St. Louis, Missouri, Relling now makes his home in the Los Angeles area. Over the past ten years he has worked as a librarian, truck driver, hospital orderly, professional musician, salesman—and just now is teaching junior high school English part time while a part-time graduate student at the University of Southern California studying cinema, TV, and dramatic writing. In his spare time Relling is working on a screenplay for "a science fiction swashbuckler." His story "The King" is a reminder that fantasy fans aren't the only ones prone to idolize (and capitalize upon) their dead heroes.

Man, that was a while ago and I still shake. But, Jesus, who wouldn't? I'm probably not ever gonna stop, not as long as I can remember what I saw. And I'm not real likely to forget.

And I haven't *even* tried to pick up the sticks since then. Kind of forced retirement, you know. I don't think I could hold onto 'em. But I haven't had much of an urge to try. And I'm not gonna for a long time. Not for a real long time.

It's not like it didn't get to anybody else who was there, like the guys in the band, or the people in that theatre, or anybody who read about it later, who really don't know what happened. But I *saw* him, and he *was* there, and Jay's dead and Tommy's dead, and I *know* it was him. I know.

'Cause I worked for him. You remember back in '69, when he made that comeback, and they did that big Vegas gig and the tour and the film of that Hawaii gig? The one that's been on TV a couple times. Well, I worked part of that tour. When they were playin' in the midwest and they did this job in Kansas City and Ronnie Tutt came down with the flu, I got hired—on account of one of the horn players knew me and we'd worked together before—until Ron got better. So I did the gigs in St. Louis and Chicago and then Ron came back. But I hung around and got paid as a percussionist, 'cause The Man liked me, you know, and wanted to keep me around. Just as a favor.

That was a great job, 'cause he paid the band real well, and everything was first class all the way. And those cats, those guys in the band, could *play*. Glen Hardin did the piano work and a lot of the arranging and he was fine, man, really fine. And James Burton, the guitar player. I never heard anybody who could play like him. Just jamming with those guys was all right. Yeah, it was all right.

But The Man himself was great. He was The King, you know, just like they said. I mean, a lot of people only knew him from the early days and "Hound Dog" and Ed Sullivan or maybe from those not-so-good flicks he made. Or they only know the last year or so before he died, when he got so bad, you know, puttin' on all that weight, and his voice goin' and all and the stories about the booze and the pills and all that other shit.

But when I knew him he was at his peak. He was at the top. He was in good shape—he worked out, you know, exercise and karate and all, two, three hours a day—and his voice was real smooth and strong. God, he could sing. Did you ever see that thing on TV from Hawaii? He was great. Just great.

And he would kill those crowds. Absolutely. Not just the chicks, either, but the guys, too. And not only the young ones, but like old ladies and housewives and little girls and all. They'd scream and faint and just wet their pants. He had 'em, man, and he knew it all the time. It was unbelievable. Like he lit a fire under every one of them. And he did, too. He did.

We could feel it, too, just playin' behind him. And he still had some of that at the end, you know. That fire, that electricity. Even when he was goin' down, when he was *dying*, they were still hangin' on him. Even though he was fat and sick and all and couldn't sing like before. But he was still The Man. He still had it, even though he was in bad shape.

Look what happened when he died.

Those people thought he was some kind of *god* or something, and they came from all over the world to that funeral. Like he was something more than an ordinary human being and not like the rest of us, you know. And really he was, in a way. He was special. And anybody who'd known him, or thought they did, or who loved him was there. There were thousands of 'em. Jesus, I was there and it was—well, like nobody out of all those people could believe it, you know, and they all felt so bad. Like he couldn't really be mortal and couldn't really die. You could feel it like a weight on your back in that crowd, that "how-can-he-do-this-to-*us*" sort of thing. He couldn't really be dead.

They're still comin' today.

When I think back on it now, maybe that was a part of what happened later. You know, all those people not accepting that he was dead, wanting him to be back, praying to him like he *was* a god—

Maybe that was part of it. That and something else.

The hustlers. The hucksters. The cheap bastards who came down like buzzards to make a buck out of all that grief, that love, that worship. It made me sick to see those guys on the streets, man, *right out in front of that goddamn tomb*, sellin' ashtrays and T-shirts and photos and records. And the people, those thousands and thousands of people were buyin' it up, just because they loved him and didn't want to let him go. Like they had to have a part of him to hold on to. I got pissed off, and punched one of those guys out, one who was sellin' necklaces of little silver coffins with his name engraved on 'em. They had to pull me off that son-of-a-bitch.

But I knew Jay, and Jay was straight about his act, and he'd even been doin' the material for a couple of years before. The Man himself had seen Jay once and then met him later a couple of times, and he really kinda dug it. He said Jay was the only guy he'd ever seen who could do him right, you know. And Jay was a big fan of his. But Jay did other stuff in his act, you know, his own material and all. And like I said, Jay had been kicking around for awhile.

So it wasn't Jay's idea, really, but Tommy Adams's, who heard Jay at a club in Knoxville. He was the one who came around with the idea for the change in the act and the offer to manage Jay if he'd go along with it. Big bucks, Tommy said.

At the time I'd been gigging with Jay for about six months. He hired me after his old drummer quit somewhere around Springfield, Illinois, and I'd been back in the midwest after knockin' around LA for a couple of years, and was just gettin' by. I wasn't workin' real steady when I met Jay and he gave me the job. Anyway, when Tommy Adams came to him with the offer that September, Jay came to me. He knew that I'd known The Man personally—like he did, too—and he wanted to know how I felt about it. So we talked.

I told him what I thought of Tommy Adams, but that I really didn't see anything wrong with the change, 'cause I knew where he—Jay, that is—was coming from, you know. A tribute, right? Kind of a memorial. The money didn't have a thing to do with it.

Oh, no.

So Jay went for it, and became Jay Redman, Crown Prince to the throne of The King. Right down to the white suit and the scarves and the sequins and the rhinestones and the Mother of Pearl inlaid acoustic guitar and the hair and the sideburns and the sneer and the jewelry and the tight pants and the swivel hips and the karate kicks. Right down to "Heartbreak Hotel" and "In the Ghetto" and "Burnin' Love" and "Jailhouse Rock" and all.

And I went right down with him.

Maybe I shouldn't say that, I don't know. At the time I didn't think it was bad at all. Jay got hot almost from the start, and Tommy was gettin' us gigs all over the south and the midwest, from Fort Lauderdale to Chicago to Atlanta to Nashville to New Orleans to St. Louis, in clubs and dinner theatres and bars and everything. It got to where by February I was pullin' down about five bills a week, just by myself. Tommy wasn't kidding when he said there'd be big bucks. For *all* of us.

But it wasn't the money.

It was real strange. We'd do the gigs, you know, at those supper clubs and all and those people, man, they were just amazing. I mean, Jay was good and he had it down and all, but he was still just Jay. He was only pretending. It was an act, right?

But the people. It was like bein' back on that old tour, with the chicks screaming and passing out and reaching up to touch Jay when he'd wiggle or smile or wink at them.

Funny. There must have been a hundred other guys around the country with the same gig, and from what I heard, it was like that for all of them. The people were just crazy for something to hold on to.

But Jay took it in stride, you know, and stayed just Jay. There was no magical transformation or anything like that, where Jay started to talk like The Man when he was off stage or was possessed or any of that other crap you might have heard about. He knew it was an act, so on stage *and* off he was always still Jay. Sure, he dug all the attention and the bread, but he was always himself.

But Tommy, whew. Tommy didn't really go crazy, at least psycho or anything like that. It was the bread, you know. The dough started rollin' in and Tommy's all the time walkin' around with these big dollar signs in his eyes. That was all it was, was the bucks. Tommy was another buzzard, just like those other guys.

What started it was when Tommy lined up this TV gig for Jay that was a kind of "head-to-head" for the seven or so best impersonators doing the act. So we do the gig in Vegas at Caesar's Palace. Very big deal, right? Much bread. We made out fine.

Except that Jay loses and finishes behind a couple of other guys who maybe looked a little more like The Man or moved more like him or sounded more like him or—like *I* said—were just better than Jay. So what? You know. We still got paid and we didn't do bad at all. Jay was good, as he always was, and we weren't gonna be workin' any less or losin'. There was enough in it for all these other cats and it wasn't like we weren't pullin' down our share.

Tommy wasn't happy, though. We're not makin' enough, he says. We gotta go all the way, he says. We need another gimmick, he says, like it isn't already gimmick enough. So he starts tryin' to talk Jay into changin' his face, for Christ's sake, like some clown in Florida did, but Jay told him to shove it.

So Tommy comes up with something else. The memorial

concert, right? In Memphis, on August 16, the anniversary of the day The Man died. And the whole time Tommy's explaining this to Jay and me and the rest of the band, I keep hearin' this *ka-ching* like a little cash register in Tommy's head, and seein' those dollar signs in his eyes again.

But we all say sure, we'll do the job, and then we don't think any more about it. Except for Danny Palmer, the bass player we picked up right about the time Jay changed the act. I'm not gonna do it, Dan tells Tommy. I'm quittin'.

This is a big surprise for all of us, you know, 'cause everything's been goin' along okay and the money's good and Dan's a good bass player. Tommy's not worried at all, though, 'cause he figures what the hell, we got a good gig, we'll pick up another bassman, no sweat. Which was true, of course. But there was something else about Danny Palmer that bothered me personally.

So I ask him, hey Daniel, how come you're splittin'?

And at first it's like, well, I got this other gig lined up and I'm kinda tired of all this, you know.

But I'm gettin' nothin' that sounds like the truth. Come on, man, I said. Be straight with me. So he tells me.

He's scared. He's scared, and he doesn't know why.

Scared? I say. Scared of what?

I don't know, he says.

And I don't know what to say to him.

Then he says, it's like this. Those people and Jay and Tommy and the rest of us. Then he stops and looks at me real funny.

Do you know what necrophilia is? he asks.

No.

He tells me about it, and how what we're all doin' is sort of foul and scary and definitely not right. Something bad is happening, he says.

And I laughed.

Then he got sort of mad and split and that's all there was to it. But it still bothered me, even though I didn't really think about it much until later on.

Anyway, we picked up Bobby Redman, who was Jay's cousin, to play bass, and went on ahead, gigging like before. There wasn't any reason for me to think there was anything wrong, no matter what Dan Palmer might tell me. Besides, he was forgotten almost as soon as he was gone.

And all day on the 16th things were fine. There were a lot of people in town, you know, and the show'd been sold out weeks in advance, so we'd booked a second one and *that* one sold out, too, just like Tommy figured it would. Jay was feelin' good and loose and we were all okay.

That afternoon Jay and Bobby and I went out to the mansion, where The Man was buried. We fell in with the crowd, which was really big—that's no surprise, I guess. But I got that same feeling I'd had before, you know, that sad and heavy kind of load, and I looked over at Jay and he was lookin' at the grave, and his eyes were real glassy and he was pale. So I said, hey, man, let's get outta here, and Jay just nodded and we split.

We went to the theatre and back into the dressing rooms and Jay was real quiet for awhile. Then, after a bit, he's okay again. Bein' at the mansion got him down, he says.

Pretty soon the rest of the band shows up and Tommy's back there with us and we're gettin' ready to go on and he's pattin' us all on the back and tellin' us how great we are and how great Jay is and all. Then it's nine o'clock.

The house lights go down and everybody except Jay hits the stage, which is pitch black. Then the p.a. starts in with "Also spracht Zarathustra"—you know, "2001." That finishes, and we break into the opening bars of "C C Rider," and the crowd is already up.

Then the spotlights are on and sweeping over the crowd and the stage, and WHAM, there's Jay leapin' in from stage left, and he's shakin' and throwin' kisses to the crowd. And he's got 'em, man, he's got 'em. The place is absolutely nuts.

We ran through that set, and each song had 'em yellin' louder than the last. But it's real strange. Like it's not even Jay anymore, but it really is THE MAN HIMSELF, and they want him so bad. It was like lyin' on a beach, you know, and lettin' the waves wash over you, and we could feel that *want* just like that, man, up on stage. And Jay was "on" like I never seen him "on" before.

We closed the show with "Girl Happy," and that crowd was just insane when Jay ran off with the rest of us. Tommy was right there in the wings, and he claps an arm around Jay's shoulder and starts to lead him away toward the dressing room. I could see Tommy's head bobbing up and down, and could imagine that little cash register going *ka-*

ching all over again. But Tommy knows his stuff, right? He knows to let that crowd build up to a point where they're gonna *explode*, and then let Jay come out by himself and do his solo and really kill 'em.

I looked down at my watch and saw it wasn't quite 10:15. Plenty of time for the encore, and then clear 'em out and set up for the second show. Plenty of time.

They cut the house lights.

The applause and the yelling was enough to shake that whole damn building like it was an earthquake. It was black out there again, and they started to hold up lit matches and cigarette lighters, and it looked like torches or stars against a night sky. That's when I heard the scream.

It came from behind me, from somewhere backstage. I squinted at Bobby, who was next to me in the dark. Did you hear that? I asked him.

What? he says.

That scream, I say.

Jesus, he says, they're *all* screamin'.

From behind me I heard somebody hiss that Jay was comin'. I turned around, and he shuffled past me real slow. I reached up to pat him on the back, but something stopped me. And I noticed a smell.

It was real sweet and sort of sickening, like if you go into a flower shop and open one of the refrigerators, where they keep the roses and the carnations and all. It was almost enough to knock me over.

It was still dark when he walked to center stage and picked up his guitar. He played the first chords to "Love Me Tender," and all of a sudden, it was so quiet. It was like being in a church.

Then he started to sing.

I'd never heard Jay sing the song like that before. Usually he did it real well, which was why he saved it for an encore. But this time it was different.

It was more than good. It was incredible. It was pain and fear and loneliness and crying and every sad thing you ever felt in your life, or could ever imagine.

And nobody in that whole place could make a sound, except for the man on stage. Nobody could even move.

He finished the song, and the place was dead silent until he put the guitar down and started to move off toward the wings.

Then it all broke loose.

We were there waiting for him and whooping, and ready to hug him and congratulate him. But when he got close enough and Bobby started for him, something froze all of us, and he walked right by like we were statues. He went down the hall backstage toward the dressing rooms, but didn't go into his. Instead he kept right on going, down the dark hallway toward the stage exit door.

Then it was like somebody turned on a switch and we could all move again. I started to run after him and called his name, but he was a good twenty feet or so in front of me by the time he reached the door. He was right under the red exit sign.

Then he turned around. He looked at me, but only for a second.

Then he was gone.

They told me later that they found me there by the exit, after they'd looked into the dressing room and seen what was left of Jay and Tommy. At first the cops even wanted to arrest me, but it didn't take 'em long to figure out that I couldn't have killed them. I just couldn't have.

At the inquest the coroner gave an "official" report, and called it a "murder-suicide." He said that Jay and Tommy died between 10:15 and 10:45. He said that it must've been closer to 10:45, since witnesses testified that Jay didn't finish his encore until almost 10:30.

But I'm the only one who knows that they died at 10:15. And I'm the only one who can tell them that it wasn't Jay who did that last encore.

But I won't.

FOOTSTEPS

Harlan Ellison

The close of 1980 saw the publication of Harlan Ellison's *Shatterday* (Houghton Mifflin), an important fantasy collection to rank alongside his other milestone collections, *Deathbird Stories* (1975) and *Strange Wine* (1978). *Shatterday*, Ellison's thirty-eighth book, includes several stories which have appeared in previous volumes of *The Year's Best Horror Stories*, in addition to his stunning semi-autobiographical fantasy, "All the Lies That Are My Life." An anthologist of note, as well as author and critic, Ellison has edited the controversial *Dangerous Visions*, *Again, Dangerous Visions*, and the long-anticipated *Last Dangerous Visions*. Born in Ohio in 1934, Ellison rose through the ranks of science-fiction fandom and transcended the parochialism of that genre to become a major modern writer. He currently resides in the Los Angeles area.

Paris is again the setting for "Footsteps" (do you *really* want to tour Europe after reading this anthology?), and Ellison's account as to how this piece was written is itself a fascinating story.

Author's Introduction

This is my most recent story. It's a little more than six months old. I wrote it between the hours of 12:00 noon and 7:30 p.m. in the front window of a bookstore in the St. Germain section of Paris on Wednesday the 14th of May, 1980.

Like Georges Simenon before me—who sat in a glass case in the window of Gallimard in Paris earlier this century (and if anyone happens to have the specific date, I'd be most grateful to receive that information) and wrote an entire novel in one week—thereby validating for lesser lights like myself the act of creating in public—I have now created before the milling throngs not only in Boston, Los Angeles, Metz (France), San Diego, London, and New York . . . but in Paris.

Simenon is gone now, but I smile to think of following in his footsteps.

The circumstances were interesting, as well as the venue. Because the journalists of Paris—television, magazine, and newspaper—were skeptical of the undertaking (hadn't they heard Simenon had done it?) and suggested it might be a put-up job, that I would either use a story already written or plot one completely the night before, I set it up in the following manner, to insure the authenticity of spontaneity.

The owners of the bookstore—Temps Futurs at 8 Rue Dante—were to think on the subject they wanted me to write about. They were to devise a basic starting point . . . a love story, a pirate adventure, a fantasy about water sprites, whatever . . . and not until I walked into the store with my trusty Olympia portable were they to tell me what the subject of my day's labors would be. When the journalists heard that, they said it was impossible to work that way, that Artists did not create in such a fashion.

When I came into Temps Futurs, Stan and Sophie Barets had me set up with a platform in the window, a heavy board laid across sawhorses, a chair . . . and Perrier.

I arranged my typewriter, paper, pipe and tobacco, my correction fluid, pens, Typit keys, and Perrier, had them put on the store's stereo system a cassette of Django Reinhardt . . . and I waited for the word.

Stan, looking sheepish, told me that during the preceding evening, when he had been trying to think of something fresh and clever for me to use as a starter, he had received a phone call from a Parisian disc jockey who called himself The Werewolf. The deejay had said if I would write a story about a werewolf, he would give the bookstore publicity all through the day and night on the radio.

And so Stan said, "I want you to write a story about a she-werewolf who is a rapist." And one of the store's clerks, hearing that, added, "And she should have long, blond hair." And Sophie chimed in, "And it should happen in Paris."

My response was not quite dismay—but something very

like it. For originality, it was both wanting and overabundant. The idea of werewolves, male or female, was ground pretty well worked over. But adding rape to it, rape of males by a female, which is virtually impossible, was almost too original to work with. The blond hair was no problem, but this was only my second trip to Paris; I barely spoke the language, and I didn't know the city at all well enough to use it in the story with any authenticity.

But I'd agreed to the terms of the endeavor, and so I said I'd do it. The mind began to function in that way I call writing, a mode that employs cunning and duplicity worthy of a Presidential candidate trying to avoid taking a position on a touchy subject.

For instance: who said the female had to rape males?

And: the bookstore is filled with Parisians who do know the city; isn't that a handy reference library for proper geography and background?

Not to mention: didn't I read somewhere that sadists who brutalize their love partners found that the penis became engorged at the moment of greatest pain or death? Was it Sade? Gilles de Rais? Sacher-Masoch? Oh, what the hell, who's to contradict, how many snuff film experts can there be out there?

So I got the basic idea for the plot, and I started writing. And through the day the journalists came and buzzed around and took their pictures, and I signed books for visitors and answered silly questions and listened to Django and smoked my pipe and drank my Perrier . . . and I wrote. The story before you.

For her, darkness never fell in the City of Light. For her, nighttime was the time of life, the time filled with moments of light brighter than all the cheap neon sullying the Champs Elysées.

Nor had night ever fallen in London; nor in Bucharest; nor in Stockholm; nor in any of the fifteen cities she had visited on this holiday. This gourmet tour of the capitals of Europe.

But night had come frequently in Los Angeles.

Precipitating flight, necessitating caution, producing pain and hunger, terrible hunger that could not be assuaged, pain that could not be driven from her body. Los Angeles had become dangerous. Too dangerous for one of the children of the night.

But Los Angeles was behind her, and all the headlines about the INSANE SLAUGHTER, about the RIPPER, about the TERRIBLE DEATHS. All that was behind her ... and so were London, Bucharest, Stockholm, and a dozen other feeding grounds. Fifteen wonderful banquet halls.

Now she was in Paris for the first time, and night was coming with all its light and all its promise.

In the Hotel des Saints Pères she bathed at great length, taking the time she always took before she went out to dine, before she went out to find passion.

She had been startled to find the hotels in France did not provide washcloths. At first she had thought the chamber maid had forgotten to leave one, but when she called down to the reception desk the girl who answered the phone could not understand what she was asking for. The receptionist's English was not good; and French was almost incomprehensible to Claire. Claire spoke Los Angeles very well: which was of no use in Paris. It was fortunate language was no barrier for Claire when she was ordering a meal. No problem at all.

They made querulous sounds at one another for ten minutes till the receptionist *finally* understood she was asking for a washcloth.

"Ah! *Oui, mademoiselle,*" the receptionist said, *"le gant de toilette!"*

Instantly, Claire knew she had hit it. "Yes, that's right ... *oui* ... *gant,* uh ... *gant* whatever you said ... *oui* ... a washcloth ..."

And after *another* ten minutes she understood that the French thought the cloth with which one washed one's body was too personal to leave in a hotel room, that the French carried their own *gants de toilette* when they traveled.

She was amazed. And somehow mildly pleased. It bespoke a foreign way of life that promised new tastes, new thrills, possibly new highs of love. What she thought of as transports of ecstasy. In the night. In the bright light of darkness.

She lingered a long time in the bath, using the shower head on a flexible metal cord to wash her long blond hair. The extremely hot bath water around her lower body, between her thighs, the cascade of hot water pouring down over her, eased the tension of the plane trip from Zurich, washed away the first signs of jet-lag that had been creeping up on her since London. She lay back in the tub and let the water flow over her. Rebirth. Rejuvenation.

And she was ferociously hungry.

But Paris was world-renowned for its cuisine.

She sat at a table outside Les Deux Magots, the cafe on the Boulevard St. Germain where Boris Vian and Sartre and Simone de Beauvoir had sat in the Forties and Fifties, thinking their thoughts and sometimes writing their words of existential loneliness. They sat there drinking their Pastis, their Pernod, and they were filled with a sense of the oneness of humanity with the universe. Claire sat and thought of her impending oneness with selected parts of humanity. . . . And the universe was of no concern to her. For the children of the night loneliness was born in the flesh. It lay at the core of the bones, it swam in the blood. For her, the idea of existential solitude was not an abstract theory; it was her way of life. From the first moment of awareness.

She had dressed for effect. Tonight the blue sky silk, slit high in the front. She sat at the edge of the crowd, facing the sidewalk, her legs crossed high, a simple glass of Perrier *avec citron* before her. She had not ordered *pâté* or *terrine*: never taint the palate before indulging in a gourmet repast. She had avoided snacking all day, keeping herself on the trembling edge of hunger.

And the moveable feast walked past.

He was in his early forties, stuffy-looking, holding himself erect like Marshal Foch in the guidebook history of France she had bought. This man wore a sincere gray suit, double-breasted, pompously cut to obscure the fact that the quality was not that good.

The man—whom Claire now thought of as Marshal Foch—walked past, caught a flicker of nylon as she crossed her legs for his benefit, glanced sidewise and met the stare of her green eyes, and bumped into an old woman with a string bag filled with greens and bread. They did a little dance trying to avoid each other, and the old woman elbowed him aside roughly, muttering an obscenity under her breath.

Claire laughed brightly, warmly, disarmingly.

Marshal Foch looked embarrassed.

"Old women have very sharp elbows," she said to him. "They stay at home with pumice stone and sharpen them every day." He stared at her, and the expression that passed over his face assured her she had him hooked.

"Do you speak English?"

He took a long moment to shift linguistic gears and took a step closer. He nodded. "Yes, I do." His voice was deep, but measured: the voice of a man who watched the sidewalk as he walked, watched to make certain he did not filthy his shoes with dog droppings.

"I'm sorry I don't speak French," she said, drawing a deep breath so the blue sky silk parted slightly at her bosom. Making certain he didn't miss it, she let a pale, slim hand drift to her breasts as if in apology. He followed the movement with his narrowed eyes. Hooked, oh yes, hooked.

"You are American?"

"Yes. From Los Angeles. You've been there?"

"Yes, oh of course. I have been in America many times. My business."

"What is your business?"

Now he stood before her table, his briefcase hanging from his left hand, his chest pulled up to conceal the soft opulence gravity and age had brought to his stomach.

"I could sit down perhaps?"

"Oh, yes, of course. Certainly. How rude of me. Do sit down."

He pulled out the metal chair beside her, pushed the briefcase under, and sat down. He crossed his legs very carefully, like Marshal Foch, making certain the creases were sharp and straight. He sucked in his stomach and said, "I am dealing in artist's prints. Very fine work of new painters, graphic artists, airbrush persons. I travel very much in the world."

Not by foot, Claire thought. *By 747, by Trans Europ Express, by chic tramp steamers carrying only a dozen curried passengers as supercargo. Not by foot. You haven't a stringy inch on your succulent body, Marshal Foch.*

"I think that sounds wonderful," Claire said. Enthusiasm. Heady wine. Doors standing open. Invitations on stiff cockleshell vellum, embossed with elegant script. And, as always, since the morning of the world—spiders and flies.

"Oh, yes, I think so," he said, chuckling with pride. He did not say *think*; he pronounced it *sink*.

Sink. Down and down into the green water of her fine cool eyes.

He offered her a drink, she said she had a drink, he offered her *another* drink, some other kind of drink, some *stronger* drink. But she said no, she had a drink, thank you. Thus did she let him know she was not a prostitute. It was always the same, in any great city. Strong drink.

She hoped he could not hear her stomach growling.

"Have you had dinner?" she asked.

He did not answer immediately. *Ah, you have a wife and children waiting for you, waiting to start dinner, perhaps in Neuilly*, she thought. *Why, you dirty middle-aged man.*

Then he said, "Ah, *non*. But I must make the phone call to break engagement of a business nature. You would care to have dinner with me, perhaps?"

"I think that would be lovely," she said, showing him, by a turn of her head, the precise angle that highlighted her excellent cheekbones. Before she had finished the sentence he was out of the chair and heading for the *cabines téléphoniques*.

She sat and sipped her Perrier, waiting for dinner to return.

That was quick, she thought, as he hustled back to her. *Let me guess what you said, darling: something important has come up . . . a buyer from Doubleday shops in America . . . he is interested in the Kawalerowicz and the Meynard prints . . . you know I hate staying in the city so late . . . but I must . . . ah, non, Françoise, don't be like zat . . . tell the children I bring them a tarte . . . stop! stop! I must stay longer . . . I will come as soon as I can . . . eat without me . . . I will not . . . argue with you . . . goodbye . . . au revoir . . . salut . . . á bientôt . . . gimme a break, will you, I want to get laid. . . . I can hear you say it now, my dear Marshal Foch.*

And she thought one thing more: *I hope they don't try to keep your dinner hot for you.*

He smiled at her but there was strain in his face. It wasn't all that good a face to contain strain. But he tried valiantly not to show the effect of the phone call. "Now we go, yes?"

She stood up slowly, letting the parts assemble in the most esthetic manner, and the smile on his face grew more placid. Oh yes: hooked.

They began walking. She had already done some walking

in the area. Be prepared, that's the Girl Scouts' marching song.

She steered him into the Rue St. Benoit, thinking she could have dinner there without attracting a crowd. But it was still too early in the evening. The night life of Paris flows through the streets till well after two A.M. and dining *al fresco* is next to impossible. Claire never liked to hurry through a meal.

There were two restaurants at the end of Rue St. Benoit, and he suggested both of them. She made a charming move and said, "Why don't we walk a little farther. I want someplace more . . . romantic." He did not argue. Down Rue St. Benoit.

Left into Rue Jacob. Too busy.

Right onto Rue des Saints Pères. Still too busy. But up ahead . . . the river. The dark Seine. in the evening.

"Can we walk down to the river?"

He looked confused. "You want dinner, yes?"

"Oh, sure. Of course. But first let's walk down to the river. It's so beautiful, so lovely at night; this is my first time in Paris; it's so *romantic*." He did not argue.

On their right the bulk of a large building lay in darkness. She looked up at it, and past it to the sky in which the full moon shone like a waiting message.

Dining under the full moon was always nice.

He said, "This building is l'École des Beaux-Arts. Very famous." He pronounced it *fay*-moose. She laughed.

Dark. Always light. Sweet full moon riding through the heavens. Dinner warm and waiting. And then there was a bridge sweeping across the dark river. And steps leading down to the bank. Ah.

"Le Pont Royal," Marshal Foch said, indicating the bridge. "Very *fay*-moose." They walked across the quay and she led him down the steps. On the bank, two meters above the languid Seine, she turned and looked to left and right. Now she leaned against him and stood on her toes and kissed him. He sucked in his stomach, but it was not to hide the rotundity. She took him by the hand and led him toward the Pont Royal.

"Under the bridge," she said.

The sound of his breathing.

The sound of her high heels on the ancient stones.

The sound of the city above them.

The sound of the full moon glowing golden and getting larger in the sky.

And there, under the bridge, swathed in darkness, she leaned against him again and took his thick head between her slim, pale hands and put her mouth against his and let the sweet smell of her wash over him. She kissed him for a long moment, nipping at his lips with her teeth, and he made a small sound, like a tiny animal being stroked. But she was ahead of him. Her passion was already aroused.

And now Claire went away, to be replaced by something else.

A child of the night.

Child of loneliness.

With the last flickering awareness of her departing humanity she perceived the instant he knew he was in the love embrace of something else, the child of the night.

It was the instant she changed.

But that instant was too short for him to free himself. Now her spine had curved, and now her mouth had filled with fangs, and now the claws had grown, and now the body beneath the blue sky silk was matted with fur, and now she was dragging him down, and now she was on top of him and now the claws were ripping the sincere gray suit from his flesh, and now one blackened claw sliced a line through his throat so he could not scream; and now it was dinnertime.

It had to be done carefully and quickly.

He was erect, his penis swollen with arrested lust. Now she had him naked and on his back, and she was on him, and settling down over him; and he entered her, even as he gurgled his life away. She rode him, bucking and sweating, while his mouth worked futilely and his eyes grew large and surrounded by white.

Her orgasm was accompanied by a howl that rose up over the Seine and was lost in the night sky above Paris where the golden sovereign of the full moon swallowed it, glowing just a bit brighter with passion.

And down in the dark, surfeited with passion, she dined elegantly.

The food in Berlin had been too starchy; in Bucharest the blood had run too thin and the taste had not risen; in Stockholm the dining was too bland; in London too stringy; in

Zurich too rich, she had been ill. Nothing to compare with the hearty fare in Los Angeles.

Nothing to compare with home cooking.... Until Paris. The French were justly famous for their cuisine.

And she ate out every night.

It was a very good week, her first week in Paris. An elegant older man with bristling white moustache who spoke of the military, right up to the end. A shampoo girl from a chic shop, who wore a kind of fluorescent purple jumpsuit and red candy-apple cowboy boots. An American student from Westfield, New York, studying at the Sorbonne, who told her he was in love with her, until the end when he said nothing. And others. Quite a few others. She was afraid her figure was going to hell.

And now it was Saturday again. *Samedi*.

She had felt like dancing. She was a good dancer. All the right rhythms at just the right times. One of her meals had said the most interesting *bôite*, at the moment, was a bar and restaurant combined with a discotheque called Les Bains-Douches, which translated as "the bath and shower" because it had formerly been a bath and shower house since the nineteenth century.

She had come to the Rue du Bourg l'Abbé and had stood before the large glass in the heavy door. A man and a woman were behind the glass, selecting who could come in and who could not. In Paris, the more one is kept out of the club, the more one wishes to enter.

The man and the woman looked at her. Both reached to unlock the door. Claire knew what she looked like; the appeal was evident to male and female alike. She had never worried for a moment about gaining access. Inside.

And now, all around her, the excitement and the color and the firm strong young flesh of Paris moved in stately passion like underwater plants.

She danced a little, she drank a little, she waited.

But not for long.

He wore a very tight T-shirt with the words 1977 NCAA Soccer Champions on it. But he was not an American, nor an Englishman. He was French and his jeans, like his shirt, were very tight. He wore motorcycle boots with little chains banding the toe. His hair was long and waved back carelessly, but he did not have the sloe eyes of a punk. The eyes were sharp and blue and too intelligent for the face in which they rested. He stared down at her.

For a few moments she was unaware of him standing there, even though he was directly in front of her table. She was watching a particularly elegant couple performing lifts at the far right side of the dance floor; and he stood there, watching her without interference.

But when she looked up and he did not turn away, when his eyes did not narrow and he did not grow nervous as she turned the full power of her personality on him, she knew tonight would very likely be the best gourmet dining she had ever had.

His name was Patrick. He was a good dancer; they danced well together; and he held her tighter than a stranger had any right to hold her. She smiled at the thought because they would not be strangers for long; soon, if the night filled with light, they would be very intimate. Eternally intimate.

And when they left he suggested his apartment in Le Marais.

They went over the river to the old section, now quite fashionable. He lived on the top floor, but he was not wealthy. He told her that. She found him quite charming.

Inside, he turned on a soft blue light and another that was recessed in the wall behind a long chrome planter box filled with fat, healthy plants.

He turned to her and she reached out to take his head between her hands. He reached up and stopped her hands, and he smiled and said, in French she could understand, "You would eat some food?" She smiled. Yes, she *was* hungry.

He went into the kitchen and came back with a tray of carrots and asparagus and shredded beets and radishes.

They sat and talked. He talked, for the most part. In a French manner that posed no problems for her. She couldn't understand that. He spoke as fast and with as much complexity as all other Frenchmen, but when others spoke to her, in the hotel, in the street, in the disco, it was gibberish; when he spoke, she understood perfectly. She thought he might have learned English somewhere and was speaking partially in her native tongue. But when her mind tried to halt one of the words she thought might be in English, it was gone too fast.

But after a while she stopped worrying about it and just let him talk.

And when she leaned toward him, finally, to kiss him on the mouth, he reached across and put his hand up under her long blond hair, up to the nape of the neck, and brought her face close.

Through the window she could see the waning moon. She smiled faintly within the kiss: it was not necessary to have a full moon. It never had been. That was where the legends were wrong. But the legend was correct about silver bullets. Silver of any kind. And therein lay the reason why a vampire cast no reflection. (Except that was merely *another* legend. There were no vampires. Only children of the night who had been badly observed.) Because Jesus had been betrayed by Judas for thirty pieces of silver, the metal had been put to an evil purpose and was therefore, thereafter, invested with the power to turn away evil. So it was not the *mirror* that cast no reflection of the children of the night, it was the silver backing. Claire could be seen in a mirror of polished steel or aluminum. She could bathe in the river and see her reflection.

But never in a silver-backed mirror.

Such as the one over the fireplace just across from where she sat on the sofa with Patrick.

A *frisson* of warning went through her.

She opened her eyes. He was looking past her.

Into the mirror.

Where he sat alone, embracing nothing.

And Claire began to leave, to be replaced by the child of the night.

Fast. She moved very fast.

Spine curves, fur mats, teeth lengthen, teeth sharpen, claws grow. And her hand that was no longer a hand came up as she shoved him away from her, raking the razoring claw across his throat.

The throat opened wide.

And the green sap flowed out. For a moment. And then the wound magically puckered, drew together, formed a white line of scar, and then vanished altogether.

He watched her as she watched him heal.

For the first time in her life she was frightened.

"Would you like me to put on some music?" he asked. But he did not speak. His mouth did not move.

And she understood why his French had not been incomprehensible to her. He was speaking inside her head, without sound.

She could not answer.

"If not music, then perhaps you'd like something to eat," he said. And he smiled.

Her hands moved in vagrant ways, without purpose. Fear and total confusion commanded her. He seemed to understand. "It's a very large world," he said. "The spirit moves in many ways, in many forms. You think you're alone, and you are. There are many of us, one of each, last of our kind, perhaps, and each of us is alone. The mists part and the children emerge, and after a while the old ones die, leaving the last of the children motherless and fatherless."

She had no idea what he was saying. She had always known she was alone. That was simply the way it was. Not the foolish concept of loneliness of Sartre or Camus, but *alone*, all alone in a universe that would kill her if it knew she existed.

"Yes," he said, "and that's why I have to do something about you. If you are the last of your kind, then this life of chances, just to satisfy your needs, must end."

"You're going to kill me. Then do it quickly. I always knew that would happen. Just do it fast, you weird son of a bitch."

He had read her thoughts.

"Don't be a fool. I know it's hard not to be paranoid; what you've been all your life programs that into you. But don't be a fool if you can stop. There's nothing of survival in stupidity. That's why so many of the last of their kind are gone."

"What the hell *are* you?!?" she demanded to know.

He smiled and offered her the tray of vegetables.

"You're a carrot, a goddam carrot!" she yelled.

"Not quite," said the voice in her head. "But from a different mother and father than you; from a different mother and father than everyone else out on the streets of Paris tonight. And neither of us will die."

"Why do you want to protect *me*?"

"The last save the last. It's simple."

"For what? For what will you protect me?"

"For yourself . . . for me."

He began to remove his clothes. Now, in the blue light, she

could see that he was very pale, not quite the shade that facial makeup had lent him; not quite white. Perhaps the faintest green tinge surging along under the firm, hard skin.

In all other respects, and superbly constructed, he was human; and tumescently male. She felt herself responding to his nakedness.

He came to her and carefully, slowly—because she did not resist—he removed her clothes; and she realized that she was Claire again, not the matted-fur child of the night. When had she changed back?

It was all happening without her control.

Since the time a very *long* time ago when she had gone on her own, she had controlled. Her life, the lives of those she met, her destiny. But now she was helpless, and she didn't mind giving over control to him. Fear had drained out of her, and something quicker had replaced it.

When they were both naked, he drew her down onto the carpet and began to make slow, careful love to her. In the planter box above them she thought she could detect the movement of the hearty green things trembling slightly, aching toward them and the power they released as they spasmed together in a ritual at once utterly new because theirs was the meeting of the unfamiliar, yet ancient as the moon.

And as the shadow of passion closed around her she heard him whisper, "There are many things to eat."

For the first time in her life, she could not hear the sound of footsteps following her.

WITHOUT RHYME OR REASON
Peter Valentine Timlett

Peter Valentine Timlett was born in London in 1933, has lived in Australia for a few years, and now makes his home in Kent. He is primarily known for his Atlantean fantasy trilogy: *The Seedbearers* (1974), *The Power of the Serpent* (1976), and *Twilight of the Serpent* (1977). More recent novels include an Arthurian trilogy and a novel based on the witchcraft trial of Father Urbain Grandier, *Nor All Thy Tears*. He has worked as a jazz musician and in the distribution department of a large British publishing house. For several years Timlett was a practicing ritual magician, until he became frustrated with the aims of the occult group to which he belonged. Timlett's interest in the occult is reflected in his *Seedbearers* trilogy, which he wrote without being aware of the heroic fantasy fad with which his trilogy was then lumped. (The U.S. paperback of *The Seedbearers* was saddled with a cover that rates as the most blatant Frazetta-Conan swipe ever.) Not one to pay heed to publishing trends, Timlett completed his Arthurian trilogy (as yet unpublished) little realizing that the market would be flooded with Arthurian novels that season. Timlett writes virtually exclusively in the novel form, and "Without Rhyme or Reason" is his only published short story. Ramsey Campbell coaxed this one out of Timlett for *New Terrors*, and I wish him success in persuading Timlett to show us a few more.

It was a large house, far bigger than she had expected. Must be five or six bedrooms at least. Not all that old, late Victorian probably, and the gardens were superb. It was set well back off a very minor road about a mile outside the village with not another house in sight, and as a consequence it was beautifully quiet and peaceful. She could be very happy here indeed.

She rang the bell and waited. After a couple of minutes she rang again. There must be someone at home, surely. Her appointment was for three o'clock, and she was punctual almost to the second.

"Yes?" said a sharp voice behind her.

She spun round, startled. "Oh, I'm sorry. I didn't hear you come up." The woman was in her late forties, tall and slimly built, with clear gray eyes that studied her firmly, almost fiercely. "I am Miss Templeton—Deborah Templeton. The agency sent me. Are you Mrs. Bates?"

The woman nodded. "You are punctual. I like that." The gray eyes swept her from head to foot. "You are also very pretty. I told the agency that you had to be pretty. I like to be surrounded by beautiful things, including people. You are not beautiful but you are very pretty. It's the dress, I think, and the hairstyle. Pretty but not beautiful."

Miss Templeton's hand strayed involuntarily to her hair. "I usually wear it down," she said.

"Yes, you should. With your hair down, a decent eyeshadow, green I think, and a daring evening gown you could look quite stunning."

The girl smiled. "It's been a long time since I dressed like that. There has been no occasion." Mrs. Bates was no advertisement for her own philosophy. She wore patched and faded jeans, muddy at the knees, and a shapeless smock-like top that did little for her figure, and her hair was pushed up under an old hat that looked as though it might have begun life a decade earlier as a chic jockey cap in a Chelsea boutique. But she had that classical facial bone structure that most women envy, giving her face a precious ageless look. Given the right clothes this woman could also look quite stunning, despite her age.

Mrs. Bates was aware of her appraisal. "One should dress to please oneself, not others," she said firmly. "When I am in the garden I dress like a gardener. In the evenings I dress like a woman, even when I'm alone." She turned and walked away. "Come into the house," she said over her shoulder.

Miss Templeton followed her around the side of the house and into a sun-lounge through a pair of French windows. A curious woman, this Mrs. Bates. The agency had been right to describe her as somewhat eccentric. But the room was beautiful. Each piece of furniture, as far as she could tell, was a genuine antique, and the woman waved her to a Victorian chaise-longue that alone would be worth a fortune by her own standards.

"As I am in my gardening clothes I will remain standing," said Mrs. Bates. "I am a wealthy woman, Miss Templeton. The contents of this house are worth far more than the house itself, and for that reason alone I have to be careful whom I invite to live with me."

"I understand."

"And there is also the question of compatible personalities." Again those gray eyes scanned her from head to toe. "I imagine that the agency told you that I am an eccentric."

"They said that you were a strongly individualistic person," said Miss Templeton carefully.

"And so I am. This is my house and thus I have the right to determine how it shall be run."

"Of course."

"I am a fanatical gardener, Miss Templeton. Summer or winter I spend most of my time in the garden. I do not want a companion, let's be clear about that. I want someone to look after the house, leaving me free to tend the garden. Anything to do with the house, anything at all, will be your province."

"So I understand. The agency gave me a list of all the duties and conditions and I find them very acceptable."

"Good. As to meals, I see to myself during the week. You will be required to cook only one meal a week, on Saturday evening, for which I trust you will join me. I am a fanatic about the garden but not about the house. Providing it is kept reasonably clean and tidy you may come and go as you please. If you like walking you will find the countryside around here quite delightful. I am not a sociable woman, Miss Templeton. I can be quite charming when I put my mind to it but basically I prefer my own company. During the week, when you are not actually engaged upon work in the house, I would be grateful if you would remain in your rooms, but I would welcome your company on the Saturday evening."

The girl nodded. "You want the house to run smoothly

without you being bothered about it, and I am to stay out of your way except on Saturdays."

The woman smiled. "Exactly. All this may sound a bit odd to you but I find that it suits me very well and I need someone who can fit in with that pattern, someone who is also quite happy with their own company most of the time. Your letter said that you are twenty-eight, an only child, and that your parents are dead. Any other attachments?"

"No, none, not even a romance."

"I see. Sorry to ask these rather personal questions but the reasons are obvious. However, I think it is only fair that I reciprocate. So, Miss Templeton, I can tell you that I am forty-eight and do not give a damn who knows it. Like yourself, my parents also died when I was young, and like yourself, I am also an only child. Because of that I was already fairly wealthy in my own right even before I married, and my husband had money as well. We were married for ten years before he ran off with a younger woman."

"Oh, I am sorry."

"To be candid so was I. It was a good marriage, or so I thought, even though there were no children."

"Why did he leave?"

For a brief moment a look of bleak hatred crossed her eyes. "Let us say that the girl in question used her physical assets to good effect. So I, too, am quite alone with no attachments whatever. Did the agency tell you the salary?"

"Yes, the money is fine."

"Good." Again those gray eyes surveyed her critically. "Well, Miss Templeton, I think we will get on very well indeed. I'll leave you for a few minutes to think about it. By all means have a look round the house. Your rooms are the first two on the right at the top of the stairs. There is a bedroom with your own bathroom attached, and a small sitting room with a connecting door. I'm sure you will be comfortable. When you are ready you'll find me in the garden," and she turned and walked out on to the patio.

Deborah Templeton continued to sit there in the sun lounge for a few moments. What a curious woman, she thought, and what an extraordinary interview. It was the sort of interview that a man might have conducted, not a woman. For a brief moment the thought crossed her mind that Mrs. Bates might have unusual tastes, hence the reason perhaps why her husband had left her for a more normal woman and hence the reason perhaps why she was so insistent that her employee be young and attractive, but she dismissed the idea almost as soon as it arose. The woman might be odd but that oddness certainly didn't stem from Sappho.

She rose and walked through the house. She had not exactly come from penurious circumstances herself, but she had never lived in such luxurious surroundings as this. The kitchen was enormous and fitted with just about every labor-saving device on the market, and the main lounge was a superb room of elegance and grace. She walked up the main staircase and directly she entered what was to be her bedroom she knew that she simply had to have this position, for there was the most gorgeous four-poster bed curtained in woven tapestry of gold and red like something out of a fairy tale. It was silly, she knew, to let such a trivial thing as a bed clinch the decision, but it had always been a fantasy of hers to sleep in a four-poster.

She looked at herself in the tall cheval mirror and pulled a wry smile. Pretty but not beautiful. An accurate but deflating description. There had been a time, oh so many years ago now, when she had been stunningly attractive, in the days when she had deliberately dressed for that effect, but the image that stared back at her from the mirror was suburbanly "mumsy" and hardly likely to stir the male libido.

She walked over to the window and stared down into the garden to where Mrs. Bates was busy weeding the flowerbeds. The woman was certainly an autocrat, but if it was true that she would not see her for most of the time then that was no real problem. And yet there was still something odd about the whole thing. It was all too good to be true. Or perhaps the oddness had more to do with Mrs. Bates herself than the position she was offering. Anyway, she would be a fool to turn it down.

The name on the list of duties that the agency had given her was Mary Elizabeth Bates, followed by an indecipherable signature. The name, Mary, was really quite apposite. "Mary, Mary, quite contrary," she murmured, "how does your garden grow?" and the answer was that it grew very well, though Mary Bates herself was certainly contrary, contrary indeed.

The girl left the room and went downstairs into the garden.
"I think I will be very happy here," she said simply.

The woman smiled. "When I read your letter and saw your photograph I was already half certain, but when I saw you standing at the door I knew that you were going to be the one. When can you come?"

"Would Monday be too soon?"

Mrs. Bates held out her hand. "Monday will be fine. I'll see you then."

Deborah had said Monday just to give herself the weekend should she wish to change her mind, but by Saturday lunch time she had given the landlady of her bedsit a week's rent in lieu of notice and was already packed and eager to go. Saturday evening and all day Sunday stretched to a seeming eternity but at last the Monday came and the taxi delivered her to her new home by noon.

Mrs. Bates, still in the same old pair of jeans, welcomed her kindly but not effusively. "You know where your rooms are. Use today to get settled in. Cook yourself a meal when you feel like it. I'll talk to you more fully, and go over the house accounts with you, tomorrow," and she turned and went back into the garden. Deborah smiled wryly and lugged her suitcases up to her rooms, and by two o'clock she was unpacked and ready to explore the house.

Her mother had always said that you could know almost everything there was to know about a woman's environment, temperament, and character by the contents of her kitchen cupboards, her wardrobe, and her laundry bin. The kitchen harbored no surprises, in view of the evidence of wealth in the rest of the house. The tins and jars and bottles in the cupboards revealed a highly expensive epicurean taste that promised a future of delightful cuisine, though no doubt it would prove a disaster to any calorie-controlled diet, and the wine rack contained a dozen or more bottles, mostly German hocks, though in amongst the array of white wine there were two bottles of Nuit St. George. Mrs. Bates obviously dined well.

The girl did not dare go into her employer's bedroom to see her wardrobe, but she did make a quick examination of the contents of the laundry bin and there met with a surprise that almost bordered on shock. There were two suspender belts, one of black and purple and one of black and scarlet, and five pairs of the scantiest briefs that she had ever seen, again in scarlet, black, and purple, and all of them lacy and highly revealing. And in addition there were two bras, one black and one red, so brief that they simply had to be quarter-bras that would make the point quite clear on any normally endowed woman. It was puzzling. These were the underclothes of a young Soho showgirl, not those of a forty-eight-year-old rural semi-recluse. Mrs. Bates was proving to be something of an intriguing mystery.

At four o'clock it began to rain and Deborah rushed to her sitting room window to see what Mrs. Bates would do. The woman hurried into the conservatory and emerged a few minutes later dressed in wellington boots, oilskin trousers, and a waterproof anorak with the hood pulled up over her head, and calmly went back to work. She really did look quite ridiculous bent over the flowerbeds with the rain drumming on her back. As it was late June the weather was still quite warm despite the rain, and if you are suitably waterproofed then there was no logical reason why you should not work in the rain, and yet it seemed ludicrous. People didn't tend their gardens in the pouring rain. It simply wasn't *done*. And how on earth could you equate that comical and eccentric figure down there in the rain with the sort of woman that wore lurid and provocative underclothes? It was delightfully mysterious.

Deborah did not see Mrs. Bates that evening, but on the following morning she found a note in the kitchen asking her to come into the library after breakfast to go over the house accounts. Well at last Deborah would see Mrs. Bates in something other than jeans, but when she entered the library the result was oddly disappointing. She was dressed in pale blue slacks and a white high-necked blouse. The outfit was simple, tasteful, and hardly in keeping with the erotic contents of the laundry bin. And Mrs. Bates proved to have a good brain, neat, precise, and logical. The house accounts were all neatly annotated and filed in alphabetical order in a proper filing cabinet in the library, and within half an hour the familiarization talk was over and Mrs. Bates changed back into her jeans and returned to the garden.

In accordance with her instructions Deborah Templeton kept out of her employer's way for the rest of that Tuesday and all day Wednesday, though Mrs. Bates in the garden was material so fine that she trailed wisps of it behind her as she moved, and it was quite staggering how little of Mrs. Bates it covered. The contrast to the wellington-booted figure in the garden was so startling that it was scarcely believable that it was the same woman.

Without even thinking about it Deborah went back into her bedroom, stripped off her cocktail dress and her underclothes, put on her evening gown, and went downstairs to serve dinner.

Neither gown was mentioned during dinner, indeed little was said at all. Mrs. Bates made an appreciative comment about the prawn cocktail, was quite complimentary in respect to the Tournedos Rossini, and said that she found the lemon sorbet to be delicious. It was only when they withdrew to the main lounge for coffee that the first mention was made. "An excellent meal, my dear," said Mrs. Bates, "and I completely withdraw my earlier remark about being merely pretty. You look quite stunning. I doubt that any man could keep his hands off you."

The girl smiled. "With you in the room I doubt that he would even see me."

Mrs. Bates looked down at herself. "Yes, men are quite stupidly physical. With a dress like this, or one like yours, a man's every instinct prompts him to reach out and remove what little there is. All female virtues are as nothing compared to the power of a revealing gown, as I know to my cost."

Deborah sipped her coffee. "The girl who took your husband?" she said softly.

The woman smiled grimly. "We entertained a lot in those days, mostly business acquaintances of my husband's, and people from his office. I did not dress then as you see me now. I used to dress elegantly and tastefully, but never revealingly. An old-fashioned attitude, perhaps, in these days of blatant sexuality, but we all have our own particular tastes and standards."

"And the girl?"

"A personal assistant to one of my husband's directors. She came to one of our dinner parties dressed in a gown almost exactly like this one and made it perfectly obvious to my husband that he need only snap his fingers for her to remove it altogether." Mrs. Bates put her coffee cup on a side table and leaned back in the armchair. "Two weeks later he left me and went off with her."

"I'm sorry," said the girl quietly.

The woman was silent for a moment. "He would have come back to me, you know, when the novelty had worn off, and I would have taken him. It was a good marriage. Men are so vulnerable to a really determined and blatant advance from an attractive woman. Few of them can resist. It is almost part of their nature, you might say."

"What happened?"

"Three weeks after he left they were both killed in a car crash in southern France, and I hope she rots in hell for all time. And it was all so unnecessary. A discreet affair would have been far better. It would have satisfied the sexual attraction and preserved the marriage."

The girl did not comment. Her sympathy was instinctively with the husband. An autocratic woman such as Mrs. Bates would not be easy to live with from any aspect, sexual or otherwise. There was probably more than one reason why he had left her.

"And all because of a revealing evening gown," said Mrs. Bates bitterly. "That girl had worked at that office for two years and I *know* that there had been nothing between them prior to that dinner party. It was the gown that did it."

Deborah sipped at her coffee again. Possible, but not likely. If it had only been a question of sex then a discreet affair would indeed have satisfied the situation. There had to be more to it than that. The way this woman kept harping on that one particular aspect seemed to suggest that Mrs. Bates felt very inadequate and inferior in that area.

"And so I went out and bought this gown, and some other clothing," said Mrs. Bates. "And do you know why?"

Deborah shook her head. She didn't like the way this was going. The woman really did have a most peculiar expression in her eyes.

Mrs. Bates stood up abruptly. "Then I will show you. Come with me," and she took the girl's hand and led her to the other end of the lounge to where a large mirror hung on the wall. "That's why," she said, pointing to the two reflections. "Having come off second best on one notable occasion I wanted to see how I would compare if I were similarly dressed."

The girl felt her spine begin to tingle. Not fear exactly, but that instinctive nervous apprehension that the sane sometimes feel in the company of the insane. By God, how long had this woman brooded on her misfortune to have produced this sort of crazy reaction? This obviously explained the long string of attractive girls. Mrs. Bates was measuring herself against them, one after the other. And then what? If the measurement was in the older woman's favor then presumably that was an end of the matter, honor having been satisfied. But what if the comparison was unfavorable?

Deborah looked at the two reflections. Mary Bates really was an attractive woman. Her body was trim and taut, and her figure was still quite superb, even without a bra, and in that wisp of a gown she looked like a high priestess of a pagan cult, sensual, uninhibited, and devastatingly provocative. Few women her age could even begin to compare. But she was forty-eight years of age, and she looked it. Nothing could hide the difference in age between the two women reflected in that mirror, and ironically the two provocative gowns served only to reveal that difference more clearly. Deborah was not vain about her own looks, but she knew that if a choice had to be made at that precise moment then most men would choose herself. Mrs. Bates simply did not compare.

The girl smiled nervously. "There's no comparison," she said lightly. "If there were any men around I wouldn't stand a chance." In the mirror she saw the woman's eyes narrow to an expression of cold hatred.

"Nonsense, my dear," said Mrs. Bates smoothly. "You are far more attractive than I. If the whole situation occurred again my husband would undoubtedly go off with you."

Deborah released her hand and walked away back to the coffee table. "You underestimate yourself, Mrs. Bates." She picked up her shawl. "I'm not attractive to men and never have been, no matter what I wear. Why do you think I live on my own? It's not by choice, I assure you." She began to move toward the door. Oh God, she simply had to escape from this stupid insanity. "Anyway, it's getting late, and the wine has given me a headache. If you'll excuse me I think I'll go to bed."

The look of hatred had vanished from the woman's eyes. "By all means," she said coldly. "Thank you for a lovely dinner, and a most entertaining evening."

The girl could not get to her room fast enough. Once inside the bedroom she leaned back against the door and closed her eyes. Her hands were trembling, and sweat had broken out over her whole body. What a weird scene! No wonder the others had left in so much of a hurry. First thing tomorrow she would see if she could get her old bedsit back again. She was not going to stay in this house with that crazy woman a minute longer than absolutely necessary. She stripped off her gown, towelled herself dry, put on her nightdress, and lay down on the bed, but her mind was in too much of a turmoil for sleep.

It was about half past eleven when she heard Mrs. Bates come up the stairs and go to her own bedroom, but an hour later Deborah was still fretfully awake. She went to the open window and stared down into the garden. It looked even more beautiful by moonlight, and the silver bells really did look silver. It was a warm night, and oppressively close. Perhaps a walk round the garden would calm her down.

Silently she opened the bedroom door and stood there listening, but all was quiet. That wretched woman must be fast asleep by now, dreaming whatever weird images would rise in such a neurotic as Mrs. Bates. She slipped on her dressing gown over her nightdress and went downstairs and out into the garden.

It was a lovely night, and for the first time during that entire evening she was able to breathe more easily. It was in many ways a dreadful shame that she had to leave. On the surface it was an ideal job in ideal surroundings, but even from the beginning it had seemed too good to be true, and so it had proved. She sighed and meandered across the lawn. Such a beautiful garden, but such a weird gardener. Even here in the garden the behavior of her employer had been decidedly odd, coming back again and again to this particular spot. Deborah looked down at the long low mound of Mrs. Bates's favorite flowerbed. "Mary, Mary, quite contrary," she murmured, "how does your garden grow? With silver bells and cockleshells, and pretty maids all in a row."

And it was then, at that precise moment, that the earlier warning bells, the odd behavior of Mrs. Bates, and the fact of the missing girls, all came together in an explosion of realization in her mind. So sudden was the revelation, and so terrifying, that for a full minute she could not move at all even though every instinct in her screamed out for her to get away, and her whole body trembled with wave after wave of piercing coldness. Then slowly she began to back away. Oh dear God, it cannot be, surely!

"Admiring the flowers in the moonlight?" said a voice behind her.

Deborah spun round and there, just a few feet away, was Mrs. Bates looking pale and ghostly in a flowing white dressing gown. This second shock, coming so close on the first, came near to causing a fatal heart attack, quite literally. The girl gave a piercing shriek of terror and fled in panic toward the house, bursting in through the French windows and flying up the stairs to her bedroom.

There was no key to the bedroom door, and no straight-backed chair to prop under the door handle. Frantically she dragged the dressing table across the carpet and rammed it against the door, and only just in time.

"What on earth is the matter, girl!" Mrs. Bates called out from the corridor, rattling the handle and pushing against the door. "Let me in. You frightened the life out of me, shrieking like that. What on earth is the matter? Let me in!"

Deborah said nothing. She picked up a pair of scissors and backed away to the middle of the room. Mrs. Bates had shoved the door open a couple of inches but could move it no more, and Deborah saw her pale hand come snaking round the edge to identify the obstruction.

"This is ridiculous!" the woman shouted. "Remove that thing and open this door!"

"Get out! Get out!" the girl shrieked.

The hand disappeared and then there was silence. Fifteen seconds passed, half a minute, and still there was no sound from the corridor.

"You forgot the connecting door," said a calm voice behind her, and a hand descended on her shoulder.

Again that shriek of hysterical terror rang out. Deborah spun round and stabbed blindly with her scissors, again and again. She stabbed the woman's eyes, and her face, and her shoulders, and fell with her to the floor, and kept on stabbing again and again, at her arms, at her breast, and again and again and again at what was left of her face, and then she sprang clear, flung away the scissors, raced through the connecting door, through the sitting room and out into the corridor, and stumbled hysterically down the stairs to the telephone.

The police arrived twenty minutes later; an inspector, a sergeant, two male constables, and a policewoman. Little sense had been made of the hysterical babble on the telephone and they had come prepared for almost anything, though hardly for what they actually found. The girl was covered in blood from head to foot, and at first they assumed that she had been attacked and savagely beaten, but as her story began bubbling out they began to realize that here was something far more grim. "They're out there, I tell you, buried in the flowerbed, murdered by that crazy woman upstairs!" she finished. "And I was to be next! If you don't believe me, go and look!" and she burst into great racking sobs.

Leaving the constables downstairs with the girl, the inspector and the sergeant went up to the bedroom. They came out two minutes later and leaned against the wall, fighting down the nausea. "You knew Mrs. Bates quite well," said the inspector at last. "Is that her?"

The sergeant wiped his brow. "How the hell can I say! It doesn't even look human!"

Presently the two men came down the stairs and walked over to the open French windows. "There should be a spade or a fork out there somewhere," said the inspector. "Take the two lads. Just dig enough to verify the story. The rest can wait."

Thirty minutes later the sergeant returned and the two men exchanged a whispered conversation, and then the inspector came over to Deborah. "Now let's take this again from the beginning."

"What more do you want!" said the girl hysterically. "You've seen what's upstairs and you've seen what's in the garden! For God's sake get me out of this place."

"I've seen you, and certainly I've seen what's upstairs," said the inspector grimly. "It's the rest of the story I don't understand."

The girl sprang to her feet. "Good God, there are six dead girls buried in the flowerbed! I've told you why and how! What else is there to understand!"

The inspector shook his head. "There is no one buried in the flowerbed, Miss Templeton," he said quietly. "No one at all. Now let's start right from the beginning—and take it very, very slowly."

DAW

SPECIAL FOR HORROR FANS

THE YEAR'S BEST HORROR STORIES: SERIES VIII
Karl Edward Wagner, editor   (UE2158—$2.95)

THE YEAR'S BEST HORROR STORIES: SERIES IX
Karl Edward Wagner, editor   (UE2159—$2.95)

THE YEAR'S BEST HORROR STORIES: SERIES X
Karl Edward Wagner, editor   (UE2160—$2.95)

THE YEAR'S BEST HORROR STORIES: SERIES XI
Karl Edward Wagner, editor   (UE2161—$2.95)

THE YEAR'S BEST HORROR STORIES: SERIES XII
Karl Edward Wagner, ed.   (UE1975—$2.95)

THE YEAR'S BEST HORROR STORIES: SERIES XIII
Karl Edward Wagner, ed.   (UE2086—$2.95)

THE YEAR'S BEST HORROR STORIES: SERIES XIV
Karl Edward Wagner   (UE2156—$3.50)

NEW AMERICAN LIBRARY
P.O. Box 999, Bergenfield, New Jersey 07621

Please send me the DAW BOOKS I have checked above. I am enclosing $_____
(check or money order—no currency or C.O.D.'s). Please include the list price plus
$1.50 per order to cover handling costs.

Name _____

Address _____

City _____ State _____ Zip Code _____
Please allow at least 4 weeks for delivery.